Quillquest Books

USA

Also by Frank Mosco

Fiction

The Whitemoon Crisis
Monkey
The Last Ghostrider
Searching for Jimmy Buffett
Cane's Gate
Hooky's Big Egg
On Still Waters

Nonfiction

Adventures in Black & White, Vol 1
People, Places & Things

Adventures in Black & White, Vol 2
Native American Dancers

Cybersafe
What you need to know to safely navigate the Internet

Film Scripts/Teleplays

Magnum P.I.
The Last Jazz
Cane's Gate
A Monkey Tale

Quillquest Books

A division of Quillquest Publishing Co. USA
279 King Arthur Ct, St. Augustine, FL 32086
Quillquest Books, Quillquest Junior Books, Quillquest Classic Books, and
the sailing quill are the exclusive trademarks of
Quillquest Publishing Co, USA.
For information or comments about this book contact
Quillquestbooks@msn.com

ISBN-10: 0-940075-25-3
ISBN-13: 978-0-940075-25-2
Copyright © 2018 by Frank Mosco

For

Ben Robinson
(a catcher of fish, females, and tall tales)

A Novel By

FRANK MOSCO

PROLOGUE

From his place in the sky, the lone pilot could see the rural Maryland landscape scarred by the ravages of war. Small towns sat destroyed and abandoned, roads, bridges, and vehicles ruined, farm homes and outbuildings burned. Then an oddity appeared. Where once large machines used to work the soil and produce crops, a lone farmer was now turning over a small patch of land using only a single mule pulling an antique plow.

We've done it again, thought the pilot as he looked about, then looked ahead to see the waters of the Chesapeake Bay in the distance. *We've thrown ourselves back into a primitive existence, into a third world existence. How do we explain this to our grandchildren?*

The man behind the plow was probably having similar thoughts about the antique aircraft overhead. He looked up briefly, his eyes following the old yellow biplane through a bright clear sky until he lost it in the glaring sun, then turned his attention back to his mule and the task at hand.

The old 1932 Stearman biplane was the only aircraft left in Boxer Bernhardt's grandfather's collection, the only one still in existence after the others were confiscated and shot down while being used as spotters and observation craft during the latter days of the war. Those planes, along with most anything else that could fly, were utilized by the military to compensate for the loss of satellite capabilities and the eventual shortage of unmanned drones and other military aircraft.

The war had drained the resources and used up the equipment on both sides and had destroyed the industrial base necessary for replenishment. This resulted in most private aircraft being confiscated for the cause, including his grandfather's old classic plane collection. It was throwback technology necessary in a modern bloody conflict that had degenerated into a defensive war of will and survival; a conflict of attrition rather than aggression with battle lines eventually settling along a narrow zone that crawled up the Chesapeake Bay extending west along the old Mason Dixon line through the Appalachian Mountains to the great Mississippi via the Ohio River. From there it followed the waterways to what was left of Chicago, one of the first cities to be nearly destroyed completely by the pre-war riots. South and west of there the country was up for grabs and though the lines west of the Mississippi had been redrawn numerous times, they were now settling uneasily between land claimed by a

Cuban led Hispanic alliance and a British backed Canada that was part of a Northern U.S. alliance. But then the battle lines were actually more wishful thinking than reality because most of the claimed ground was determined by its character, be it urban, suburban or rural and how badly the opposing factors desired it at the time.

The first time Boxer Bernhardt, the Stearman pilot, had ever flown he was an eight-year-old boy. It was just before the turn of the century when his grandfather, the U.S. Senator from Pennsylvania and Korean War hero Navy fighter pilot, took him up in this very same aircraft. That first experience with his flying ace grandfather introduced him to the lure and wonder of open cockpit flight that impressed him so much that two years later the talented twelve year old Boxer was a certified licensed pilot who gained notoriety while flying solo across the continent. Soon after, as a teen out of high school, he carried on the family tradition and entered the United States Naval Academy where he graduated with honors, shipped off to flight school, and was on his way to becoming a top notch aviator and an exceptional achiever in phenomenal aircraft such as the F-18 Super Hornet and F-35 Joint Strike Fighter.

Now, many years later as the war was winding down, he and the rest of a battle weary world began to settle in behind newly drawn blood stained geographic borders, to lick their wounds and contemplate the results of their insanity. At his war's end Boxer retreated to the family's ancestral two-hundred-fifty year old Pennsylvania farm.

There he resolved to spend his final days mourning the loss of his friends, his loved ones, his son, and the loss of his country as he had always known it. It was to the family farm he brought two now fatherless children and their mothers to begin what he hoped to be a safe new life. And it was there soon after retiring with them to the farm he discovered his treasured old Stearman biplane hidden in the barn, covered with canvas and hay behind a wall of old milking machines and other rusty equipment.

Boxer was thrilled. He saw and accepted the plane as a welcomed old constant in a new world where so many people had lost all forms of their past, lost those things that gave them any sense of security; a world that left them with little faith in the future.

On the side of the fuselage of the faded yellow plane, just below and to the rear of the open cockpit was the crest of a pair of boxing gloves over a pale blue circle bordered with the words *Boxer's Baby.* He had painted the art there himself the day after the Senator had given him the plane to celebrate his acceptance into the Naval Academy.

Now shortly after discovering the hidden plane, he replaced a few struts and wires, spent a few hard days breathing life back into the old bird's engine, then flew a few successful short test flights. At present the current older Boxer Bernhardt found himself flying low over the countryside along the Susquehanna River, following it until he reached the upper Chesapeake Bay. The water below glistened from the glare of the sun as he hugged the Chesapeake's eastern shore, heading south. Hearing and feeling only the strong throated vibration of the old engine, he looked down on a shoreline littered with the scars of conflict and remnants of war. He viewed the rusting ruins of destroyed and sunken military craft protruding from the water. As he continued along the bay, he could see destroyed landing craft, and on land, various disabled or mangled military vehicles sitting lifeless among bomb craters that littered the Kent County shoreline.

In some areas the battlefield extended as far as a mile or more inland of the peninsula to where the fighting had stalled, becoming too costly for both sides to continue. At some locations amidst the scarred battleground, the tools and machines of war sat as burned out useless monuments surrounding open fields full of white crosses where those who died opposing each other in battle were paradoxically buried together as brothers of the same nation. Boxer knew there were similar sights further south along the bay, including the location of the huge battle of Dorchester, but he didn't intend to venture that far. These places, he recalled, were evidence of how the war had regressed from high-tech battles in the sky and strategic sophisticated strikes on land to old war tactics full of not much more than men, desire, and wishful thinking. The opposition fighting with men who were beginning to doubt their convictions and on his side, men like him, who were just tired of the fight and heartbreak.

He continued until he came upon the skeletal remnants of the nearly four-and-a-half mile long Chesapeake Bay Bridge. Though current rules of a cease-fire treaty forbade it, he turned his plane west, flying just under the radar a few meters above the surface of the water alongside the broken twisted half-submerged steel and concrete of the bridge, then south until he reached the mouth of the Severn River. There on the river's shore where it met the bay stood his beloved Naval Academy and the city of Annapolis, most all of which now serving as a rapid response military base. If any of the occupying personnel there saw him they must not have cared enough to report it. Seeing a group of curious soldiers looking up he simply tipped his wings and they smiled and waved in return. After all, they probably thought it was just some joy rider in an old antique plane and why not, except for a few occasional light skirmishes the war had pretty much ended nearly two years prior.

He was surprised to see the Academy was for the most part still intact, the chapel dome still prominent above its skyline as was the Maryland State Capitol building. Apparently, the academy's alumni who served on the wrong side had enough respect and fond memories to avoid its destruction. Along with the naval air station across the river, the Academy now served as a military base and domicile.

He turned southwest; flying until he reached the Potomac River then banked and followed it with the intended destination being Washington. Whenever he came upon a military unit or populated area he would throw the Stearman into a barrel roll or some other acrobatic maneuver, leading them to view him as entertainment rather than a possible threat. Then

Washington finally appeared on the horizon and though most of it still lay destroyed just as it had been at the start of the current cease-fire, he could see that portions of the once abandoned city were now occupied and under repair and reconstruction. Still neglected were mostly the residential areas, much of them burned out during the pre-war riots. They were now a massive dark charred grave of a former civilization.

In the distance could be seen additional residential areas destroyed during the close-in urban combat that led to losing the Capital altogether. They sat as endless empty shells and carcasses of anonymous homes and townhouses, lost along with their many decades of family history and memories. The work now taking place was selective, demonstrating the priorities of the new government that claimed it. They wanted to bring back the landmarks and show the world who occupied the prize. Boxer had trouble dealing with the fact that the Capitol was now occupied by people who claimed to be another country altogether; becoming their paraded center of power. Their actual Capital, was the city of Atlanta not Washington. Washington was now only a trophy. He also had difficulty accepting that the new center of power of what was left of the original United States was now, as it had been when it was newly formed, in Philadelphia.

He climbed slightly, banked the Stearman away from the river to the heart of the city below and throttled back. He saw the Lincoln Memorial had been completely restored. In addition, it sported large multiple flags of its new owners, the now familiar red flag featuring a clenched fist over a broad rainbow. The grassy park area surrounding the reflecting pool in front of the Memorial was now a graveyard with each of the thousands of graves marked with a one-foot square cut granite block. The blocks lay flat on the ground engraved with only a number, each designating the remains of a civilian or soldier. They now lay anonymous as individuals destined to be remembered only as a group involved in a movement that led to their death but not the side on which they fought.

Boxer continued flying in a wide arc that brought him over the reflecting pool and then leveled off and headed for Capitol Hill. His old plane buzzed over what was left of the great obelisk of the Washington Monument; much of its original 555 feet lying in fractured sections, its large blocks sprawled over the grassy downgrade toward the heavily battle-damaged World War II memorial. Immediately to his left sat the charred destroyed remains of the White House, hardly recognizable as the once grand mansion and world famous seat of power of the United States Presidency. To his right across the tidal pond, the Jefferson Memorial remained intact, but serving as a base for the radar ears of a nearby abandoned STA missile battery, abandoned because there were no longer any missiles to launch, the supply having been long ago depleted.

Flying toward the Capitol on the hill, he could see many of the buildings behind and along the National Mall sat severely damaged, pocked and shattered by small arms fire, glaring evidence of how they had been used as opposing fortresses rather than offices or museums. It was there across the mall and around all of the Capital city where the urban battle had ended, where the last of the civilian patriots and a hand full of remaining U.S. military heroically held out in defense of their national city and it's treasures; fighting, falling back, and dying to preserve the Capital and symbol of U.S. power, to defend their republic. In the end they lost the city and their lives.

As he skimmed above what was left of the old trees along the grassy mall he viewed a cluster of construction equipment and what appeared to be makeshift barracks. Workers on the ground looked up and waved, others just stared at the old yellow biplane, not sure what to make of it. The sight of all this tore at Boxer's emotions when he flew low over what was left of the Capitol building, seeing one entire wing of the building no more than a pile of rubble, and a full half of its majestic dome and main structure destroyed and gaping open like some great suffering beast. Boxer, the hard core fighter jock and retired Admiral, came to tears. He pushed up the old goggles, wiped his eyes clear and circled the hill for another pass. A few men on the steps of the Supreme Court building paused and looked up. The scene reminded him of a time years ago. Looking down on the Capitol steps, he remembered the time as a young boy when he spent an entire workday with his grandfather the Senator. Standing with him and looking about on those same steps the young Boxer expressed his first impression of what he saw. "It looks like Rome. It's like the Roman empire," observed the young boy, impressed by the grandeur of the buildings and the architecture with its many columns.

"No, not an empire," he remembered his grandfather saying. "A republic. The people's republic. By definition an empire has an emperor, king or queen. However, if an empire can be defined by size and might then I suppose you might be correct. In this day and age it's a hazy gray line that separates the two. You might say our Republic, or empire as some may see it, being as great and mighty as it is, is like a fine crystal chalice. It's strong enough to hold much more than its own weight in balance but will easily shatter if tapped or tipped on its side. Don't ever let these huge columns and great noble buildings or the might of our nation fool you. It's a fragile crystal empire that's only as strong as its people. And if there's anything more threatening to a great nation it is its own people, the loss of faith of its people and the loss of direction by its leaders."

"I don't understand," the young Boxer replied.

"It's the nature of the beast," said the Senator. "Greed, ignorance, misguided values, complacency, dependency, a lust for power; these are the recurring characteristics of the human race that have brought down empires great and small. That's why some of us come and serve here in this place, not to rule and regulate but to preserve the republic, to act as the finger in the dike, sort of speak, and prevent a flood of self-destruction. Unfortunately, there are also those here who have less noble ideas. Do you understand what I'm saying?"

"I'm not sure," Boxer remembered saying to his grandfather. "What kind of other ideas?"

"No time to explain now. Got to get to a meeting but we'll talk about this again some time. You'll understand then and if not I'm sure you'll understand eventually," concluded the Senator with a smile.

The Senator was always the patient teacher, always the leader. That was a good day, Boxer remembered, thinking it was as though it were just yesterday; a cool sunny spring day much like the one he was flying in now and a day that ended with a ride in this same old Stearman. Piloting the plane now, he was so occupied with his memories and disturbed by what he was seeing that he neglected to notice the American Socialist Union Blackhawk helicopter that had popped up behind him.

Boxer's old biplane had no national markings, only its original old registration numbers. Nor did it have any communications gear and so the ASU chopper pilot could not raise him on the radio for identification and to order and escort him out of their no fly zone. Therefore, according to ASU defense protocol the assumption was made it was a U.S. North Country spy craft. As a consequence the ASU Blackhawk's pilot fired a rocket to bring it down. At that same moment however Boxer happened to bank for his return to the bay. The rocket closely missed and careened into the remnants of the Capitol dome, adding additional damage and insult to what the national landmark had already suffered in the war. The sound of the explosion was enhanced as it echoed through the smoke off the huge shell, off what was left of the gaping bell shaped dome.

The near miss and explosion snapped Boxer back to the reality of the moment and he reacted quickly, immediately taking evasive action. He flew wildly, knowing the old aircraft could not avoid for long the armaments of the ASU chopper. Like an air show flyer with extraordinary skills, the experienced old fighter pilot flew through, in, and out of canyons of office buildings, low along tree-lined avenues, and under freeway overpasses, outrunning and hiding in motion at speed, finally losing the chopper.

Temporarily free of his pursuer, he quickly decided to head for an old familiar refuge in Maryland located midway between Annapolis and DC. As he would do when he was a boy, he found the narrow winding Patuxent River and followed it for a few miles then cut away for a brief distance until he reached an old familiar sight, his grandfather's small private airstrip next to the old Senator's estate home. It was where Boxer first learned to fly. He carefully put the plane down on the neglected runway, avoiding some debris and trash as he taxied until arriving at a dilapidated tin hangar. The hanger's roof was partially collapsed but with just enough room to stash the Stearman underneath. In he went, parking the aircraft and quickly covering it with old tarps and fallen pieces of the tin wreckage. In the distance he could hear what he was sure were now two ASU choppers cruising along the river. He listened to make sure they were not coming in his direction and after assuring himself they had passed; he rushed off to a nearby narrow gravel road that led into a growth of trees. The short narrow road brought him to the rear of what was left of a large barn.

A few minutes later Boxer stood on the porch of the large old federal style house. It was the house that was purchased by his grandfather not long after his election and arrival in Washington. Such was the old man's confidence that his first term as senator was just the beginning. Boxer passed over an open threshold, the door long since gone, entering to discover a wrecked empty shell. Most everything of value that survived the fighting had been looted. Lying on the floor near the fireplace hearth was a charred family group photo in a broken frame taken during one of their gatherings on a Christmas day or was it a wedding. Boxer wasn't quite sure. It was discolored and faded by years of exposure to the weather. He picked it up and set it on the mantel where it belonged, where it had sat for so many years. Then as a second thought, decided to keep it and stuffed it in his jacket.

The grand house was the main building of the estate that became the family hub and the boyhood home of Boxer's father. It now sat destroyed beyond recovery, the majority of its upper level gone, ravaged by ground combat during the war. Most of the out buildings were destroyed as well but the smaller original farm dwelling built of stone that later became a guesthouse, except for being scarred by bullets and having most of the windows shattered, was still intact. Boxer often thought of the old guesthouse as his own private domain, gifted to him by the Senator whenever he was visiting. "Off to your castle," the old man would say to the small boy, "and ply your dreams and schemes."

It was in that guesthouse Boxer would read and relish the stories of the great aviators of the past, where he would watch and watch again all the great movies that featured aviation, and where he would impatiently plan his own future. In fact, it was even there in the guesthouse that Boxer lost his virginity to the daughter of a French diplomat he met at a reception. She was a few years older than he and the more experienced aggressor in the affair which of course raised no exceptions from Boxer. The rendezvous was a milestone in his life that took place during one of the many summers he spent there with his grandparents, the same summer he served as a young Congressional Page. A few years later it was there he would spend occasional weekends to relax and shed the cumulative stress serving as a midshipman while attending the Naval Academy in nearby Annapolis.

Boxer walked about, looking at the destroyed main house and deserted estate and remembered that it was here during one of those festive Christmas holidays many years ago that he first learned of the events that would send the world into disorder and chaos.

The sun began to set and an older, worn and tired Boxer Bernhardt had made his way to sit in the shadow of a large oak tree recalling what he had seen that day while flying over Washington. Intermingled were the many memories he had of the same city as a boy when he would spend entire days in the Air and Space Museum, those times and events in the city as a young man, and later as a senior Naval Officer. Then there came the very harshest recollection of all, the memory of the day his grandfather, the wise old fox and eventual majority leader of the United States Senate, was killed; of that day 19 years ago when the war began. As he remembered these things he felt the weight of his age and the accumulation of the years of conflict and grief. *Could so much have taken place during such a short time in the life of mankind*, he wondered? *Could the world have changed so quickly and irrevocably?* He leaned back against the tree, listening to the choppers that searched for him in the far distance and reflected on his life, trying to make sense of it all, recalling the nightmare back in 2019, the politics and the national dilemma that led to riots, and then a revolt which escalated into a domestic war that subsequently led to the demise of his country with consequences that changed the world. He closed his eyes and asked of himself only one simple question – *why*?

His eyes closed in an effort to find those pleasant memories of family, of a less complicated time, a time of peace. But with those memories came the reality of the nightmare.

CHAPTER 1 _____

20 YEARS EARLIER

BERNHARDT ESTATE – DEC. 22, 2018

"I still don't believe you. No matter how many times I hear you tell people, I still think it's just bullshit," said Antwan Ellis to Boxer Bernhardt as he watched Senator Jesse Bernhardt, the family patriarch, on the other side of the room clowning and making a fool of himself with his grandchildren as they decorated the Christmas tree. The old senator then took his leave, retiring to his library study and leaving generations of spirited members of the Bernhardt clan to laugh and enjoy the holiday and meander about the big house.

"Dimmit Antwan," replied Boxer, "I told you back when they first roomed us together at the Academy, and the story hasn't changed. Get it straight for once will ya? Family picnic. Boxing gloves. I was eight years old. I beat the shit out of my cousin who was bigger and three years older than me and they've been calling me Boxer ever since."

"Oh no, buddy. That *ain't* the way your sister tells it."

"My sister? What the hell you mean my sister? She doesn't know. She wasn't even there."

"Now why would she lie? Especially to me?"

"What, you think just because you're married to her that she wouldn't bullshit you? Hey, man, that's *my* sister remember? The one who works in the State Department press office and bullshits for a living. The one who sugared the gas tank when you and I wouldn't take her with us to Vegas remember? She's just jealous and wants to make me look bad that's all. Always been that way."

"Nah, don't think so. No lies in the bedroom, my man. Not in our house. She damn near cracked a rib laughing and telling me how you got that name. And you forget, I've seen the scar. We were roommates at the Academy remember? Fess up and come clean, man. Come on now remember that honor system there, Commander Bernhardt. Tell the truth. Were you bit on the ass by a boxer dog named Peaches or not? Hey, don't worry. My lips are sealed. I promise I won't start any scuttlebutt. I'm family now and the father of your two beautiful twin nieces... and a navy aviator of the fighter breed of the highest quality who sure as Hell doesn't want to be associated with or related to some dude who was bested by some little mutt named *Peaches*."

"You tell anybody that story and I'll flame your black ass at sea and nobody will ever find the pieces," threatened the seemingly very serious Boxer Bernhardt.

"Uh oh, there you go. Playing the bad-ass racist again," laughed Antwan. "Hey, white boy, you don't have it in you. You know you can't pull off that shit;

especially with me your brother in law, and you know you love me more than your lawnmower. And, I might add, you don't actually think you can out-fly my Afro ass. Cold day in Hell when that'll happen - *Peach meat.*"

"No contest roomie, no contest. You forget what I did to you at Miramar."

"And you forget about the punch out over the Med last year. Like maybe you had a senior moment or something," laughed Antwan.

"Hey, come on man... a low blow. That was a mechanical, damnit. Everybody knows that," argued Boxer.

"Oh, what a tangled web we weave..." smiled Antwan as he reached out and straightened Boxer's tie, then tightened it with a jerk. "When are you white boys gonna learn to tell the truth?"

Just then Antwan's twin daughters, Dinese and Sian, scooted up, each taking one of his hands.

"Daddy," they said, stepping all over each other's words, "you have to come and see what we put on the Christmas tree."

"This isn't over," declared Boxer, while loosening his tie. "You and me on deck tomorrow with the gloves. High noon."

"Peaches," laughed Antwan as he was being pulled away.

"Come on Dad," insisted the girls.

"Okay, okay, I'm coming. Oh, hey girls, did I ever tell you how your Uncle Boxer got his name?"

"We already know that," said Sian as she pulled her father away. "He got bit on the butt by a dog. Mom told us."

Boxer threw up his hands and turned for the bar where he found his father acting as bartender. His father, the soon to retire Admiral Allen Bernhardt, smiled. He had overheard their conversation. "Thirty-five years old and still defending that nickname. Hah, you really don't expect your sister to keep any secrets do you? Especially about you? Maybe for the State Department but not about you. Just be glad she doesn't tell the one about how you barfed on the rocket ride at that carnival when you were eight years old. No way in hell a fighter jock could live that down."

"Payback is a bitch," laughed Boxer. "Someday..."

"Yeah, right. So how's everything up in the wild blue yonder these days?' asked the Admiral.

"Well, you won't believe this Pop, but there's still lot's of sky left up there and they're still making clouds in spite of what the climate change doodahs claim. It's still climate change now, right? Or is it global warming again or global freezing again or whatever? I forget."

"I think they've settled on the phrase *climate change* for a few more decades. It's a safe all encompassing phrase. That way they're covered when they change their minds...again. More like global ignorance, you ask me. If those so-called scientists knew as much about the weather as we sailors they'd all just shut the hell up and go fishing," chuckled the Admiral as he poured Boxer a glass of eggnog. "It's all about money anyway. We got it…everybody else wants it. Like we're some kind of world welfare store or something."

"Isn't it always?" replied Boxer.

"Here, put a little fuel in that tank. It will brighten the evening."

"No thanks," refused Boxer. "Think I'll go for something a little stronger."

"This will do. Take it," ordered the Admiral. "I tripled the rum content when your mother wasn't looking. Just make sure the kids don't drink any."

"You spiked it again? Why am I not surprised?" laughed Boxer as he accepted the drink. He took a long gulp and his eyes fluttered as the strong white rum-spiked traditional Christmas drink hit his gullet. "Wow," he smiled, "You could use this stuff for jet fuel."

"The way those idiots in Washington keep messing with the fossil fuel industry we just might have to some day."

They both laughed then the Admiral grew serious. "Drink it down and have another. You might need it in a minute. We're going in to have a word with the old man. Apparently there's some serious shit going on. Said, 'he wants to give us a heads up'."

"More defense budget cuts?" speculated Boxer.

"Not likely. The old man and the new administration have a pretty good handle on that now. But who knows? Could be anything where politics is involved," said the Admiral as he finished and refilled his mug of eggnog. "You and I are fortunate men. We live in a simple world where we follow orders. For us it's win or lose, kill or be killed. Those people on the hill, the politicians, their world isn't so clear. They function in a constant fluctuating state of mollified deceit, confusion and ambition. Up there on the hill you can get killed five times a week. I don't know how the old man put up with it so long. You know him, all that shit runs against his nature."

"Don't you think the Senator is way overdue for retirement?" asked Boxer as he strolled along with his father. "Most folks his age are in a home drooling their oatmeal."

"Nah, not the old man. Don't be so quick to put him out to pasture. Not as long as he can spit and shit and thinks there's unfinished business to take care of… which means he'll never retire. Hell, there's always unfinished crap up on the hill. That damn place is like a perpetual motion machine of unfinished business. It's like a pit full of snakes all crawlin' around trying to make up their minds about shit they don't know anything about and stuff they shouldn't be messing with anyway. They call it politics. You ask me it's just a big clusterfuck. I hate it, but unfortunately I have to be more diplomatic now days… one of the drawbacks of rank, unlike the old man." The Admiral took a long swig of his eggnog and continued. "In the worst of circumstances he somehow keeps his cool and maintains a sense of humor while he plows on through it all. Patience… forbearance… that's how he copes with those idiots in government."

"Politicians...sometimes I wonder if maybe that word *idiot* isn't a more adequate description. The word *statesman* doesn't seem to apply very well anymore."

"You know, just once I'd like to see somebody run for office by swearing to never do a damn thing. Sure as hell he'd get my vote," laughed the Admiral. "At least he wouldn't have to lie about doing nothing while in office."

"Then we'd be paying them all for nothing," observed Boxer.

"Doing that anyway aren't we?" replied the Admiral.

"Yeah, well, *you* won't have to worry about the DC dance much longer, Pop," smiled Boxer. "If I remember correctly you have twenty-two days and a wake up. Then it's retirement with sunny days on the bay fishing and early morning easy putts on early morning dew covered greens... eighteen holes a day. But don't you think it's strange, you retiring before your father?"

"Not from my end. Looking forward to it. Some people just aren't made for retirement though. Their work is their life. Like your grandfather. They thrive on the challenge. Have to be busy, productive, challenged. That's what made him a great aviator. He grew up on a farm and doesn't know any different, wouldn't know what to do with his time; especially with your grandmother pressing him to quit. And you know that's one woman you don't disagree with. Gotta hand it to him, he's one tough old bastard."

"But you intend to retire, correct?"

"Oh, hell yeah. I would think thirty years in uniform is enough for anybody, wouldn't you son? Sure I intend to retire. But in between fishing and golf I'll have to listen to your mother bitch because I don't want to tag along on her antique safaris. Good thing you kids have children to create a diversion and keep her occupied," said the Admiral before finishing off his holiday drink with a nice long gulp. "Speaking of grandchildren; what's up with Junior over there?" asked the Admiral, directing his glass in the direction of Boxer's boy, Carson, who had just joined Antwan and the twins by the Christmas tree. "Does that cute little girl over in the Severn School still have his head turned inside out about a media career or has he decided to live in the real world with the rest of us?"

"Hell, who really knows what they want at that age. Well, actually we do know but don't like to think about the consequences. Besides, I hear she broke his heart. Started dating a lacrosse star. He considers it treason because he's all about football and wrestling. He started asking me about the Academy the other day though."

"Well, maybe that's a good sign. I guess he could do worse."

"I don't know. He's talking about the Marine Corps."

"Oh, hell, she really did break his heart didn't she? Maybe even messed up his head a bit. Marines, hell, that's like joining the French Foreign Legion. Definitely a violation of the family tradition," laughed the Admiral. "But then hey, maybe that's not a bad idea. Maybe I'll join him. Marine Corps sounds a lot better than endless antique safaris. I wouldn't worry about him though. He's a good egg and still has a few years to decide."

"Like I said," laughed Boxer, "payback is a bitch. You dragged Mom all over the globe, now it's her turn. Dragging you to antique markets. That's payback."

"It wasn't me. It was the Navy."

"Oh right. Blame it on the Navy. Like you got drafted or Shanghaied for life and had no choice?" said a smiling Boxer. "If you didn't out rank me, Admiral, I'd kick you in the ass for violating that Academy Honor Code that Antwan was slapping me with a little while ago."

The two men, their spiked eggnog glasses in hand, laughed as they strolled into the Senator's library where they found the old man settled back in a leather-bound high-back chair, his feet propped up on his desk. In his hands was a thick folder, the contents of which changed his expression from that of the relaxed elder with a house full of family and holiday cheer to that of the seriously concerned statesman.

"Uh oh, last time I saw that face was when Reagan was shot. This must be serious," the Admiral said softly.

"They were good friends, right?" asked Boxer.

"Yeah, but that's not what bothered him. VP George Bush owed him five hundred bucks from a bet on a college bowl game that they made back when Pop was assigned to the White House as the Navy Attaché. He was afraid Reagan would die and that George would become President before he paid up. Bush was always fair and diplomatic about most everything. Didn't think a President should show favor or a preference when it came to American sports teams or social issues. Thought that it wouldn't look good if it was known he paid on a football bet."

"Doesn't sound like a big deal to me."

"Reagan didn't think so either. He owed the old man five hundred on the same game. So, you see, the Senator could have lost a cool grand as well as a favored president with one shot. It's a point of pride kind of thing. We're a very competitive family in case you haven't noticed."

"Oh, I've definitely noticed," smiled Boxer.

"And it wasn't just the thousand bucks. The old man and Reagan were damn good friends," continued the Admiral. "The President often affectionately referred to him as 'that young Squid who kept him from being all at sea, lost regarding the Navy.' And I think there were some regular poker games in there somewhere also, but the old man would never cop to it. Mom disapproved."

"Young?"

"Yeah, don't forget, Reagan was no spring chicken and back then your grandfather was in his 40's finishing up his navy career. To Reagan everybody under sixty was a kid. Nothing wrong with that as far as I'm concerned. Tell ya the truth; I think we could do well to amend the Constitution to require that no presidential candidate should be less than the social security retirement age. Hopefully, that would guarantee more wisdom and maturity and less bullshit emanating from over there in the big house. Might keep them from continually adding years to the social security retirement age as well. Hell, older execs couldn't do any worse. Seems all these young guys just keep fucking up the works. More ambition than brains ya might say."

"Oh I don't know. Sometimes some of the older ones aren't much better."

"Copy that, my observant young Commander," agreed the Admiral. "But hopefully they wouldn't have the stamina to maintain their idiocy, or once being elected would realize that life is too damn short to fuck it up on a grand scale just for the sake of party politics and political survival."

The Senator glanced up and offered a slight smile to acknowledge their arrival. "You know I can hear what you guys are saying,"

"So, did I get anything wrong?" asked the Admiral.

"Actually, no," replied the Senator. "Accept Bush owed me a cool one-thousand not five hundred." The smile was quickly lost when he looked back to the contents of the leather bound folder. "I see you've spiked the eggnog again," he said without looking back up.

"My duty to the men of the family," declared the Admiral.

"Uh huh. And you've been performing that duty since you were, what, 14 years old?" returned the Senator. "You think I didn't know?"

"I had my suspicions," laughed the Admiral. "Especially since you always drank most of it. I take it that's not *Dicken's Christmas Carol* you're reading there," said the Admiral as he plopped into one of the overstuffed chairs in the room. Boxer leaned back against the built in bookcases on the wall.

"I wish it was," said the Senator with a cursory smile.

"It's the report from the budget and economy wonks. Combine it with the international intel work-ups from the NSA, CIA, and the State Department, especially the crap that's going on in China, and we've got one hell of an economic mess with little or no wiggle room." He looked up as he tossed the folder to the desk, dropped his feet to the floor and leaning forward saying with all sincerity, "Boys, we're in one serious world of shit."

"I know the last administration sold us down the river and left one hell of an international and economic mess, but I thought you said we could eventually recover, that we were on the road to recovery, that the Republicans were at the helm again," observed the Admiral.

"Yes, sir, I thought things were turning around," chimed in Boxer as he took a seat across the room.

"That's true and would pretty much hold true, wouldn't be easy, but would hold true as long as we stay the course, cut the in-fighting, and don't hit any major road blocks such as the one in this intel report from State."

"How bad could it be?" asked Boxer.

His father, the Admiral, turned to Boxer to offer his take on what he thought the Senator was about to reveal. "I'm assuming he's referencing the current Chinese regime having lost power to the Ling Toa group, a bunch of old-school commies that believe China doing business with the rest of the world is bringing down the house and circumventing the chain of power, destroying China's noble heritage. Or should I say, China's communist heritage. Not to mention their ability to control a few billion of their own people who have started to get a taste of liberty with their newfound individual wealth. At least that's what I gather from the recent ticks coming across my desk."

"That's about it," entered the Senator. "Throw on top of that the fact that the Chinese have overspent and overbuilt leaving their economy severely strained and about to tank because of decades of their currency manipulation and we've got a problem. Those old-school bastards are professing a desire to implement a freeze on foreign investments and start calling in their notes to rebuild their cash flow. They hold trillions in U.S. notes and if we can't pay up then the shit's going to hit the fan. Our petty differences over Taiwan, human rights, computer hacking, North Korea, and patent infringements will seem like a sunny day on the beach compared to what might happen. They need cash so they can continue to build their navy and space program; necessary to fulfill their ambitions of complete dominance or control of Asia. They haven't joined the space age and been building world class subs and super carriers for nothing, and they've long since proven they sure as hell aren't shy about throwing a few million bodies at any chosen foe. Therefore, they have no reason to be shy about economic demands. They have spread their chips and influence around the world thanks to WalMart money and the like, and now they may intend to cash in. Or in our case, collect."

"That's insane," observed Boxer. "Our country is their biggest source of income. Why cut it off?"

"That's correct and there are so many business and industrial tie-ins that if you tried to diagram them all it would look like that damn bird nest stadium they built for the Olympics. I wouldn't venture to try and understand the Oriental mind, son," said the Senator. "I saw them throw a half-million soldiers across the border in Korea without so much as a wink or the slightest concern about the loss of life. They've always had population problems. Hell, who's to say they might not just consider a war to be a good thing, a simple solution to thinning out the chicken house sort of speak. Wars have been fought for stranger or lesser reasons and in spite of all the theories and strategy, the outcome of war is a simple concept. The side with the most of everything wins. Think about how much it would take to defeat millions of screaming Chinese souls in uniform pouring into our West Coast. What would those yuppie bastards do, hit 'em with rock and roll tunes and movie deals? How the hell do you think the Russians beat back the Nazis. They had more bodies to sacrifice and they didn't hesitate to do it...by the millions. And thanks to outsourcing - mostly to China I might add - our industrial complex isn't quite what it used to be. This isn't the 1940s when we had the finest industrial base in the world, it's the 21st century. Everything is faster and much of the rest of the world has caught up. Our future industrial work force has been turned into a mass of dull headed movie and rock star wannabes living on government freebies. And many of those left in the labor force have been coddled by corrupt unions. They won't even take a piss without getting paid for it first. Do you think we can adjust quickly enough as a people and a nation to produce enough to support and sustain a full-out war against a military of that size backed by their own natural resources and established manufacturing complex with an unlimited work force? And we sure as hell wouldn't have the time to adjust for it like we did in the 40s. It seems everyone in the world has learned from our past except us."

"Not to mention the big stick," entered the Admiral.

"Big stick?" said Boxer.

"Nukes," clarified the Admiral.

"Not to worry boys, at least not right away. In *that* we still have an advantage...if you can call it that. And the major players like China have had the good sense to practice restraint in that regard. Mutual destruction is not very appealing. Even to the Chinese." The Senator sank back in his chair and took an exhausted pause before he continued. "I'm sure we can negotiate something when it comes to their economic ball and chain. They'll have to realize the folly of calling in all notes at once. In doing that they'll get a lot of nothing and diminish their future earnings, the equivalent of shooting themselves in the foot... or the head. The real problem is that the last administration emasculated this country, cut back defense, bloated the government, devalued the dollar, strangled our energy industry, increased the population of dependant citizens, and left us broke and in debt up to our short and curlies. Not to mention the embarrassment of a truckload of scandals and constitutional violations to be cleaned up and remedied."

"Quite a rosy picture," said Boxer.

"It was amateur night with those guys, a goddamn self-serving circus full of vengeance and ignorance," continued the Senator. "What I'm really worried about is…well… even if we reach an amicable agreement with the Chinese other invested countries and entities will get the word, see the writing on the wall, get antsy and start to cash in their chips as well. It will be an international run on our bank you might say. And who's to say it wouldn't be contagious and cause runs on other free world countries. The world economy is screwed up enough already. The consequences are frightening to say the least. And like I said, we've devalued the dollar and it's going to take time and a lot of faith to bring it back up."

"What about our gold reserves?" asked the Admiral. "I've heard there's a movement to return to the gold standard."

"Not as easy as you might think. Most likely impossible. Gold reserves? All there? Partially depleted? All gone? Who the hell knows? They won't even let God know what's up with that dog. What's there probably isn't enough to back our world-wide debt and circulated currency anyway. Our currency is based on faith and there's not a lot of that going around lately thanks to the last administration. Those idiots at the FED have been printing money and slowly emptying the piggy bank to cover their asses for years. Should have shot those autonomous bastards long ago," the Senator said with disdain. "By the way, that statement isn't for public consumption for obvious reasons. The dems would have a field day with it, even though it's their mess."

"What about the new budget deal? I thought that was going to put us in the black in a few years," asked Boxer.

"It was and it can, but even working as well as it is it will appear to be nothing but smoke and mirrors if there's a panic looming on the horizon. It'll certainly help but our only hope is to cut even more spending and that means serious cuts to the social programs, the so-called *entitlement* programs. We can't cut any off of national defense, just the opposite, and we've already eliminated a great deal of the feel good funding and pork crap. We're closing more than half of our overseas military installations and are eliminating most of our foreign aid outlay which means we'll be losing fair-weather international friends at a rapid rate. Who the hell knows what kind of crap that will stir up and who will move in to fill the void? More like the Russians or some other overly ambitious country like Russia that's eager to fill the vacuum and cash in on some world power? It will be another cold war." The Senator pushed back into his chair and continued, "The only thing left to cut is entitlements which are the worst of the problem anyway. Entitlements – now there's a contradiction in terms for you. Over the years the liberals have convinced the masses that they are entitled to a free lunch, like it's some sort of God given or constitutional right. This suckling from the federal tit has got to stop. It's simple, the math just doesn't work and besides, it simply isn't an element of our national DNA. It's Socialism, clear and simple... Marxism, Communism... call it what you will. It doesn't work and it's wrong."

"Phasing out those programs will sure as hell ruffle some feathers," observed the Admiral. "Millions of them."

"It's more serious than that because I'm not talking about cutting back;" replied the Senator. "I'm talking about cutting some of them altogether. Of course the improving economy due to lowering corporate and individual taxes, and eliminating the choking business and manufacturing regulations compensates us by putting lots of those folks to work. But how long will it take until they realize that, until they actually realize the positive reality of it, I mean? Even most of the dems in congress have finally come around to realize that we have no alternative and with that change of philosophy, they well know, will most likely end their public careers. They'd like you to think they're being honest and noble. Truth is they would rather go out losing an election after doing what's right than appear as though they're jumping ship, which is exactly what they're doing."

"You're painting a pretty bleak picture there gramps," said Boxer.

"We've come together, had every genius in the country work the numbers and the conclusion is always the same; we have to outright eliminate the entitlement programs except for Social Security, which may suffer a temporary cut back or a freeze and probably should be privatized for the younger generations. And Medicare, we'll try to somehow maintain the Medicare program but it's a hell of a mismanaged mess. And after all, the people paid for it and they deserve it. Medicaid, however, another social freebie, is a damn disastrous economic ball and chain that's gotta go or be reinvented, even after wiping out that damn Affordable Care Act fiasco that we inherited from the last administration. Even then, after all that, the national debt will take years to eliminate. We're broke, gentlemen. We've become a pseudo socialist nation of consumers as opposed to producers, a nation with too many spoon-fed parasites dependent on the government which in turn is dependent on what it takes from those that aren't; on what it takes from all those hard working middle class folks in various industries and professions that are hog tied and dying off because of unions, government regulations, and taxes," said the Senator. "Excuse my ranting, boys. I know Christmas isn't the best time for this conversation but it's just that I'm so god damn frustrated."

"That's a dark scenario, indeed. Didn't think it was that bad," said the Admiral as he leaned back in his chair. "I've always focused mainly on the military part of the budget pie. Now cutting the assistance programs - do you realize the social implications of what you're saying, the possible public reaction? A nightmare for sure. A riotous nightmare."

"Of course you didn't think it was that bad, that's because my opposite party colleagues and even some of our own on the hill have been feeding bullshit to the public for so long the people have become numb to the truth or have reached the point to where they can't even recognize it. They invent a crisis that doesn't exist to get elected then create real crisis to keep their inept asses in office. Nearly a century of lies upon lies and wheels within wheels, building a fragile house of cards that is about to crash. For more than half a century it's become a regular cycle. The liberals screw it up and the conservatives from whatever party fix it, except this time I'm afraid all of the Progressives' mess might not be fixable. Even though emergency legislation will be introduced right after the holidays to hopefully head off this possible Chinese mess, it may not be enough. They'll spin it as a fix-all but the new Chinese regime likely won't buy into it mainly because of their short term desires. And if they don't buy into it then the rest of the world won't either and the snowball will begin to roll and grow. And you can't blame them. I mean, it's not like our last president left the world with a lot of faith in our system."

"Are you serious? There's no alternative, no remedy at all? Nothing to be done?" asked Boxer.

"Nothing of consequence in the short term that we can really hang our hats on…short of drastic national fasting. Just bigger and bigger band aids. Except…well, Jean Stephenson, Senator from California, has come up with something. Says she's been talking to big corporate money people in the private sector, wheeling and dealing to get them to form a coalition or consortium of sorts to buy up most or all of our national debt, consolidate it in

American hands to keep it in house and within our boarders, sort of speak, until we can crawl out from under this mess."

"I wouldn't think there'd be enough private money available to pull off something like that," observed Boxer. "It would be an unimaginable amount."

"Well they keep printing it so the shit's gotta be out there somewhere. It sure as hell isn't on Main Street. I can't pretend to understand it all. And who's to say the currency of the deal will be in the form of money anyway? Those kinds of people don't always deal in currency but in value concepts and futures and market controls and who the hell knows what? It's another world and to be honest it gives me the creeps. I've always known there were controlling forces beyond that of governments and nations, but I suppose like everyone else I was arrogant enough to believe that at least the U.S. was in control of its own destiny. But like your grandmother used to say; quoting Jesus Christ, *'Beware the money changers.'*

Jean Stephenson is a financial genius, a corporate lawyer and all that, and she seems to know the principle characters that can make it happen. I believe that with bipartisan backing she might pull it off on the political end. Hell, any republican who can get herself elected to the senate from California must have their shit wrapped pretty tight; at least enough to pull off something like that. Not that California is a prime example of fiscal responsibility. They're a failed state bigger than most countries, a bankrupt state that can't seem to get out of its own way. My concern, however, is that we would still be in debt, but in debt to who, and more importantly, in debt with what obligations. A country managed by some damn shadow government corporate board of directors with back room unofficial veto power over Congress? Hardly constitutional and it could end up being some sort of nightmarish Faustian deal. And regardless of her success, which may actually stabilize the debt situation, it won't remedy the immediate spending problem. We still need to cut back if for no other reason than to pay off the debt. That means nearly eliminating or drastically shrinking bloated, and I might add, bothersome megalithic entities such as the predatory Environmental Protection Agency and the Department of Education and others. Radically scaling down the Departments of Agriculture, Energy, NASA, the IRS and eliminating a dozen worthless other bureaucracies altogether. To be honest, I think that would make a lot of people across the country quite happy, me included. Everybody except the damn Service Employees International Union that is. Believe me, I won't lose any sleep over sticking that damn bunch in the ass. The biggest screw up JFK ever made was allowing the existence of unions in the government. The entire damn country has been going downhill ever since. Can you imagine; an *international* union calling the shots and making demands in the government work place – in *our* government? Could there be anything more idiotic or threatening to our national security? Anything? Yet that's what we have. Those bastards gotta go."

"You've been trying to rid the government of unions for years," said the Admiral. "A lone voice in the wilderness."

"That's right. And it damn near cost me a few elections. They tend to play real dirty, those unions. Even had my life threatened a few times."

"There's no doubt. If you want to cut spending, you're going to have to wipe out the unions. You remember the mess some of the states went through with that. That'll be one hell of a nasty fight, Pop, and I have to ask - are you up to it?"

"I've been there before. There's legislation in the works, but now isn't the time to introduce it. Maybe after things settle down a bit. Government can be a nasty business. Hell, if they don't like it the most they can do is bump me off," laughed the Senator as he rose slowly from his comfortable chair. "And I've got one foot in the grave already so bring it on. Then you boys can just box my ass and ship me back to ol' PA. And after you've done that know that it wouldn't hurt my feelings one bit if you happened to have a loan of a couple F-14s and blow the shit out of the SEIU HQ."

As the three generations of Bernhardt men exited the study the old Senator quickly restored and maintained his holiday face for the benefit of the rest of the family, but on more than one occasion during the evening Boxer noticed the elder Senator briefly looking with concern to the children and he knew what was on his mind - an uncertain future with an uncertain outcome.

THE PENTAGON – DEC. 23, 2018

Army Captain Beverly Qualin was pissed off. She had been forced to cancel her Christmas leave because, as the General had informed her, she was the only one capable of completing the task in time for its inclusion in the Status of Arms Report. Punching computers at the Pentagon was the last thing in the world Qualin wanted to do with her career when she entered the military academy at West Point. She wanted to fly and she wanted to fly the biggest birds in the Army arsenal, but soon after graduating West Point and entering the flight training program they discovered she had developed a depth perception problem which ended her dream altogether. From there, with the help of a family friend with connections and in spite of her eye problem, she got into the airborne infantry program. Surprisingly, having successfully completed jump school they snatched her up and assigned her to the Pentagon. *Four years at the Academy and all the pain of jump school and now here I am sitting on my ass,* she would think nearly each and every day.

Office bound as she has been for the past five months, pulling and compiling data for this report or that, putting together briefing material that amounted to nothing more than scripts for the General for his dog and pony shows and appearances in front of just about every committee and every other elected bonehead in Washington. Reports and stats that she knew were only being read and maybe digested by congressional staffers. Reports with information most likely condensed by those same staffers to a sixth grade level for quick easy perusal by their elected idiot bosses, and then eventually manipulated to fit some political agenda. This was known as *gisting*, a necessary condensation function in some areas of government but mostly done just to save elected officials time and mental effort, if not mental anguish, leaving them time for fundraising, socializing, traveling or just bullshitting in front of the media. Such gisting, she thought, taught the elected species just enough to be dangerous and to give the appearance at opportune times that they actually knew what the hell they were talking about.

Captain Qualin was always amazed at the transition of language in Washington and how the most simple of concepts could somehow become the most complicated incomprehensive government babbling, and in a like manner how the most important complicated issues could be misrepresented by being condensed to a ridiculously simple blurb or catch phrase sound bite. Most likely, she thought, to cover up the fact that most of the elected layman and bullshit artist on the hill didn't understand the language or couldn't begin to comprehend it.

Qualin was a quick study and it didn't take long for her to figure out the chain of information flow and evolution of the facts and figures on the Capitol scene because she was present at most of the General's meetings. But in fact, all it actually took was a few weeks of dating a senate staffer, a political gister by profession, who found it necessary to run his mouth in order to impress her about pretty much everything he and his fellow workers did. All she did was ask for the sake of small talk during their dates and out would flow a cornucopia of information. She started to feel like she should be working for the CIA instead of the DOD because it was so easy to glean information from him. She dated one other man after that who turned out to be another boastful soft-handed self-serving ambitious namedropping Ivy League overachiever. *Are they all like this,* she thought. After that she decided that dating in DC was about as exciting as eating a heart healthy diet. The alternative was dating within the Pentagon, which was out of the question for any number of reasons, but mostly because she preferred the type of kick-ass fellow Airborne head cases she met at jump school. They were cut and dry and you pretty much always knew where you stood with them. There were no games. They wore their hearts and ambitions on their sleeves.

The Pentagon crowd, however, were different animals altogether that seemed to be always walking on eggs. To Captain Qualin, even though she was a woman, she felt she would be safer in the more physically dangerous world of combat than the swamp that was Washington. She recalled someone once telling her that before this town came to be, it was a lowland swamp known as

Foggy Bottom. *Yeah,* a *rose by any other name,* she thought to herself.

The Army knew she was an academic achiever and computer whiz. She, in fact, led all of her classmates in all of the high-tech and cyber war courses. She was a natural and easily sailed through every computer course the Academy threw at her, so the Army wasted no time in diverting her and her skills to where they thought she would do the most good. In fact, she excelled in most all things at West Point and comfortably placed in the top five percent of her graduating class. But the staff job she had now she hated for a number of reasons. First, it was tedious, reminding her of when she used to do inventory at the Walmart big box store during that year between high school and when she entered the Academy, the year she decided to become a career officer and pilot. Another reason was that she thought she had been betrayed after having been given the hope that she might have another shot at flight school after successfully correcting her vision problem with laser eye surgery.

At the Pentagon they assigned her to the Army Chief of Staff and told her it was a real opportunity for advancement, a job anyone would give their eye teeth to get. Captain Beverly Qualin wasn't shy. She thought the great opportunity line was a crock of shit and said as much, claiming she had been chosen simply because she was a looker with nice legs, and that she fully expected she would be defending her ass and supposed virtue at every turn from the advances of a bunch of intimidating higher-ups.

Upon arrival at the Pentagon when the General asked her how she felt about the assignment, Qualin did as she had always done and spoke her mind. "It sucks, sir," she told the General. "I'm a soldier, not a damn coffee gopher or secretary."

The General laughed, telling her that he had enough gophers and that secretaries were a dime a dozen. Instead, he wanted a dependable confidant individual, preferably one who could kick ass and take names, and that she fit the bill, reminding her of her martial arts black belt and an incident at West Point when she broke the nose and two ribs of an upper classman who tried to molest her. He then told her that if she kept her shit together and stuck with it through his tenure as Army Chief of Staff she would emerge with rank and a transfer to the job of her choice which could include flight school.

"Do I have a choice now?" she asked of the General.

"Of course," he laughed. "You have the choice to shut the hell up and do your job or get shot."

She was impressed by his humor and familiarity with her past, and from that point on a mutual respect for each other's frankness proved they got along just fine. Captain Qualin functioned as his Special Duties and Projects Coordinator, which involved mostly researching and preparing confidential reports and planning road shows, a Major's slot for which she would be promoted as soon as she was eligible.

Captain Qualin's boss, Army Chief of Staff, General H. Conrad Lewis, was what some people referred to as a self-made man, which in military terms means he wasn't connected. He began as an enlisted man serving in Special Ops when he gained the attention of the higher-ups who suggested he attend Officer Candidate School. To their surprise, he made it known he would prefer to attend the Military Academy at West Point and he got his wish. His career was meteoric, with distinguishing service in various covert operations and leadership with command roles in both Iraq and Afghanistan. His climb in the ranks also included touching all the bases with studies at Harvard and successful stints at the military command schools and the War College. In addition, he had a flare for politics and was often called on to smooth over hot issues during hearings on Capitol Hill. Now, as a senior officer, he ruled the Army roost and many say he is one of the best ever to hold the position. He was also the only member of the Joint Chiefs to be held over from the last administration.

General H. Conrad Lewis was the product of a mixed marriage between a white immigrant British oil executive father and an African American dancer mother. His father, killed in an auto accident when the General was very young, left him to struggle with his identity while his mother, a beautiful, educated, and sophisticated but emotionally frail woman, sank into depression after the accident, forgoing her promising career in ballet. For the most part, the fatherless young Lewis was on his own but still managed to be an achiever in all things leading to an obviously successful future. All things, that is, except social acceptance, or at least that's what he was told by a black activist minister named Jamison Johnson who, for a time, had an extra marital affair with Lewis's mother. Johnson stayed in touch with Conrad Lewis because the boy needed a father figure in his life, and because he was cultivating a promising young man for future purposes.

General Lewis gave his staff two days off for Christmas, which included Captain Qualin. To compensate for the short holiday most all of the staff finished their work and cut out early. Qualin however, was facing a lot more work after the two-day break and wanted to get as much of it done as possible before leaving. She wanted to at least get the mass of needed stats downloaded and ready for compilation upon her return to the office. Not that losing that half day really mattered. She was pretty much a loner and her folks lived in Texas so she had no time or plans to visit them. Her Christmas would consist of a few phone calls to friends and family, a microwavable holiday meal and probably a newly released movie at a multi-cinema.

She sat alone in the office and popped away at her computer keyboard with an occasional smile as she remembered taking a digital phone photo of her Charlie Brown Christmas tree. It was nothing more than a single evergreen branch decorated with a single red bulb that she and her roommate had set up on the dining table in their townhouse apartment. Her roommate, a data processor at the Department of Energy, was out of town for the holidays but left one small gift sitting under the tree and made Beverly Qualin promise not to open it until Christmas morning. Qualin had sent the photo to her mother, a symbol of her lonely uneventful holiday. She smiled because her mother in turn circulated the photo by way of social media and e-mail, showing all of her friends how her poor little girl was sacrificing her holiday on behalf of the country. Qualin thought it embarrassing, but tolerated such things simply to please her mother.

It was during these thoughts the info she was to compile for the General started rolling in from the Pentagon mainframe. There were great lists of armaments and personnel strengths from American military installations all around the country and the world. Her job would be to compare this data on file at the Pentagon with that she had received from the various military facilities to find discrepancies and determine the final numbers for the report. A daunting task for which she only had a week after Christmas.

Walmart, she thought to herself, *I'm back in goddamn Walmart.*

Glancing at the material as it printed she noticed that much of the information was not only that which she had requested through the authority of the Army Chief of Staff, but also included was similar info from Air Force and Navy installations as well. She thought it odd, then thought that perhaps someone ordered the additional information to be included for a more substantial inter-service report of which she hadn't been informed. She stored it along with that of the Army data, dismissing it with the intention to follow up after the holiday.

After the downloads were complete she put the printed copies in the safe and then took up her coat and hat, flipped off the lights, made the long walk through the halls of the Pentagon, and headed into the cold crisp December dusk. Driving away, heading for her townhouse apartment in Arlington, she once again thought of the excess of information that inadvertently downloaded to her computer. *Boys keeping track of their toys,* she thought. Then her train of thought was quickly and easily diverted when she noticed large heavy snowflakes beginning to hit the windshield of her car. She liked the snow, not having experienced much of it until she attended the Academy at West Point. *It was special,* she thought, *one of the miracles of our planet.* She especially liked the way it muffled sounds and made everything white and clean. Though cold and crisp, it somehow made her feel emotionally warm and peaceful. She smiled, anticipating a beautiful white Christmas.

CHAPTER 3 _____

Senator Jean Stephenson sat impatiently in an uncomfortable intricately hand carved chair, one of only three in the large empty 16th century ballroom. The sound of each of her movements carried and echoed throughout the room, be it a slight crick from the old chair or just the setting down of her briefcase on the marble floor. The room was enormous, making her feel as though she was sitting in an empty coliseum, feeling like the only fan that showed up for an NBA game on the wrong night.

Geneva? she thought. *Why the hell Geneva? Why not Jackson Hole, Wyoming, as she had originally suggested?*

She looked to the ceiling, 20 or 25 feet high, a masterpiece of imagination and artisanship depicting some historic Swiss event of which she couldn't begin to imagine where or when it took place. It reminded her of one of those incredibly difficult jigsaw puzzles that she and her late father used to do on long winter nights. It seemed the puzzles always took forever, nearly impossible to complete. She would often want to give up, preferring to do something else or be somewhere else, but her father refused to let her. "Your efforts are best appreciated only if you complete the task," he would tell her. It was a lesson well taken.

Sitting, staring up, it crossed her mind that one could spend endless hours just studying the ball room ceiling and endless days pouring over the details of the rest of the room with its intricately carved gilded trim and large framed art that included dozens of large portraits and landscapes. She had already spent a day piddling away the hours in a hotel where she stood looking out over Lake Geneva to the mountains beyond while waiting for the call. Sure, it was beautiful and perhaps someday she would vacation here and take in all the sights, but just now she was not a tourist and she was impatient, not being one to waste time for any reason.

Her interest kept returning to the large portrait in front of her of a man on a horse with a raised sword. It just didn't work, she thought, at least not to her American eye, not to the judgment of a western girl who knew horses and the real men who rode them. The man in the portrait seemed too effeminate, too fragile to wield a sword on or off a horse.

Probably just another inbred royal wimp posing for self-satisfaction, she thought. *A portrait to perpetuate a false image as has been done over the centuries by countless royals.*

Jean Stephenson was a practical farm girl, the product of the reality of working the land with a lineage that went back to the struggles of her stubborn Oklahoma Boomer family of the 19th century. People who were eventually forced to relocate during the drought of the great depression and to start a new life in the California Valley. She wasn't big on European history but had read enough to know Geneva originated with the Celts and that guy on a horse didn't look much like any Celt. She pictured Celts as long tall muscular blondes, Viking types who didn't take any crap from anyone, the rugged cowboys of their day.

Wasn't there some American Midwestern Scandinavian or Celt or something in her family tree on her mother's side? She seemed to remember someone mentioning it. Did they even ride horses, she wondered.

And then, there were the Romans and the French and who the heck knows who else ruled this place at one time or another.

Yeah, she thought, *the wimpy guy on the horse had to be French. Maybe he should be riding a wooly haired sheep.*

She had been sitting there now for nearly a half hour. A U.S. Senator kept waiting that long; hardly indicative of the Swiss. *But then she wasn't supposed to be meeting with the Swiss and it was her meeting*, she thought, *her call, until that is, when someone circumvented the agenda. But who had the clout to do so? And why the hell am I sitting out here waiting for them?*

She looked down at her watch, then to the floor to discover that even the intricately inlayed marble floor could pass as the detailed work of some famous past master. She wondered how difficult it would be to frame and hang such a floor if there were even a wall large enough to hold it. She began to imagine what it would take to build such a wall. Jean Stephenson's mind often worked that way, always exploring the possibilities, creating challenges in her mind and solving them. There were no limits, no tasks too big, too daunting, or too challenging to put her off. That's how she ended up in the U.S. Senate in the first place. The ballsiest senator on the hill is how she was often referred by her colleagues. A reputation that stemmed from her incessant will, western earthy character, and her track record.

Senator Stephenson hated the political dancing involved with every issue and every piece of legislature that came down the pike. *"Just do it or screw it,"* she would often say to her colleagues in the Senate. *"Stop blowing sunshine up my ass, cut all the hypothetical bullshit, government double-speak and self-serving crap, and just get the job done."* She rubbed most everyone, especially the opposition, the wrong way and for the most part they ignored her until the republicans took over the majority in the last election. After that they had to live with her forceful common sense approach to government, especially after Majority Leader Jesse Bernhardt took over the senate. He recognized her talents and ability to get things done and gave her much more responsibility and influence. She headed up committees and was pivotal in cleaning up much of the mess made by the last administration and a senate that was ruled like a dictatorship by its former Progressive leader from Nevada. She was doing it as methodically as a high-speed snowplow, all the while giving her fellow senators the choice to hitch a ride and be a part of the solution or just get the hell out of the way.

Prior to her political life, Jean Stephenson was a practicing corporate lawyer of humble beginnings, coming from an agricultural community. Early in her legal career she gained a reputation for negotiating very successful and lucrative corporate and international contracts and agreements. She did it in countries and with people and organizations that had usually been considered impossible to deal with. As a result, she made billions for corporations both old and new and millions for herself and the law firm she created. Then one day an old childhood friend appeared with an appeal for help.

She and Ramone Pena had grown up on neighboring farms in the Central Valley of California. As children, they attended school together, played together, swam together, and worked together on their families' farms. She often thought of him as the brother she always wanted but didn't have. It was Ramone who planned to become a lawyer until an auto accident that nearly killed two people and a charge of drunk driving put him in a courtroom. The judge gave him an option to join the military or suffer the consequences of severe punishment. Jean Stephenson was also in the car and told the court that, yes; they had been drinking but that the accident was the fault of the other driver in the oncoming vehicle that had swerved across the road into their lane. She was telling the truth and others had witnessed and testified the same thing, but the occupants of the other car had money and influence, political influence, and high priced legal representation - and they lied. Angered by the injustice she had seen, Stephenson decided to take on Ramone's dream of becoming a lawyer. She went off to college and law school while Ramone went off to war in the Middle East, resulting in the loss of a leg in combat.

And so he had come to stand in her Sacramento office years later with a request for help and a story of government lunacy that was killing their valley. The government, he told her, had cut off the water diverted from the San Joaquin that supplied the farms of the valley. The valley known as the most fertile and productive in the country and was the source of a quarter of the nation's fruits and vegetables. It was already suffering from three years of drought and an economic recession, and without the water it was fast turning into a dry wasteland. Millions of acres of orchards and farmland were dying and no crops could be grown resulting in a loss of billions of dollars and 50,000 jobs. It seemed the government, in the form of the Environmental Protection Agency, claimed to have done this simply to save a small obscure three-inch long fish known as the Delta Smelt. They had determined it was an endangered species, threatened because it only existed in the main river water source that ran through the center of the valley. They claimed the diversion of water from the river was killing off the fish, but their ruling resulted in the loss of water to the valley and was destroying the land and the livelihood of thousands of people, not to mention eliminating many millions of dollars in commerce.

Jean Stephenson took on the case, implementing every legal means possible to get the pumps turned back on. After nearly two full years, and in spite of having the backing of the farmers, the public, and the fast gaining backing of the entire nation thanks to national media coverage, she continued to lose to the EPA at every turn. The agency seemed to be immune to the law and completely ignored the will and needs of the people, often even ignoring the rulings of the courts. She simply could not resolve the situation even after many appeals to Congress and the President. At wits end, Stephenson, along with lifelong friend Ramone, fellow farmers, the mayors of the valley towns, and friends of the cause, defied all government orders and took matters into their own hands. They challenged the Governor of California to a meeting at the site of the pumps that had been shut down in hopes of finally settling the matter.

Stephenson had brought in the media and upon the Governor's arrival, challenged him to support his state, his people, the farmers of the devastated valley, and to restore the economy by defying the EPA and turning on the pumps. When he refused, saying it was a federal matter and he didn't have the authority, she decided to do it herself. In front of the entire world, she ripped off the seals, opened the valves and the water began to flow. The action gained her great popularity among the voters but resulted in her arrest and disbarment. Eventually, however, her right to practice law was restored when many of the most powerful lawyers in the country came to her aid and took up her cause. Like her decision to take up law at the sight of injustice, Jean Stephenson then decided to take on the bureaucracies that had become more powerful than the people they were created to serve.

She did this not in the courtroom but by getting elected to the U.S. Senate.

Two huge doors at the end of the cavernous ballroom in Geneva opened and a well-dressed man emerged, stood at attention and motioned for her to enter.

"It's about damn time," she whispered to herself as she collected her purse and briefcase, rose from the chair, and started across the large empty room, each step echoing throughout, making the great hall seem even larger. As she passed through the doorway into another large room she failed to offer a smile or even recognition to the man who called her in. *She wasn't there to make friends*, she reminded herself, *she was there to pitch a deal, perhaps one of the biggest financial deals in history.*

When she saw the faces of the six people sitting around the conference table she immediately understood why she was in Geneva and she didn't like it one damn bit. More importantly, included in the group was an individual she would rather run over with a tractor than conduct, or even so much as discuss business - any kind of business. Having her druthers, she wouldn't so much as negotiate the financial future of a chicken farm with the man, much less the financial future of her country.

Dammit, she thought, *I should have known. Dammit to hell!*

CHAPTER 4 _____

DULLES INTERNATIONAL AIRPORT, - JAN. 7, 2019

Those bastards blindsided me, thought Senator Jean Stephenson as she finished off her bloody Mary. *Why didn't I see it coming? Dammit, I should have known the minute they changed the location of the meeting.*

They claimed they wanted to avoid the prying eyes of the media, which was why she chose to make the trip alone. Alone without any staff, no one was likely to think of her departure as anything other than one of her many rendezvous with her husband, a commercial airline pilot.

The passenger jetliner cleared the Virginia hills at Washington Dulles International then lined up and descended to the runway. The pilot exhaled just as the heavy aircraft's wheels screeched and smoked on contact with the thick concrete tarmac. Dulles was not a favorite destination for some pilots because of the difficult approach. The airport sat outside the Washington beltway in a broad Virginia valley surrounded by high hills that had to be avoided and negotiated, leaving little time or distance for an average long comfortable approach. Senator Stephenson, sitting in first class, knew this as well because her husband was a pilot and often complained about having to fly into Dulles, although he did prefer it to flying into Reagan National on the shores of the Potomac. The Dulles approach didn't bother her that much, however, because she subscribed to the theory that, like her, few if any pilots were eager to die and therefore did their damn best to fly safely. The rest, she often said, was simple fate and she and more than 23 million other passengers flew in and out of Dulles International each year, concerned only with the unhappy thought and displeasure of being charged for their luggage, squeezed into obscenely narrow uncomfortable seats, and arriving on time.

Jean Stephenson wasn't concerned about seat size however, simply because on this trip, like most others, she upgraded to the wide seat comfort of first class. Upgrading was supposed to be a no-no for government employees, even senators, but given the fact she usually declined the option of using more expensive private government aircraft, especially when on the business of the Senate, her choice of first class accommodations saved a good bit of the tax payer's money, something of which too many of her colleagues in the senate were rarely concerned. On many occasions she flew for free when she used the airline for which her husband flew. She kept that to a minimum however, not wanting to appear as though she were receiving preferred treatment because she was a senator. Then again, the entire concept of saving a few dollars as a servant of the people was sometimes laughable considering how her colleagues thought nothing of spending billions of taxpayer money at the drop of a hat.

As the aircraft taxied across the tarmac, Senator Stephenson sat stewing in anger, silently reviewing over and over in her mind the exploratory meeting in Geneva, angry because she knew the individuals with whom she met were indeed probably the only people in the world who could bring off the deal she had proposed. They weren't all Americans and as such didn't represent an exclusive collection of U.S. financial institutions as she had desired. She concluded, however, it was better to see the real face of the beast now than to pretend all the money involved would have actually been domestic in the first place. It was the way of the world, the way the big money and big money power existed. Money in motion, all intertwined, melded together with a single purpose – to make more money. Be it the Euro, the Pound, the Dollar, the Japanese Yen, or the Chinese Renminbi, it was all the same and passed through the same hands. She recalled a quote by Thomas Jefferson that she had used as the subject title of one of her college term papers that dealt with international trade; *"A merchant has no country,"* said Jefferson. *"The mere spot they stand on does not constitute so strong an attachment as that from which they draw their gains."* Only her favorite founding father such as Jefferson could say or imply so much with so few words such as *"A merchant has no country."* To her Jefferson was a rock star, his success clearly derived from an exceptionally logical mind and uncanny understanding of the human psyche. Jefferson's declaration concerning merchants was a simple fact, she thought, as well as a prediction of things to come, and just as likely… it could have been a warning.

Senator Stephenson was well aware of who those people at the Geneva meeting were. She had dealt with some of them before and had studied their histories, which was extensive, going back to the days of the Roman Empire. They were the *merchant bankers* of the world, the descendants of the founders of today's banking systems and standards, though today there are institutions often referred to as Merchant Banks they are not the same thing and in fact are derivatives of the truly powerful original Merchant Bankers, many of whom still exist. A few of their names are familiar such as Rothschild and Barings. They are truly the movers and shakers of the world, underwriting, financing, and facilitating massive business and financial deals around the planet. In the past, they have financed kings and kingdoms, wars and postwar reconstruction. In fact, it was the merchant banker Barings teamed with Hope & Co. that facilitated the Louisiana Purchase in 1803 that doubled the size of the United States. They profited and shaped the way the world did business millennia before the high tech communications and computers of today, and some might say, more efficiently. Any individual who knows and understands the existence of the merchant bankers knows then the true meaning of the phrase, *new world order*, but has to question if it is indeed new.

Even today, there isn't a corner of the world for which they don't have full access and influence. A single merchant banker or member of a merchant banking family may sit behind a small desk in a small office in London with nothing but his knowledge, his memory, and a single telephone, and from there trade, finance, insure, or simply guarantee deals involving billions of dollars in a single day. Stories abound about merchant bankers who, with only a single communiqué, secured safe passage of valuable cargo laden ships through dangerous war torn areas of oceans, and with a single request to warring factions prevented the destruction of a particular city or landmark structure. There were stories of merchant bankers that bailed out kings and financed entire countries. Such legends and stories were abundant.

Jean Stephenson sat back comfortably as the plane taxied to the terminal, comfortable but still fuming about the meeting. She recalled having once flown to London to meet with one such merchant banker. A call came in just as she sat in front of his desk. He apologized profusely for having to take the call, explaining it was a time sensitive matter that had just come to his attention. It seemed a well known world-wide shipping magnet had two ships sitting idle in Hong Kong loaded with a half billion dollars of cargo. The ships were held up due to their cargo being under-insured and the complications of the insurance writer dealing with the individuals concerned would hold the ships up for three days. The catch was that if the ships didn't depart that day and deliver the cargo on time, they would miss picking up an even more valuable cargo at their port of destination, representing hundreds of millions of dollars in lost revenue not to mention a late delivery penalty and a loss of credibility of the shipping line. The merchant banker, somehow having already committed to memory the complete financial status and rating of the shipping tycoon and the exact tonnage and value of all of his ships and cargos in question, without hesitation guaranteed him that the ships would depart Hong Kong that very same day. He achieved this with a single phone call to the concerned party in Hong Kong, stating that he would guarantee the cargo and the ships, and he would very much appreciate their immediate release. No papers, no lawyers, no contracts ever crossed any desk. The merchant banker's name was all that was needed and his word was his collateral. It was that simple. The merchant banker's profit end was a set percentage of the amount of the guarantee.

This particular family member of that particular merchant Bank was responsible for his own part of the world, which was why Jean Stephenson was there, to facilitate a major project. She liked to deal with people face to face much like her father the western farmer. After all, this was a multi-billion dollar arrangement. She felt dealing in person gave her an edge, a chance to look into people's eyes and get a feel for their character and decide if they could be trusted and to demonstrate that she was a party of trust as well. On this occasion however, the merchant banker surprised her. He offered her a choice of tea or wine, came from behind his desk to sit next to her and questioned with all sincerity why she had bothered to fly halfway around the world to meet with him. She explained that as the mediator of the deal and legal representative of the parties involved, she thought the personal visit was only fitting, especially since they were dealing with the financing of a very large, extensive and expensive project in a developing Asian country. He explained he was quite familiar with every aspect of the project and the principal parties involved and in fact even knew everything there was to know about her as well. He then smiled and said he would approve and back the project. "After all, it's only the building of an international airport." he said in a manner of reserve typical to an Englishman in a classic dark pinstripe suit.

Such was the credibility, power, and resources of the merchant bankers, thought Senator Stephenson. With a simple handshake or a phone call they somehow ruled the financial world. But certainly all was not always roses in that world, not so considering there was a bad apple who had somehow managed to insert himself into the mix. She had gotten the impression that others who attended the meeting felt the same way but somehow managed to overlook or tolerate his presence as they looked at the potential profits of the deal. His name was Arisztid Bakos and he seemed to be a little too chummy with John Latham who along with Senator Stephenson was the American architect of the effort to secure and consolidate the U.S. debt. She had dealt with Latham on other occasions throughout her career and was more than impressed by his acumen for structuring and making deals. In fact, she thought of him as a damn genius when it came to the art of creative international financing which is why she brought him in on the deal in the first place and, until this very moment had complete faith in him.

With a little thought she quickly understood the necessity of involving merchant bankers, but what the hell was he doing bringing in Arisztid Bakos? With that man involved, she suddenly felt like she was walking into a spider web and didn't like it one damn bit.

Her usually pleasant face now carried a scowl, adding a few years to her appearance. This was not something she welcomed as she was facing her upcoming 55th birthday. Realizing she was no longer a spring chicken was something she dealt with maturely and even humorously at times, but she also realized that some of that aging process was a direct result of her existence and position in the government where there were always unwanted surprises and complications at every turn, a never-ending roller coaster ride requiring a maximum of tolerance and caution just to get through the day. *At least I haven't sunk to coloring my hair,* she would say to herself each morning. *Not yet, anyway.*

Arisztid Bakos was a Hungarian born American citizen and one of the richest men in the world. He began his career working with a merchant banker and showed exceptional promise, but having learned most all he could from them he spun off on his own. Known to some as a sainted philanthropist and to others as an international financial pirate, who bought, sold, and manipulated currency on the FOREX (foreign exchange) and anything else that would turn a profit, Arisztid Bakos was a driven individual with very definite ideas of what the world should be. As an individual, he was personally worth trillions of dollars but as a financier with various joint interests, he controlled funds mounting well in the multi-trillions.

Jean Stephenson had no problem with anyone who could accumulate wealth but understood that what a person does with that wealth and influence is something else altogether. Bakos had more than once been accused of manipulating markets and entire national economies to generate massive profits on the FOREX. However, in the process of his business fun and games on the FOREX and elsewhere, he often mixed in political and social agendas. He claimed to desire his own kind of new world order with open borders and an open society where everyone could participate in government and free enterprise equally. Not an uncommon desire in many camps around the planet except he wanted to achieve this in all countries even at the expense of the rest of the world.

Though he often spoke of a one world currency, he privately professed to prefer that each nation maintain its own currency. This, thought Jean Stephenson, was the hitch in his giddy up. Different currencies meant he could still manipulate economies for fun and profit. To Senator Stephenson, Bakos was just another power hungry control freak and in fact, based on his often-stated dislike for the United States and its influence around the world, she flat out considered him to be a traitor in every sense of the word. Especially after watching him encourage and support progressive socialism within the American political system. This he did through his many NGOs and indirect multilevel financial schemes to support progressive goals. She once explored the idea of bringing him up on charges, arguing to anyone who would listen that there is a point where freedom of speech and its related actions cross the line and become treasonous and threaten our existence under the constitution. Especially when supported with his kind of resources.

Jean Stephenson had never thought of John Latham in political terms. They never even discussed politics. He was just damn good at what he did and that was good enough for her. Now she had to question his motives and actions, especially since it involved Arisztid Bakos. Had he been bought by Bakos? What were they up to? Could Bakos be so gutsy as to outwardly attempt to control the federal government's monetary system or was he inserting himself into the mix along with his well-known far left, new world order agenda in order to kill or poison the deal and weaken the U.S. economy?

She had cornered Latham after the meeting in Geneva and more than let him know of her displeasure. She threatened to pull him out of the deal altogether. After all, she told him, she brought him in and she could and probably would take him out. He said little or nothing in his own defense, offering only a confident, if not arrogant smile. She informed him she would discover whose agenda for which he was aligned and if they were in fact trying to derail the deal. She declared, "When I'm done with you, you'll be lucky to get a job making change at a burger joint." She stomped out, decided she couldn't move the deal forward without finding out what Latham and Bakos were up to and knew just who to call to start the ball rolling.

The aircraft came to a stop, attached to the jet way, and the door opened. Passengers were streaming out, first class first and then the coach passengers from the rear of the plane waiting to move past her. She remained in her first class seat as she often did, waiting for the aircraft to empty of passengers.

"Senator Stephenson, do you need some assistance?" said the pleasant voice of a man.

She glanced up, first noticing the warm smile. She recognized him as the man who had been sitting across the aisle from her. They had exchanged a few pleasantries, nothing extensive. "Oh, I'm fine. Thank you. Not in a big hurry."

"Can I offer you a ride," ask the man. "I have a limo waiting."

"That's very kind, but someone is meeting me. Thank you all the same," she replied with a courteous smile. It was then she noticed the man more closely. He was tall, well dressed, in his late thirties and had incredibly bright piercing blue eyes.

"Well then, you have a nice weekend, Senator," he said, extending his hand.

She accepted, shook his hand and nodded with a smile, "Thank you. And you as well," she replied.

He tucked his brief case and small travel bag in front of him and moved forward.

Senator Stephenson pulled her cell phone out of her bag and hit the speed dial. Her call went through and after the first ring she put the phone to her ear. She then looked up just in time to see the man looking back at her as he turned to exit the plane. He paused, smiled, and nodded, seeming to be waiting for some response. At that time it dawned on her that she had never introduced herself and found it curious that he knew who she was. Suddenly she felt a strange sensation in her hand, warm then hot, then it moved quickly up her arm and became a striking, jolting pain. She dropped the phone as the pain shot quickly to her chest… and heart.

In a matter of seconds, Senator Jean Stephenson fell dead into the aisle.

The man's smile faded as he quickly exited the plane.

Over the excitement of the passengers and voices of the plane's crew who were trying to revive her, no one heard the distant little voice from the small speaker of her cell phone that had fallen under the seat. "White House switchboard. How may I direct your call?" said the voice. "Hello, hello. White House switchboard…"

The man with the piercing blue eyes looked about cautiously as he walked from the airport and entered a waiting limousine. Immediately after the door was closed he opened his brief case, pulled out a pair of tweezers and used them to carefully remove a skin colored patch from the palm of his hand, the patch containing the very lethal topical poison that just took the life of Senator Jean Stephenson. He placed the patch in a small plastic Ziploc bag then put the bag in the case. Next he pulled out a cell phone, punched up a speed dial number and when the call was answered, said simply, "It's done."

CHAPTER 5

NEW ORLEANS, LOUISIANA – JAN. 7, 2019

"No, I won't supply arms. It has to be organic. It has to be natural and spontaneous in appearance as well as fact," insisted the elderly man with the strange accent. "I assure you this will not be a problem," he continued. The old man's eyes were unchanging and piercing, his words full of finality. Having to explain this irritated him. He obviously was not accustomed to being questioned or challenged.

Farin Dupré was growing angry. He wasn't as confident as the old man and was adamant about having a backup plan that included weapons and personnel. He was also uncomfortable with the two very large armed security guards in the room; well-trained mercenary types that protected and answered to this strange man only. Dupré had heard of this guy. The word *wealthy* didn't even begin to describe him. He was worth trillions and that was only what he admitted too, only what was publicly known. There were so many sources to his wealth that he as a professional was difficult to define. The best anyone could say was he was a successful international investor, a word that just about covered everything. His world of finance had so many layers that even his own people had trouble keeping up. So reportedly he controlled trillions of dollars around the world, but what really made Dupré cautious was the *why* he was even here? In spite of this man's philanthropic reputation and many humanitarian accomplishments around the globe, *why the hell*, wondered Dupré, *why the hell would this guy give a damn about the plight of the American black man, men like himself, or any man for that matter? It didn't take a genius to see this white bastard was cold and heartless, driven by something other than compassion for humanity.* He's a one per-center, thought Dupré. *Hell, he's in the top one percent of the one per centers.* To Dupré that translated as just another greedy white guy, a calculating user, not unlike himself except with the benefit of being white.

Rumor had it the old man hated the world because the world he knew as a child destroyed everything and everyone he loved. That his journey of survival as a Jewish child in Europe during WWII was so obscene and demeaning that he grew to hate all forms of religion, governments, military, and power.

As a wealthy man, he once even tried to bring down the entire economy of England by manipulating its currency and he nearly succeeded. He then set out to fuel the fires of multiple conflicts between the Muslim world and the countries of the west and the free world in general because he firmly believed that to create his preferred version of the world he would first have to break down what currently exist. At present it would appear he was succeeding, but due to the covert methods he employed, the measure of his success in that regard was still ongoing, known only to him. In addition, there were rumbles of his involvement in Africa, South America, and Asia, sowing the seeds of discontent around the world. What was true and what wasn't about this man didn't matter to Farin Dupré, only whether or not the man's money was good.

Thought a cautious Dupré, *what the hell could this guy want so badly that he would do this?* Despite his doubts and questions, Dupré saw a silver lining for himself in the form of a large amount of money that came in the form of operational funds that he could skim. There would be no accounting as long as he produced results. He actually didn't give a damn about the old man's cause or anybody else's other than his own.

Dupré was again about to argue his case for guns and men and to object to even having to deal with the rich white guy with the strange accent sitting across from him in this luxury hotel suite, when a pacing Jamison Johnson paused and placed a hand on his shoulder, instructing him to calm down and remain silent.

"I agree," said the tall confident Johnson. "All we need is the right words at the right time. The weapons will take care of themselves when the time comes. If we begin with an organized well-armed force then we might lose the media and we certainly can't achieve anything without it. The event might be seen and labeled by the press as terrorism and reported as such. Or it might appear as some far out radical bullshit like that Occupy Wall Street fiasco a few years back. We need the national media's compassion to portray this as an honest organic uprising born of the people and derived from the people's anger, real people, not a bunch of self-serving grungy street bums or paid mercenaries who do nothing but smash windows and shit on cop cars. The news and information outlets on the internet that we already own or control won't be enough," he emphasized. "Even with all of your financial outlay and influence," he said to the old man, "it can't produce the sufficient credibility and provide the impact we'll need to generate a chain reaction nationwide. Not like it will on the basic TV networks, cable news networks and broadcast outlets in real time. It must be widespread, angry and inspired... motivating, like when Martin's assassination caused spontaneous riots all across the country."

Jamison Johnson was a black civil rights activist from the old days of the Martin Luther King marches. A radical in his youth, he has since become a more mature and subtle man as an elder. Under the façade of being an ordained minister, however, he is a bitter man with memories such as the time in St. Augustine, Florida, when the owner of a motel tried to deny him and other young black marchers access to his motel swimming pool by putting acid in the water. And remembering being assaulted by police dogs and fire hoses on what was intended to be peaceful demonstrations. Since then, without Martin Luther King to real him in, most of his life has been dedicated to preaching a twisted social gospel that cultivates separatism and racism and social paranoia rather than harmony.

Now Johnson thrives financially after having established a coalition of like-minded souls who use nonprofit organizations and a free society system to take advantage of white guilt and decent people's fear of appearing to be or labeled to be racist. Essentially, Johnson and company conducted large-scale veiled acts of extortion on corporations by organizing or threatening boycotts of their products or services to generate bad press that would denigrate their businesses. The pay off comes in the form of large donations to his so-called non-profit causes. As a professed minister, it made him a rich and well-known man who travels with an entourage on a personal aircraft, yet he remains an angry man who takes advantage of every high profile news incident or issue that involves black citizens; always spinning such events or issues to be one of racism and oppression. Unfortunately, his lying antics are all too often accepted and exploited by the national media who usually go along for the same reason the corporations give in and pay up. They want to appear open minded and racially accepting, to be politically correct to a fault as opposed to the possibility of even the slightest appearance of racism. No matter how many facts are omitted or twisted, or how much truth is sacrificed, the mainstream media wants to *appear* they are on the right side, right or wrong, and in doing so they too are often legitimizing what is clearly Johnson's own prejudice and preposterous rhetoric.

Farin Dupré on the other hand, is a new generation angry black man, motivated by hate, the product of years of the rhetoric of men like Johnson who have come to blame all of their peoples' failings on the straw man of an imagined wide-spread conspiracy of white oppression. Of a generation, many of whom after being given every opportunity to gain success and take advantage of the American way of life, still choose to go against the grain, a generation that too often wants instant economic rewards and gratification without personal dedication, work, or sacrifice. Farin Dupré was the type that simply can't forgive and forget and move on just as countless other oppressed people around the world have done for thousands of years. He is part of a generation that lays the blame of their personal failures on everyone except themselves and wants everything because they were told it's owed to them simply because of their heritage, their legacy, or simply because they're a minority.

The impatient and untrusting Dupré, the son of a dockworker father and a midwife mother, was once a law enforcement officer in the New Orleans police department. Everyone pegged him for success and he played along. He proved to be quick to learn, bright and eager, looking sharp and appearing to tow the line. He got his card punched at every opportunity, took all the courses and kissed all the proper asses as he climbed the ladder of success. Some even pegged him for political success due to his impressive and persuasive communication and motivational skills. But he served in a corrupt system in a corrupt city and the exposure to the benefits of such corruption eventually led him to decide that the wrong way was the right way to go, offering more immediate financial reward.

Somehow, unlike some of his fellow officers, he emerged clean after not one but two separate FBI investigations into broad implications of corruption throughout the New Orleans law enforcement community. He was that good at hiding his illegal activities that included trafficking in drugs, prostitution, and the extortion and protection game. That is until hurricane Katrina arrived and he was caught along with his band of brother police officers not serving and helping citizens in peril, but systematically looting everything from luxury automobiles to high priced jewelry and even high priced booze. He was summarily convicted and after serving a short stint in prison, he now passes himself off as a born-again Christian and motivational speaker who even has his own infomercial and bestselling, but controversial book. There are some who think the book is more a disguised guide for black revolution than a personal self-help work of inspiration and self-improvement as he professes it to be. In reality, Farin Dupré is impatient and angry, yet careful, calculating, and manipulative, willing to use any means or anyone, including his own people, to gain whatever he desires. As smart as he is however, he has no idea just how widespread, how grand the plans are that will require his talents. He doesn't know what the rich white guy and Jamison Johnson know and what they want, and he doesn't really care. He is focused only on personal gain and obtaining the power to control his own small piece of the world.

"You saw what happened here after Katrina," said Johnson. "These people will need little motivation when they hear they will no longer be getting any more government assistance. *You* are the backup plan Dupré.

We can't just have them go nuts and start tearing the world apart. What the hell good will that do other than destroy their own homes and communities. That would be counterproductive to say the least. I saw that shit in California. No, we certainly can't have that. That's where you come in. We need you to direct their anger, direct it at the government. Control and direct the message to your black brethren. A made for TV event, designed to anger, inspire, spread, and grow."

"I still think we'll need weapons and men," argued Dupré. "What good is all that shit if you can't back it up with force and fire power?"

"You will have what you need and you'll have it when you need it, when the time comes, more than you can imagine," said the older man as he rose to take his leave. "Much more than you can possibly imagine," he repeated for emphasis. "You don't actually believe you'll be alone in this venture do you, Mr. Dupré?" The older man paused as he looked at his watch then looked to Johnson in a way as to show he was apprehensive regarding Dupré. "I will call you," he said to Johnson. "It's late. I have just returned from Geneva and I'm tired. I have to get some rest and leave for Hong Kong in the morning. We begin a new year soon, one that will be eventful and long remembered to be sure. Have a pleasant holiday and new year, gentlemen," he said as he exited the room along with his two security men.

Following the man's exit, Dupré went to the bar and poured a drink. "I don't trust that white bastard," he said to Johnson, angrily.

"Your impatience and impertinence is going to cost you dearly some day," replied a displeased Jamison Johnson.

Dupré was the only one who insisted on an armed force. Johnson had met with others around the country and all were cooperative, understanding their place and role in the planned upcoming events. But Dupré was the most important, being he was to be the spark to ignite the fire, the first to generate headlines and lead-in stories on the airways. Johnson considered him to be the best of them all for this purpose but his concern was that Dupré was obviously the most volatile and certainly the most cunning and ambitious. Johnson decided he would have to initiate some form of control to keep him reigned in. But then, how do you control an angry storm?

"Well, just how the hell am I supposed to kick ass without any fuckin' fire power?" questioned Dupré.

"Like the man said, there's a great deal you don't know. It's bigger than you think, complicated. You'll find out when the time comes," replied Johnson as he rose to depart. "Better that way."

"Damn well better be. I don't like dancin' to no white man's music."

"Be patient… and keep your damn mouth shut about all of this."

"Okay," said Dupré. He gulped down his drink and slammed the glass down on the bar. "That old white fucker wants a show then I'll be givin' him a show. A Farin Dupré reality show he'll never forget."

YORKTOWN, VIRGINIA, JAN. 12, 2019

Senator Jesse Bernhardt walked slowly along the deserted narrow street. Along the walkway a chest high faded old lichen and moss covered brick wall separated him from the much older small colonial Grace Episcopal Church. The small house of worship stood high on a hill along with the rest of the small quant landmark colonial town. It stood like a dignified old lady, overlooking the York River, still strong in spirit and knowledge but with her obvious age partially hidden with multiple centuries of repairs and recovery cosmetics. Built in 1697, it had survived the ravages of conflict through two sieges of Yorktown, one during the revolution in 1781 and again during the civil war in 1862. Her marled walls had even survived the great fire of 1814. Even more interesting were the graves on both sides of the structure that lay beneath the tall old trees, ancient graves in the context of American history, graves that even predated the church building they surrounded.

The Senator slowed to a halt and looked over the wall to the shadows of a large oak tree that stood amid the oldest graves. There he saw a lone figure of a man wearing a grey touring cap and long British style dark blue wool bench warmer coat. He was an older man, equal in age to the Senator. Catching a bit of a chill, the man looked up beyond the tree's branches to the gray mid day sky. He tucked his blue and green Tartan scarf into the top of his coat and adjusted it around his neck to fend off the effect of the cold. When he looked across the churchyard, he discovered the Senator gazing over the wall and he immediately offered up an eager but nervous smile.

"I wasn't sure you would remember this place," said George Stanley as the Senator approached after rounding the wall and entering the churchyard.

"How could I forget? It was one hell of a weekend and could have damn near been a very costly one if we hadn't got so lucky."

"Shall we just chalk that one up as youthful indiscretion?" laughed George Stanley.

"Chalk it up as anything you like just as long as you keep it to yourself," laughed the Senator, extending his gloved hand. "But damn, what a weekend that was, eh George?"

George Stanley took the Senator's hand in both of his. "Damn sure was, wasn't it?" he said with a nervous smile.

The two men, former classmates from their prep school days all the way through the Naval Academy, and later shipmates stationed at Norfolk, were referring to a wild and crazy weekend they spent with a couple of fun girls from Newport News. The weekend road trip had somehow ended up there in the graveyard of the old Grace Church with a drunken George Stanley introducing his likewise inebriated friends to his family ghosts and ancestors. However, dancing and carousing in a graveyard in the sleepy little historic berg of Yorktown didn't fare well with local law enforcement and resulted in all four of them being incarcerated. Fortunately, as demonstrated by some of the graves, George Stanley's roots and influence in the community ran exceptionally deep and they were all soon released. Had they not been released, both Bernhardt and Stanley would have missed their deployment to the Korean War the next day which would have pretty much ruined their Navy careers. As it happened, they made it back to their ship in Norfolk in time, subsequently resulting in Jesse Bernhardt becoming a flying ace combat hero and later a U.S. Senator, and his friend George Stanley moving on after leaving the Navy to eventually become an assistant director in the Central Intelligence Agency.

Stanley chuckled as he remembered that long ago weekend in 1950. He then turned to seriously face what surely must have been the oldest two graves in the churchyard.

Retired CIA Assistant Director George Stanley was a jovial man by nature, which was a difficult personality trait to maintain in that line of work and during his time with that particular agency. Not because of the stress of the job but more the stress of the politics of a job where total paranoia was served up for lunch each day. And in the intelligence world, especially on the level he had served in the CIA, mistrust and ambition seemed to take on an entirely different meaning.

"You're fortunate," said George Stanley. "Fortunate to be a senator, I mean... no age limits, no unspoken mandatory retirement, no overly ambitious wannabes looking over your shoulder, jumping at each opportunity to do you in and move up the ladder. Treating you like you're some kind of damn dinosaur without a brain."

"Hate to burst your bubble old man, but actually you've just described the profession of politics in a nut shell. Except in politics you can bite back if you have the wherewithal."

"I wasn't sure you'd come. We haven't kept in touch very often over the last few years," said Stanley.

"Sorry, George. I'm afraid that's my fault. You know what kind of Hell the last administration put us through."

"I can imagine," agreed Stanley. "But damn, Jesse, at your age? How the hell do you keep up?"

"I'm thinking it must also be the curse of our age. You retired and got more time on your hands. But it seems the longer I stay in the senate the more I have to do and less time to do it. You know, I think there's some kind of mysterious force in the universe that makes time go faster with each additional decade we live. I wonder if Einstein ever got a handle on that one."

"Yeah," replied Stanley as he turned and strolled among the graves. "Certainly seems that way doesn't it?"

"You know, I haven't even taken the time to kick your ass on the golf course. I think we'll have to remedy that this spring. In fact, I promise to do exactly that," said the Senator. "Maybe take a week and head down to Hilton Head when the weather warms up. But I'm not so sure we'll be able to handle it. We *ain't no* spring chickens ya know."

Stanley paused next to two very old graves. "This is where it all began for me. With these two people here in this ground."

The graves to which he referred sat side by side in the typical 17th century manner, each topped with a full length raised brick sarcophagus type box structure topped with a flat slab of sandstone. A quarter of the stone cover on the grave of the wife was broken and missing and that end of the box had been re-bricked many years ago to compensate for the missing piece. George Stanley quoted from memory the words chiseled into the man's cover stone, *"Here lyeth intered Coll Robert Benjamin Stanley Esqr who was born ye 25th day October in ye yeare of our Lord 1608 and deceased October 1674 he being in the 66th yr of his age."* He moved slowly to another nearby grave. "My father brought me here quite a few times and made me memorize the names and histories of our family members. Old Robert Stanley there started it all for our family when he came over from London. He was a member of the Colonial Council, Secretary of the Colony, and served as an Acting Governor. Can you imagine the guts it took to make that journey knowing that what was waiting was just a blank slate of wilderness, and that any opportunity for a better life was all on your own shoulders? Look at them all, strong, self-reliant, independent minded revolutionaries. One a signer of the Declaration of Independence and even George Washington's original American ancestors lie here." Stanley looked over the small cemetery, let out a regretful sigh and continued, "The inscriptions on their stones are noble, saying so much in so few words. Each in their own way leaving legacies that become more important with each century. I'm almost ashamed to walk among them. What have I done? What the hell have I done to equal them?"

Senator Bernhardt was growing concerned, wondering why his old friend had sent him the message requesting they meet here. He listened intently for some expressed revelation as to the reason for George Stanley's obvious depression.

"They gave us a great country, Jesse, and we fucked it up. I fucked it up."

"I'm not sure I'm following you, George."

"We're going to lose it. Our country I mean. No... no, we've lost it and no amount of statesmanship or diplomacy or common sense reasoning is going to get it back. It's gone too far."

"George, what the hell are you talking about?"

"I'm sorry. I'm so damn sorry Jesse. I saw it years ago and didn't... I mean, I tried to tell them. At the agency, I tried but..." George Stanley turned and sat slowly on the cold ground, leaning against the grave of his ancestor. He put his face in his hands and began to weep.

Senator Bernhardt knelt beside him, placing a hand on his shoulder. He felt uncomfortable at the sight of his old friend in such a state. He never thought of George Stanley as emotionally weak or vulnerable. In fact, he never even thought of George or himself as old. They had spent their youth together, went through the hell of combat together, and fed off each other's strength and courage. That's how he still thought of himself and his friend George Stanley. Through hard times and fun times together, and never did he see an ounce of doubt or weakness in this man. But here he was now looking at an elderly defeated individual.

Is this what retirement does, wondered the Senator. *When they put you out to pasture, is this what you become, a rambling regretful old man?*

It began to snow. The flakes were large and heavy, the kind you could actually hear when they touched the leaves and cold ground. But for the most part there was only dead silence; no wind to disturb the snow as it fell and increased with each minute.

George Stanley looked up and across the small cemetery where the snow was beginning to settle on the stone markers. "My father lies over there. Remember? Remember when we put him there?"

The Senator nodded a yes. "I remember. It was the spring of '79. And your mother a year later. She lies next to him. I remember."

"Don't let them put me here. Not here. I don't deserve it. I don't deserve to be here with these people. I'm so sorry, Jesse."

"I think it's a little too soon to start worrying about where your final resting place is going to be. Don't you agree old buddy?" The Senator bent and took Stanley by the arm and started to help him up. "What say we go down the road a bit and catch a hot cup of coffee?"

As they stood, Stanley reached into the large pocket on the side of his coat, pulled out a computer flash drive and handed it to the Senator. "It's there. It's all on there," he said. "I'm so sorry, Jesse. I thought I was working on a hypothetical. But when I realized the truth it was too late. Oh God. What have I done? What have I created? What... what have I destroyed?"

The Senator looked down to the palm of his brown leather gloved hand where he accepted the small computer drive. "George, what the hell is...?" When he looked back to Stanley, he was hit with a lightning flash of fear, freezing his senses just long enough to keep him from quickly reacting to what he saw.

George Stanley had stepped back, reached into the other pocket of his coat, pulled out a snub-nosed .38 revolver and put it under his chin.

"I'm sorry, Jesse. Please tell them all I'm sorry," he said tearfully and he pulled the trigger.

CHAPTER 7

The DC cab pulled over on G-Street next to the Georgetown Law School and discharged Vincent Stagliano. The man was tall, late thirties, with some premature gray hair starting to show under the sides of a well-worn tan colored New England Patriots ball cap. He was dressed for comfort in brown suede shoes, a near matching waist length suede bomber jacket and a knit tie over a plaid shirt. The addition of the corduroy slacks made him look like some throwback 50s or 60s preppy university egghead. Nothing could be further from the truth, however, as evidenced by the well-toned athletic body on which it was all draped.

He withdrew and lit a cigarette while he stared at the departing taxi as it pulled away. He was trying to place the accent of the vehicle's driver but finally had to admit to himself that for the first time he pulled a blank. He made the cabbie to be some mix of Middle Eastern and Russian with extremely poor English that was probably learned in some little known third world place from some non-Anglo English speaking missionary. Placing accents was a pastime or game he often played as he made his way around town, and in this town there was no shortage of challenges.

Washington DC, was truly an international city when it came to people, as much because it was the national capital as because the government was an equal opportunity employer that considered almost every new type of immigrant and pretty much everyone else except an average white American male to be an equal opportunity priority employable minority. It therefore acted as an employment magnet to immigrants, the result being the capital city's service industry often resembled the biblical Tower of Babble in terms of dialect.

Vincent Stagliano tossed a faded old circa WWII canvas army backpack over his shoulder, something he had picked up in a war surplus store when he was a boy. He preferred it over the average briefcase or newer nylon back packs for sentimental reasons and because he thought it had character. He was about to turn to enter the Georgetown Law School when a black town car honked and pulled up beside him. He turned and stared curiously into the back window, but the dark tint prevented any view inside. He did, however, catch a glimpse of the government tag on the front of the vehicle as he approached. He tapped on the glass of the vehicle and the rear power window slid open.

"Welcome to McDonald's. May I take your order?" Stagliano asked with a broad smile.

"I need to talk to you. Get in," said Senator Bernhardt.

"Would you like fries with that?" asked Stagliano.

"Funny Stag," replied the Senator. "Just get your ass in the car, quick. And toss that damn cigarette. You know better than to tempt me with those things. Tough enough for me to just sneak my pipe now and then. The old lady has a nose like a bloodhound."

The door opened and Senator Bernhardt slid across the seat to make room. Stagliano flipped away his cigarette, tossed in the backpack and took a seat, getting the door closed just as the vehicle pulled back out into traffic.

Smoking was something Stagliano had picked up during his former profession, deciding then that since he was just as likely to die as to live on any given day then why the hell should any associated health issues influence the habit. And being the honest outspoken type, often characteristic of men of that same profession, he was not hesitant to inform those who expressed displeasure with his smoking that it was something he quietly enjoyed as opposed to, say... butting a disapproving nose into other folk's pastimes or habits.

"I've got a lecture in fifteen minutes," said Stagliano. "So don't try anything hinky, I'm not that kind of girl. And I don't do back seat Lewinskis."

"That's what I like about you, Stag, a sense of humor in all situations, no matter how dire. But the Lewinski thing's a little gross. Don't you think?"

"Sorry, Senator. It's this town. It tends to mess with your mind. Hard to generate good humor in a place where almost everything that takes place is a joke."

"So, you have a lecture? On what, thirty ways to kill a lawyer?" asked the Senator.

"Now you know better than that. That was another Vincent Stagliano. You're now talking to Vincent Stagliano, Adjunct Professor of Law of the prodigious Georgetown Law School. And I would never kill a lawyer because... *I are one.*"

"Bullshit. You know as well as I that if it weren't for that inoperable damn piece of shrapnel lodged in your spine you'd still be working with the spec ops teams. And what the hell's with those damn rags. Are you going through some kind of throwback mid-life crisis or something?"

"You question my wardrobe? I knew it was a mistake to attend that black tie political shindig of yours. I looked so damn good you now think I should be some kind of James Bond, running around in a tux all the time. In case you haven't noticed this is what over-educated over-qualified under-paid public servants and college profs around this town wear. It's like this town is in a time warp or something, infested with yuppies, preppies, WASPY white breaders, and loafer lovers, but it works for me. Comfortable, ya know? Unlike you high profile overpaid society types. Hell, I got nobody to impress except my mother. But I have to admit I draw the line at sporting a fanny pack. Besides, they don't make one that comfortably cradles my Beretta. Difference with me is I'm not some half-ass anemic vegan who thinks scientific theory and rabbit food can fill my stomach. Give me a three-quarter pound T-bone and a tater anytime. Now what can I do for my favorite Senator?"

"Well, you can start by shutting the hell up," Senator Bernhardt chuckled then lost his smile and took a deep breath, saying seriously, "You heard about George Stanley?"

"Only that he died. Sorry. I know he was a friend of yours."

"A lifelong friend," emphasized Senator Bernhardt. "He committed suicide. The story was muted by the CIA even though he was retired. Bad for business and all that."

"I noticed. There was just a short blurb buried way back on page three or four."

"Yeah, it was suicide. I was with him when he shot himself. He called me and we met in Yorktown. He was extremely distraught, regretful, as though he'd done something terrible. Kept talking about losing the country. Like I said, we were lifelong friends and I'd never seen him like that and never knew him to exaggerate except as a joke."

"Suicide? That sure as hell isn't any joke. Odd, there was no mention of a suicide in the paper."

"Like I said, the agency muted it, kept it low key."

"And you're telling me this why?"

"He gave me a flash drive with a bunch of encrypted stuff on it. Tons of stuff from what we can tell. I don't know. My folks got only so far trying to read it but hit a wall and I'm not any good with all that computer crap, ya know? And nobody on my staff can get past the encryption."

"So why don't you just take it to the spooks at Langley or the NSA? Cryptography's their thing. Piece of cake for those guys."

"Because of what he said, that he tried to tell the agency but something went wrong. That's why I'm coming to you. You're well connected over there at Langley and I know you work for them on occasion."

"Stagliano, perked. How'd you know that?"

"Oh hell, Major, who do you think got you in there in the first place. You told me you were going to Alaska to become a bush pilot. Shit, you didn't think I was going to let all that covert ops talent and experience go to waste did you? Wasn't rocket science. I just made your recruitment deal contingent with my vote approving the appointment of the new CIA director. Tit for tat and all that."

"What? You sold your vote for me?" replied a surprised Stagliano. "Wow, I'm so impressed…and, well, maybe disappointed that you would do a thing like that."

"Don't be too flattered. I was going to vote for the guy anyway. Just didn't want to see you *fade away*, as a famous old general once said."

"No wonder you run the senate. Sneaky old bastard. So what do you need?"

"Here, I made a copy of the flash drive. The original is securely locked in my office," explained the Senator as he handed it over to him. "I need you to find out what's on it. I imagine it's something that only the CIA can decipher because it's most likely a CIA encryption and I'm assuming, knowing how you operate, that you know someone over there that can break this thing down without going through the chain of command. Someone who will keep their mouth shut after the fact. I know whatever it is that's on this thing was disturbing enough to make my good friend George Stanley kill himself. I trust you to find out, keep it confidential and get back to me."

"You might not like what's on it," suggested Stagliano. "The best kept secrets are often bad news."

"Well, we won't know until you crack it open."

"You got it, boss. Now would you please drop me off at school? I have a classroom full of sweet young things that are just dying to absorb my wisdom and, um...other mature attributes."

"You're despicable, Major Stagliano."

"Easy there, Senator. This professor only deals with *legal* matters. If you know what I mean."

Former army Major Vincent Stagliano and Senator Bernhardt first met during the second Iraq War when the Senator was there on a fact-finding trip. While traveling a narrow street through the north end of Samarra near the Mosque Abdullah bin Masood, the senator and company came under attack. They were about to be captured when out of the cover of a nearby graveyard just east of the ambush there came the cavalry in the form of a then young Captain Vincent Stagliano and his band of Delta Force boys. It was all over in less than a minute with the Senator finding himself lying on the dusty ground looking up at a tall confident sweaty smiling young captain who asked with great authority, "And just who the fuck are you?"

The Senator told him who he was and explained he was there with Iraqi escorts to visit and inspect the results of a multi-million dollar community project, a rebuilding of a hospital. They wanted to put to rest a rumor going around Baghdad and Washington that the project and its money had morphed into an operations and arms center for the insurgents. Captain Stagliano informed the Senator that he didn't believe there was any way in hell the Senator was supposed to live long enough to see anything at all, much less a hospital.

When asked what he meant, Captain Stagliano grabbed the Senator's senior Iraqi escort, the one with the radio, threw him to the ground, and without hesitation shot him in the leg. His delta team quickly secured the others of the Iraqi escort party.

"You're riding in bad company, Senator," said Stagliano. He then said something in Farsi to the man on the ground he had shot. When the man refused to talk Stagliano pointed his weapon at the other leg. The man then immediately started talking and confirming that the ambush was planned and the Senator was the target. Stagliano kicked him in his injured leg, aimed his weapon at the man's crotch and demanded information about the hospital. The man then described the insurgent's covert security at the hospital along with the fact there was a large underground weapons cache. It turned out the Senator was indeed being led to his death or perhaps his capture that would have resulted in a publicized beheading on the internet.

"These men, my escorts, were assigned by the Iraqi government. I agreed, to demonstrate our trust in them, declining our own American security. This guy is their commander," said the Senator, nodding toward the man on the ground that was holding his leg and rolling in pain.

"The word *trust* doesn't carry much weight in this part of the world, Senator," Captain Stagliano told him. "You speak Farsi?"

"Of course not."

Stagliano bent down and took the radio from the man on the ground. When the man objected, Stagliano kicked him again.

"Well, some of my boys and myself have a working understanding of it. We picked up on this guy's com chatter. He was talking to the bad guys while he was sitting right next to you. Leading a lamb to the slaughter, you might say. Protocol demands that we should have called it in and waited for instructions, but hell... if we'd have done that then by the time the higher ups got up off their brains with recommended action you would have been on your way to meet Allah."

The Senator grew angry, bent down and picked up one of the Iraqi weapons, an AK-47, and checked to see if it was locked and loaded. He then looked with a great deal of heated contempt to the traitor on the ground and said, "Captain, would you be so kind as to leave us alone for a minute?"

Captain Stagliano laughed, reached over and took the weapon away from the Senator, saying, "Now Senator, I know they say 'what happens in the field stays in the field' but trust me, nothing really stays in the field forever, especially if it involves a U.S. Senator. Not even a flying ace hero of a Senator. Yeah, that's right. I know about you and I'm pretty sure you wouldn't hesitate to pull the trigger on this piece of shit, but for your sake…well, let's just not go there." He handed the weapon to one of his men, turned back to Senator Bernhardt, patted him on the back and said, "Let's just say it's the thought that counts. Besides, looks like that bastard's gonna bleed to death anyway."

The Iraqi escorts, now prisoners, were turned over to troops from the 1st ID. The Senator then accompanied Stagliano's Delta team to the hospital where he watched them take out the insurgent's and confiscate their armaments. He was more than impressed with this young officer's confidence and autonomous leadership and offered to recommend commendations for him and his men. Captain Stagliano smiled and quickly declined, stating simply, "Appreciate that, sir, but then I'd have to explain why I shot that bastard hodgie in the leg and well…in today's *kinder, gentler* Army that's not quite politically correct - if you know what I mean."

After that incident, Senator Bernhardt used his position and contacts to follow Stagliano's career, surprised to learn that the Special Ops soldier had started his life in the army as a JAG Officer, a top of his class lawyer. Overcome by boredom, he qualified and transferred to the Rangers then to Delta Force. When eventually Major Stagliano suffered an injury during a subsequent tour in Afghanistan that ended his promising career and he was retired. As Stagliano had just discovered, it was the Senator that paved the way to a sometimes active advisory position with the CIA.

Vincent Stagliano exited the Senator's town car and watched it pull away. Indicated by the small cloud of steam when he exhaled, he noticed there had been a quick drop in the temperature. He adjusted his jacket then looked at the flash drive. After a moment he shoved it in his pocket. He then pulled out a cigarette, popped it between his lips, withdrew an Army Airborne engraved Zippo lighter from his pocket and lit up, all the while pretending he didn't notice the dark blue SUV with two occupants that had been following the Senator's car and was now parked down the street observing him. He adjusted his hat, tossed the canvas pack over his shoulder and strolled the half block to the law school. With a final quick glance back at the SUV, Stagliano thought...*this is going to be fun.*

CHAPTER 8

NORTH ATLANTIC SKY – JAN. 14, 2019

Captain Beverly Qualin was in that place between reality and nowhere; that strange place in the universe where nothing exists except flights of emotion and unconnected visions. Both of which were fogged with a split desire to somehow remain in the quiet comfort of unconsciousness or to rejoin the physical world. But she was aware of something interfering, something odd in the distance, something repetitive, something continuous.

Could she hear it or just feel it? She wondered, *was it a sound, a vibration?* She finally concluded it was both but what? *Was she asleep? Was she dreaming?*

Her eyes were moving but they were shut. Her eyelids so heavy she couldn't open them.

Why? she thought. *Why dark. Why so dark?* Her arms were heavy and numb. Then a memory, a vision. She was remembering now. *In a car. I was in the car. Who was that in the car? He asked her to wait there. No, he ordered her to wait. The General. It was the General...on the way to the Capitol. A stop off and then...another officer...eyes, a man with deep blue eyes...and another man, the driver. He opened the door and...oh God!* She remembered! *He stuck me with something. A needle. A syringe! After that nothing. But...before the car? Something before the car.*

Qualin couldn't move. She was paralyzed, drugged, but gradually, very slowly becoming conscious and remembering. The more she recalled the more excited she became and the more adrenaline shot through her system helping her to counter the drug and become aware, to remember more from that day, the first day back at work after the short Christmas break. She recalled General Lewis inquiring about her progress on the status report and her telling him she was ahead of schedule. Then something else. A nervous look on his face. It came when she questioned the additional information about the other armed forces' status information with the mysterious reference codes. Informing him that if he wanted it included in the report it might set her back a day or two. He seemed surprised, said nothing, then turned and went to his office. A few minutes later he returned and told her to come with him; that he wanted her to sit in at a meeting up on Capitol Hill. She at first thought it odd because she wasn't aware of any scheduled meeting and thought most of the Congress was out for the holiday, but she simply shrugged it off.

Now she lay there, confused, still unable to open her eyes but again becoming aware of the strange vibration and a constant droning. And cold, it was cold. She was prone, lying on something hard, metal, cold metal, and there was something uncomfortable.

Something...around my waist, my hands. Where am I? What's that sound?

She forced the memories to run through her mind again. "Wait in the car," he said. "I'll be right back, he said."

No sooner had he said that as he exited the vehicle then the driver opened the opposite door, grabbed and held her and the other man, the one with the blue eyes, an officer, the one with the syringe... *who was he? Where did he come from? What did he inject in me? Where am I?*

Suddenly there came a loud mechanical noise followed by wind and cold. *It's getting colder!* she thought. *Freezing cold! So cold!* She slowly turned her head to the sound of the wind, her body stiffening from the sudden shock of a blast of bitter wind, her lungs sucking in the icy cold air. The shock helped her finally manage to open her eyes and when she did she saw the boots and legs of someone in an insulated one piece flight suit. Becoming conscious, she came to be more aware of her surroundings!

Where am I? she wondered. *So cold!*

She tried to move and sit up but discovered her hands were cuffed behind her back with a plastic zip tie. Another weak move and she realized there was one around her ankles as well. She looked up and another man came in to view. Both men were in black flight suits with no unit patches, name tags, or markings of any kind, and wearing black ski mask. One also wore a coat with a fur-lined hood. She could now see she was in a plane, some kind of cargo plane, military, and realized the constant drone and vibration was from the turbo prop engines. There was a red light blinking, intermittently filling the empty aircraft with a dim glow. She knew planes like this. It was the kind she had jumped from when she took her airborne training at Fort Benning. *It was a C-130 or C-126,* she thought. *Yes that's it. Why am I on a plane?*

The two men reached down, one grabbing her at the feet and the other at the shoulders. They lifted and began carrying her to the rear of the aircraft.

"Who are you?" she asked, barely able to speak. "What...what the hell's going on here?"

Neither man spoke as they carried her toward the gaping cold and windy cargo opening at the tail end of the air craft. Captain Qualin saw the opening and quickly deduced what they were about to do.

"Wait! No wait! What the hell are you doing?"

Again, there was no reply.

"Damn it, you can't do this! Who the hell are you? Why are you...?" She wanted to fight but was still weak from the drug and could only manage to struggle by writhing back and forth like a hooked fish on a line. She had never felt so helpless. *Is this a dream? A nightmare?*

The two men held tight, moving carefully now as they neared the end of the ramp. There they dropped her and she struck her head. Qualin was stunned by the impact, temporally hazed then came around facing the windy cargo opening. Outside there was only the black freezing night sky. Her heart raced with fear with the realization that she was hopelessly facing death. She wanted to fight to save her life but knew she couldn't. Just the same, she struggled uselessly against the tight zip ties and tried to sit up.

The drug, she thought. *The damn drug was still doing its work.*

She looked back at her captors, silently pleading with desperate eyes but getting only a workman's stare in return, especially from the taller of the two men. He pulled off the black ski mask and stared at her with unemotional cold blue eyes. Captain Beverly Qualin resolved herself to her fate and tears chilled on her cheeks.

"Oh please. You can't do this," she begged. "Please."

The tall man stepped forward, extended his leg and shoved her down the ramp with his foot. Weak from the drug, she was unable to resist the inertia of rolling down and out of the plane. She fell helplessly through the dark night, tumbling through the bitter, biting, freezing cold. Falling and falling forever until the altitude and cold finally and mercifully sent her into unconsciousness; falling from eight-thousand feet over the North Atlantic Ocean, never to know why.

CHAPTER 9

The red 1969 convertible Camaro slid to a halt in front of Keenan Ashley's home, its radio blasting the latest rap release by 3J-Cat. The base beat of the rap music seemed to permeate the entire neighborhood of classic southern antebellum homes surrounded with tall oaks, pines, and azaleas. The driver, Damarius Mayfield, laid heavy on the horn and was about to do it again when the front door of the house flew open and out stepped Keenan's little sister, Diddy, a feisty 10 year old who scooted across the broad covered porch, down the steps, and dashed to stand next to Damarius who sat impatiently behind the wheel.

"You better turn that rap crap down. You know that old lady across the street'll call the cops," said Diddy in a motherly tone. "And you know that old bitty don't like black folks no way."

Damarius reached over and scaled down the volume of the vehicles sound system to a point where everything within 100 feet didn't vibrate with every throbbing boom. "Yeah, well. That's that ol' bitch's problem not mine. So, wass'up with you, lil sista?" said Damarius with a wide smile.

"It's gonna cost ya," she said.

"What? What's gonna cost me?"

"I know," she said with a sly grin.

"Know what?" asked Damarius.

"Bout those girls over in Quitman. I know all 'bout em."

"So we be seein' some girls in Quitman. So what?"

"So Keen is on restriction. Not s'posa be datin' any girls at all til after graduation cause of that trouble with that other girl who thought she was maybe pregnant and all. Daddy says he ain't takin' any chances of Keen losin' that football scholarship to Georgia Tech jus cause of some girl and cause of Keen not keepin' his pecker in his pants."

"So why's it gonna cost me?"

"Cause I know, that's why. And if I tell Daddy then you boys ain't goin' nowhere. And then the great Valdosta High School famous salt and pepper team Yellow Jackets ain't gonna be goin' no place for the rest of the school year. Least wise Keen ain't anyway."

"Now what kina sista'd do that?"

"The smart kind," smiled Diddy.

"Well you gonna have ta collect from Keen cause I be needin' my money for gas."

"Already collected from Keen. Now it's your turn."

"Damn girl. You be one heartless little bitch, that's what you be," said Damarius as he dug into his pocket and pulled out a wad of money, peeled off a dollar and handed it to Diddy. "Here, now go get Keen. I don't wanna be late."

"I got three bucks from Keen."

"Dat's cause Keen's an idiot. Now go get'em you damn little extortionist."

Just then Keenan trotted out the door, down the steps and hopped over the car door to land in the bucket seat next to Damarius. "Wass up my man?"

"Yo sista's a damn gangster."

"Hah, you just now findin' that out?"

"Damarius is a cheap ass. Only coughed up a buck," said an unhappy Diddy. "Think maybe I just might have a talk with Daddy bout those girls over in Quitman anyway."

"Diddy, you watch your mouth and get your ass in the house. And you better keep your mouth shut 'bout Quitman or by all the saints I swear I'll burn everything you own and hold dear in this world," threatened her brother Keenan.

Diddy stepped away from the car and meandered back up the steps of the front porch where she turned and said, "Next time I expect a full payment of three bucks Mr. Damarius Mayfield. Or else. And that ain't no empty promise." With that she turned and ran into the house, the screen door slamming behind her.

"You poor sum'bitch. You actually gotta live wit dat?" said Damarius as he threw the car in gear.

"She only does that 'cause she likes ya, Big D. You know that. You been her dream boy ever since she was six years old."

"Yeah, well, that ain't healthy blackmailin' people like dat. Young thing like dat. Ain't healthy."

The Camaro squealed away down the street and around the corner.

"I be only another big brother for her, dats all. Who be teachin' her to snipe money like dat anyhow?"

Keenan laughed and looked across to Damarius.

"What... What... Oh, I get it" said Damarius. "Hey man, you ain't paid Diddy no three bucks did ya?"

Keenan's eyes widened as he stomped his feet and clapped his hands, saying as he continued laughing, "Hah haaah, she gotcha again, dumbass."

"Oh...oh...that's, that's nasty. That's like organized crime or some shit like dat. That's what it is, organized crime. Conspiracy, extortion, shit and like dat. But hey, dass okay, bro, 'cause I'll get yo ass. You jus wait. Don't be thinkin' you gettin' away wit' dis shit," laughed Demarius as he jammed the stick into high gear. "And I gots lots a time too 'cause we both headin' fo Geogia Tech. You jus wait. I'll get'yo ass. A dollar. Yo lil sissa chumped me for a dollar, man. So your buyin' the gas smart ass."

Friends since childhood, Damarius Mayfield, or Big D as he was called, and Keenan "Keen" Ashley had been running and playing together ever since Damarius' father was assigned to Moody Air Force Base located just a few miles out of town. Liking the town, the family stayed there while his father was stationed not just here but at other bases around the world. He was back now and assigned as the base commander. Damarius was the youngest of three children, and like Keenan, was going to graduate from high school soon. They had also completed yet another of Valdosta High School's state and national championship football seasons. The winning season afforded the two of them all the necessary attention to get scholarships to Georgia Tech, which was their final choice made after both received multiple offers from other universities. Georgia Tech was the only one that offered them a full ride and the ability to stay together.

Friends since the very first day of Pop Warner football at eight years old, the two boys were all but physically joined at the hip with an allegiance more binding than that of biological twins. As such, they had even planned their future together which was simple by intent. They would, as many young boys assume, be professional football players, but failing that they would return home and together start a construction company. This alternative future being the result of their summer jobs during the past three years working construction, as well as their anticipated engineering degrees from Georgia Tech.

In a small restaurant across town Damarius Mayfield's father, Colonel Floyd Mayfield, was sitting down to a cup of coffee when he was joined by a man who had flown to town to deliver a package.

"How are you today, Colonel?" asked the man as he sat and slid the large brown envelope across the table. He was amiable yet not overly friendly; making it obvious he was not just there to be sociable.

"I'm doing just fine. Thinking of taking in some golf today. Care to join me?"

"Wish I could. Got a plane waiting. Got more deliveries to make. Your not the only wheel that needs to be greased you know," he seemed to say as both a joke and some serious point of fact.

"And how's our mutual friend? All is well and coming together as planned I hope," said Colonel Mayfield as he casually placed the thick envelope on the chair beside him, then added some cream to his coffee. "Do you have time for a cup of coffee and a bite to eat? This place makes a great club sandwich. Last time you were here I believe you said you might try one next time out."

The man agreed and the Colonel ordered two club sandwiches and another coffee. They traded small talk as they consumed their lunch while speaking of everything from the weather to the most recent season of the Atlanta Falcons. Just as casually, the Colonel tossed out the comment that there would be a full complement of hogs in the pen when needed. This wasn't a statement that had anything to do with football or weather or even hog farming. It was a message to be carried back to the source of the big envelope lying in the chair next to him. The hog reference dealt with Moody Fields compliment of flying hogs, officially known in the U.S. Air Force as the A-10 Thunderbolt Warthog, a seriously fierce heavy duty, heavily armed combat aircraft specifically designed to deal with enemy ground forces and any type of tanks and vehicles those forces might employ.

When the two men finished their lunch they exited the diner, shook hands and went their separate way. Colonel Mayfield climbed in behind the wheel of his SUV and strapped himself in. Once comfortable, he took up and ripped open the package he had received from the visiting currier. Out of the thick brown envelope he withdrew a computer thumb drive that included instructions, dates, times, contacts, targets, and other objectives. The package also included four very large bundles of hundred dollar bills. Mayfield tossed the notebook and money on the passenger seat then turned the large envelope upside down. Out slid a ring with three keys attached that he immediately tucked in his pocket. He stuffed the money and notebook back in the envelope, tossed it on the floor on the passenger's side, started the vehicle, and drove off. As he did he recalled that this was his fourth meeting with the man in the diner and he still did not know his name. Then he wondered if indeed he should.

CHAPTER 10

ABERDEEN PROVING GROUND – JAN. 16, 2019

Army Specialist Linda Singer was given her marching orders less than thirty minutes ago and she was confused.

"No questions, Singer," her First Sergeant had said. "Just take the damn dispatch and get your ass over to the field before that chopper lifts off."

"But, Top…" she began to protest. "Why…"

"Sorry, soldier. Special request. Asked for you by name. There's a driver waiting. You tell him if he doesn't get you there in time, his ass is seriously grassed."

This is bullshit, thought Singer as she pulled herself up into the waiting Hummer. *It's the 21*st *century, the age of high tech communication, overnight delivery, and they got my ass hand-carrying dispatches all the way to Georgia. What bullshit.*

Twenty-five minutes later, after swinging by her barracks to pack an overnight bag, the hummer slid to a halt next to a helipad at Aberdeen. Specialist Singer was a finance clerk and for the life of her she couldn't figure out why she was chosen to hand-carry a dispatch from Maryland all the way to Fort Benning, Georgia. To make things worse it was Friday and she had plans to pop up just across the Delaware state line for a weekend with her boyfriend who worked at the Dover Downs Casino. Her First Sergeant never said anything about a ride back home, just that someone would meet her to accept the dispatch and make further arrangements.

Two Sikorsky UH-60 Black Hawk helicopters were sitting on the pad. One with its crew completing a pre-flight while the other was the object of discussion between an officer and the chopper's pilot in front of a small group of what appeared to be civilians or members of the media. Singer recognized the officer as a Captain from the public information office. She had seen him on various occasions that involved visitors, VIPs, or the press, and Aberdeen Proving Ground certainly had its fair share of all three. Aberdeen was where they tested everything from tanks to rubber bullets and often romanced the government budget and media crowd with demonstrations of anything that needed funding or good PR.

The Captain concluded his conversation which consisted of briefing the pilot who would be briefing their guest. He then turned, said goodbye to their media visitors, introduced them to the Chief Warrant Officer pilot, and departed the pad.

Singer decided and hoped to avoid whatever event was happening with the media and instead approached the pilot of the other aircraft who was sitting in the cockpit running down his preflight checklist. He looked over and pushed the door open just as she approached. Before she could speak, he asked, "You the courier?"

"Yes, sir," she replied. "Is this my ride?"

"Nope," said the pilot as he removed his sunglasses and scrutinized her with more than the usual amount of curiosity. "Over there," he said, pointing to the other aircraft. "You're with the zoo crowd."

Singer nodded with a smile, finding herself drawn to his deep blue eyes. She then turned away and walked to settle behind the group of reporters where the pilot was introducing them to the aircraft on which they were about to fly.

"As you know, this is a UH-60 Black Hawk four-bladed, twin-engine, medium-lift utility helicopter manufactured by Sikorsky Aircraft. And before you ask, the answer is – yes, just like in the movie Black Hawk Down. However, a great many upgrades and technological advances and improvements have been made to this aircraft since then. They are far too many and it would be too time consuming to get into those at this time, otherwise we would miss our lift off schedule. And besides, most of those changes are classified. Therefore, I will only point out the obvious changes that I noticed caught your attention and had some of you looking at earlier, being of course, those large tanks above your heads on both sides of the aircraft. The UH-60 can be equipped with stub wings such as those you see at the top of the fuselage. They allow us to carry tanks or various armaments. No, those are not napalm bombs like you see in the movies. We are no longer permitted to use napalm due to the kinder gentler rules of war. They are auxiliary fuel tanks that will enable us to reach our destination without having to refuel. This stub wing system is called the External Stores Support System, or ESSS. It has two pylons on each wing to carry two 230

US gallon and two 450 US gallon tanks in total. You will find all this information in the printed material we gave you. Information important for your understanding of the aircraft system you are about to observe, but most of which isn't why you are here today. You are here today to observe the capabilities of the newly developed engine that has been incorporated into our sister ship that is sitting next to us. And as a special treat you will be among the first non-government folks to observe the new *Serpentine* laser based pulse weapons system. You'll see the amazing capabilities of the new engine during our flight south and get to observe the new weapons system during combat maneuvers at Fort Benning."

The members of the media group instinctively turned and looked at the other aircraft. Then one turned back with a question.

"I've read that this is basically the same aircraft used by SEAL Team 6 in the assault that killed Bin Laden in Pakistan. But if it was, then why…"

"Yes sir. Essentially it is the very same aircraft but the aircraft you are referring to had a great number of modifications, none of which I am permitted to discuss at this time."

"I have a question," said Specialist Singer. "Is this the bus to Columbus?"

The pilot laughed. "You must be our tag along courier. Yes, this is the bus to Columbus, Specialist, and we are departing now. So folks please climb aboard and follow the crew chief's instructions at all times. Next stop Fort Benning, Georgia. Thank you."

Thirty minutes later the two choppers were cruising a mile high in the sky at a steady comfortable 120 mph. They were heading south along the eastern edge of the Appalachian Mountains when they both suddenly banked right. In a matter of minutes, they flew into the range of the Appalachians known as the Blue Ridge. It was through the Blue Ridge that the media was going to get the first part of the show. The pilot of the Black Hawk aircraft flying beside them appeared to have put the pedal to the metal, as they say, when his aircraft fell back then leapfrogged ahead of them and entered into a high speed roller coaster ride. It flew around the mountain tops, through the saddles, and dove into the valleys only to shoot up the sides of mountains and actually circled around the host aircraft, all at an incredible speed not common to a chopper of its size. It was a regular air show type of demonstration and all for the benefit of the few specialized aviation journalists sitting on board with Specialist Singer, and of course, with the hopes of obtaining positive PR to generate more funding adequate to convert all of the Army's Black Hawks with similar new engines.

To make the experience even more enjoyable for the press, the host chopper's pilot started a milder version of a roller coaster ride of his own, being careful not to overdo it for fear of later hearing his crew chief complain about cleaning up the barf left behind by one or more of their guests. Contrary to popular opinion, helicopters aren't belly bombers but just the same, an inexperienced passenger can actually think their way into a spell of regurgitation. Down he flew, in and out of the valleys, up and over the hills, hugging the treetops and back up again.

Specialist Singer smiled. She was actually enjoying the ride and the scenery, something far different from the urban neighborhood in which she grew up and the drudgery of the dull finance office where she worked at Aberdeen. She was quickly forgetting her lost weekend date at the Dover Downs Casino Hotel.

When their pilot decided they had enough, he leveled off over a vast portion of undeveloped unoccupied mountains. Looking out, the mountains seemed to go on for mile after endless mile in each direction. It was beautiful, natural, and in the distance it was indeed blue as in the name. It was the trees that put the blue in the Blue Ridge from the isoprene released into the atmosphere contributing to the characteristic haze on the mountains. The pilot knew this from the days he spent hiking the Appalachian Trail as an Eagle Scout. Something he would like to do again with his son if he could ever get the time.

The pilot of the other aircraft followed. He had never been an Eagle Scout nor was his mind on the scenery. He was still mulling his orders around in his head. He knew what he and his specially chosen crew was supposed to do, but when remembering the innocent attractive face on Specialist Singer there was a quick flash of doubt. It lasted only seconds however, until his dedication to his mission took priority. "Okay gentlemen," he said to his crew through the aircraft's com system. "I supposed this is as good a place as we're going to find."

On the other aircraft, Singer was sitting with her back to the cockpit behind the co-pilot, looking out the window as the other chopper flew up beside them. She looked across and caught the face of the other chopper's pilot. Framed by his flight helmet and even behind his tinted sunglasses he appeared serious and intense. He stared back at her, focused only on her for a long moment, then looked forward as he banked the Black Hawk away in a wide circle to settle a safe distance behind them.

"Are we system ready?" he asked of his co-pilot.

"Roger that," came the answer.

The pilot armed the new advanced weapons system mounted forward underneath his aircraft, the new weapon that required more power, hence the real reason for the more powerful engine. In a single second it immediately scanned, identified, and evaluated the speed, distance, and structural vulnerability of the aircraft ahead. Once seeing this in the weapons control display, the pilot locked the laser onto the other Black Hawk. He took a deep breath and as he exhaled, he let lose the new pulse gun. His aircraft shuttered just slightly as it shot the powerful pulse of energy. He quickly pulled away to avoid the blowback. Looking over to his left, he watched the aircraft carrying Specialist Singer, the members of the media, and the Black Hawk's entire crew, disintegrate in mid-air. The entire aircraft, its inboard and exterior fuel tanks became firebombs, ripping and incinerating everything in a flaming red ball of Hell, then raining down over the trees of the mountainside and valley below. A cloud of smaller bits of flame began to spread over an area of miles.

Assuring himself there was no trace of the destroyed aircraft to be seen from the air, the killer pilot nodded to his co-pilot who then went on the radio falsely identifying himself as the downed aircraft's commander and calling in a mayday. Two minutes later the pilot reported witnessing the incident of an unexplainable mid-air explosion and calling for downed aircraft assistance.

The downed Army UH-60 Black Hawk was big news all over the country, especially since it included the deaths of civilian media, but the story lasted only as long as the search of the crash site and survivors continued. According to Army sources, what was eventually found were varied and small pieces of aircraft and only a very few unidentifiable body parts. With so little search success and the eyewitness reports of the other Black Hawk crew the matter was soon closed.

The Army news releases stated only that the aircraft had suffered a mechanical failure, presumably in the fuel system, accounting for the near total incineration of the crew and passengers. After notifying the families, they listed the deceased names of the aircraft's crew, the five aviation media members, and a military courier named *Captain Beverly Qualin*, of the Army Chief of Staff's office, Pentagon, not Specialist Linda Singer. They further stated that only two crew members' remains plus that of Captain Qualin had been identified by DNA.

Specialist Linda Singer's First Sergeant and Commanding Officer were told that she had been replaced at the last minute by Captain Qualin. False reports were then circulated that Specialist Singer had a serious falling out over the weekend with her boyfriend at the Dover Downs Casino Hotel, accounting for her not reporting back to work on the base the following Monday. It was assumed the incident affected her emotionally and made her a prime suspect in the death of her boyfriend who was later found murdered in his car on the side of a small country road. Singer would later be listed as AWOL and a fugitive from the law, never to be found.

CHAPTER 11 _____

SENATE BUILDING, WASHINGTON – JAN. 16, 2019

In his office in the Russell Senate Building, Senator Bernhardt pushed away from his desk and leaned back in his chair noticing a gurgling hollowness in his stomach that made him wish he hadn't skipped breakfast. "Are you sure of this?" he asked his youngest staffer, Jimmy Britton.

"Yes sir. Positive," replied the nervous young man standing in front of the desk.

James L. Britton was less than a year out of the University Of Pennsylvania School Of Law and was intentionally careful about passing on information that had not been verified by at least two sources as he had been taught. Getting two or even three sources wasn't just something he learned as a law student but something he also deemed necessary because he was always excessively paranoid and deadly afraid of screwing up. In this case however, there was only a single source and even though it was an impeccable source if ever there was one, he was a nervous wreck about bringing it to Senator Bernhardt's attention.

"How did you come by this?" asked the Senator.

"Well…uh. Actually…"

"Spit it out, Jimmy."

"Pillow talk. He's dating Armand's daughter," said Janet Healy from her comfortable perch in a chair across the office. Healy was Senator Berhardt's senior staffer and, as he often put it, 'the leader of the pack.' She had been with the Senator through the good times and bad and was as tough as they come when it comes to campaigns, politics, and the usual business on Capitol Hill. She was also very well known for her direct and candid approach to all things and all people; a personality trait she picked up from her Marine Corps Command Sergeant Major father during her military brat upbringing.

"You're dating a Democrat?" asked the Senator.

"More than just dating is what I hear," offered Janet Healy.

"Janet, you guys have any donuts left out there in the bullpen?" asked the Senator.

"You're not supposed to know about those," she replied.

"I *haven't* known about those donuts for years. Especially the chocolate frosted ones. I especially like not knowing about the chocolate frosted ones," replied the Senator.

"I promised your wife – no donuts."

"I *haven't* known that for years also," admitted the Senator.

"Then I refuse to be responsible," declared Janet Healy.

"Good. You're not responsible. Now would you be so kind as to snatch me a chocolate frosted before they're all gone. I made the mistake of skipping breakfast this morning. I promise I'll put you in my will to show my appreciation. I've got to eat something before we head to my office in the Capitol."

"Oh sure. Promises, promises. But if your wife asks, it wasn't me," mumbled Healy as she went to the outer offices to get the donut.

"That true, Jimmy?" the Senator asked, turning his attention back to his young staffer. "You swapping spit with Senator Armand's baby girl?"

"Well...uh, um...actually she's 23 years old, sir."

"Jimmy, it's quite alright," laughed Senator Bernhardt. "You're job description doesn't include any form of dating restrictions and I'm sure not going to tell you who the hell you can and cannot exchange bodily fluids with, other than affairs with other species that is. Most folks frown on that sort of thing - even in Washington."

Janet Healy re-entered the office with a jelly donut on a napkin and placed it on the desk. "Aren't democrats a different species?" she asked.

Jimmy chuckled nervously, not sure if she was serious or joking.

"It's alright Jimmy," she laughed. "Hell, I actually dated a democratic congressman for a while back in the day. Can you imagine that, a democrat and me? Until I caught him in bed with someone else, that is."

"Hey, this is jelly," observed Senator Bernhardt.

"No kidding. It was the last one in the box. You're lucky to get that one," said Healy. "Don't complain or I'll tell your wife."

"Oh, sorry," Jimmy said to Healy. "Your boyfriend, I mean, not the donut. I mean yeah, I'm sorry it's not a chocolate frosted but I mean I bet that was tough – about your boyfriend, I mean."

"You can say that again. It was one of his campaign workers and the *young man* was under age. You can imagine how that made me feel."

"Oh wow. What did you do?" asked Jimmy.

"Well, let's just say there's a former U.S. Representative from Wisconsin who still walks a little askew and isn't likely to be fathering any children."

"Ouch," winced Jimmy.

"Okay, enough with the confessionals. Let's get back on track here. How do we know this info is legit?" asked the Senator as he inspected, then bit into the jelly donut. A small bit of filling oozed onto his finger and he licked it off. "Hmm, blueberry. Not too bad."

"It's legit, sir. Senator Armand brought his family together for a weekend at the Greenbrier and while they were there he told them. He said he's going to announce at a press conference this week in order to get a few days of media play and then head up to New York and hit all the network news sit-downs on Sunday. But that's not the problem."

"I'd say it's not. That idiot won't even survive the primaries," said Janet Healy. "Hell, the Presidential election is two years down the road. He'll need that much time to get his shit together that's for sure. Not to mention some brain surgery. Probably run out of ideas in a week. He's not exactly Einstein."

"So tell me Jimmy, why are we concerned about this?" asked the Senator.

"He's going to use our entitlements restructuring as his reason for running. He's going to spin them as disastrous cuts, end of the world stuff with starving children and dying old folks and entire races of people living in cardboard boxes under bridges. You know the usual liberal scare strategy. He's going to claim that we're going to kill the programs altogether, then he's going to claim he's the only one who can save them."

"I've heard that song before," said the Senator.

"That son of a bitch," blurted Janet Healy. "He's on the budget committee. He agreed to the revamp of those programs, even lobbied members of his own party in the House and Senate for support."

"That's the two faces of politics, Janet. You know that as well as anyone," said Senator Bernhardt. "One face for his colleagues and one for the press and his constituents. You know, that Machiavellian stuff," said the Senator as he rose, rounded the desk and looked directly into Jimmy's eyes. "You have any idea why he's chosen this particular time for this?"

"No, sir. But I'm pretty sure this came as a complete surprise to his family. Veevee... I mean, Victoria, his daughter, said she has never known him to show any ambitions or interest in the White House. Said her mother was completely taken by surprise as well and in fact isn't very fond of the idea at all."

Senator Bernhardt leaned back on the front of his desk; finished off the donut, patted away the powdered sugar from his fingers, gave them a lick, and shoved his hands in his pockets. "I was hoping we could hold off on the news of the entitlement reform particulars until we had approved written proposed legislation out of committee, and hopefully until we could marry it with any good news coming out of Senator Stephenson's work on that debt deal. I haven't heard from her, but if she's successful then all we have to do is restructure with very few cuts. If Armand goes public with the impression that we're going to just butcher entitlements wholesale then the press and people's imaginations will run wild. There's no telling what the hell will happen. I simply don't understand this. Armand was on board with everything. Hell, he was the leading democratic advocate for privatizing Social Security and Medicare after we killed the Affordable Health Care Act. I know he's not the brightest candle on the cake, but he knows enough to understand how sensitive an issue this is and how important it is to so many people."

"Then somebody got to him," offered Healy. "I'll check with my source at the DNC and find out where they are on this. If he's jumping out on his own then there must be some outside force involved, some big money of some kind I'd suspect. I don't believe there's any way in Hell Armand could normally generate the funds to sustain an adequate campaign for the White House. Hell, he could hardly manage his senate campaign. Tell you the truth; I don't think he could beat out a known serial killer for city dog catcher, much less the Presidency."

"The party carried him to the Senate out of desperation and there's no doubt he'll be history next time around," said Bernhardt. "My guess is he's being tossed out there to muddy the waters but for the life of me I can't imagine why they would choose him. Check with the DNC. Let's get some solid info on this thing before it gets out of hand."

"It's taken us two years to begin getting this government back on track and a lot of people bit the dust in the process, democrats and republicans," said Healy. "Armand's always played it safe and somehow reaped the rewards and survived. Now all of a sudden he's gotten ambition? Nope, I don't buy it. He's guaranteed to blow it so something's not quite kosher you ask me. It will cause political chaos for sure."

"Political chaos? That's nothing new. So see what you can find out," said Senator Bernhardt. "Meanwhile, Jimmy, I want you to get the gang together some time after lunch for some brainstorming. We've only got a few days to head this thing off before Armand screws the pooch for all of us. Healy, call the Speaker and set up a private one-on-one lunch. Tell him it's important and time sensitive, a must meet. Oh, and I want a total gag order on this. Make sure none of this gets past our staff. Understand? Not one word. I don't want to start having to answer questions from the media about rumors and imaginary or hypothetical entitlement crap."

"Yes sir," replied Jimmy. "And...um, I'm sorry... about Victoria, I mean."

"Sorry? Son, are you serious," smiled Bernhardt. "Hell, I've met the girl. She's a real piece of work, that one. You've got damn good taste you ask me. If I were your age I would have beat you to the punch a long time ago. As it is, I'm old enough to be her... well, whatever. Now get to work."

"Yes, sir," smiled Jimmy Britton as he turned and exited the Senator's office.

After the door closed, the Senator quickly lost his smile and reached for the phone. With his free hand he reached over and punched number one on his auto dial. An answer on the other end came quickly after only a single ring.

"This is Senator Bernhardt," he said into the phone. "Would you please ask the President to call me on a secure line at his convenience? Thank you."

He replaced the phone in its cradle and waited. Less than a minute later the private cell phone in his pocket rang. He pulled it out and answered, knowing the conversation would be scrambled. "Sorry to bother you, Mr. President, but I believe we have a problem that requires immediate attention." He paused as the President spoke on the other end and then he replied, "Of course. No problem. I can be there within the hour," said the Senator. "Have to stop by my Capitol office on the way. Thank you, Mr. President."

CHAPTER 12 _____

EAST OF NEWFOUNDLAND – JAN. 17, 2019

"Maybe you managed to con the brass at the ACP but you sure as hell ain't foolin' this dude," declared Aircraft Commander Harry Shields, laughing as he looked over his shoulder to Senior Chief John Fortune. He then looked to his co-pilot, threw a thumb over his shoulder back toward Crew Chief Fortune, shook his head and continued. "Some day this horny bastard is gonna get us all busted and tossed in the brig. I'm thinking maybe he could use a transfer down Antarctica way."

"No sweat boss," smiled Senior Chief Fortune. "They've all been cleared through the ACP and the CG R&D Center in New London. It's all part of the program. Hey, you got the memo, right? Signed, sealed, and delivered just like always. By the book, right?"

"By the book, my ass. Your book maybe. You're full of shit, Chief," replied Aircraft Commander Shields. "I know you used that little stint as a substitute instructor to work this into the program. And don't think they don't know what you're doing at the R&D Center either. Truth is they don't care. It's just one more day they don't have to babysit." He looked to the co-pilot, "Oh, but then what the hell do I know? I'm just the damn pilot and aircraft commander. I'm only responsible for every soul and every damn thing that has anything to do with this aircraft, its crew, and its mission, right? Why would I need the added responsibility of six civilian passengers?"

Chief Fortune eased up closer between the two pilots to emphasize his words and to insure the rest of the crew wouldn't hear what he was saying. "Gentlemen, am I to be faulted because you two fine pilot officers chose domestic and marital bliss as opposed to the ability and opportunity to continually sample the abundant unclaimed and unexplored beauty and ecstasy of the opposite sex?"

"Not as long as you keep your sampling restricted to the ground and not here on my aircraft," replied the co-pilot.

"Are you faulting us for being honorable and responsible sailors, husbands, and fathers, Chief?" asked Commander Shields.

"Oh, hell no, sir. I would never do that. Although you must admit that regardless of popular opinion, all marriages, no matter what gender combination they may be, are always a same sex marriage because – well, let's face it, it's always the same sex with the same person. I'm simply saying that some of us in the United States Coast Guard appreciate the fact there are, um…shall we say…a great many fish in the sea. Variety is the spice of life, as they say. It's all a matter of taste. You know, like, one man's beer is another man's Champaign. Or is that the other way round? Know what I mean, sir?"

"Chief, I suggest you stow that shithouse philosophy of yours and get back there and take care of our guests.

And I'm talking about *educating* them, not…*entertaining* them. You copy?"

"Okay, boss, if you insist."

"Should reach the berg's last reported coordinates in about fifteen minutes, Chief," added the co-pilot."

"Roger that, sir," replied the Senior Chief as he turned and headed to the rear of the aircraft.

The characteristic red on the tail and broad red stripe on the fore-section of the fuselage set the white C-130 aircraft apart from all others in the sky and made it easily recognizable as belonging to the United States Coast Guard. This particular Coast Guard aircraft, along with three others like it based in New London, had a special mission, that of the International Ice Patrol. The IIP was operated by the United States Coast Guard but was funded by 13 nations. Its current mission is one of monitoring the presence of icebergs in the Atlantic and Arctic Oceans and reporting their movements for safety purposes; a mission necessary due to the many ships damaged and hundreds of ships lost over the centuries, the most noted of which being the RMS Titanic. The job became a primary mission of the U.S.C.G. ships and planes with international backing after World War II, eventually being performed solely by aircraft in the mid '80s.

Aircraft crew chief, Coast Guard Senior Chief John Fortune, made his way to the belly of the plane where he put on his best front as an experienced academic while informing their guest on this flight of the purpose of their mission and the history that brought it to be. It was his time to shine, not only to demonstrate the value of their place in the sky over the north Atlantic but also to especially impress, with his knowledge and experience, the attractive girl with the auburn hair and Irish accent. She was one of an international group of six postgraduate interns assigned to the Coast Guard Research and Development Center in New London, Connecticut. Each year a new group of interns would arrive, always seeming to include some lovely young girls and inevitably one that would immediately become the object of Chief Fortune's attention. The predatory Senior Chief's well-established connections were what enabled him to circumvent the system and arrange an excursion for the new arrivals during one of their flights, somehow veiled as part of the curriculum. It was during such excursions when he closed the deal by impressing the hell out of his chosen target such as this trip's cute Irish girl with auburn hair.

"Our mission today is to find, observe, verify, and evaluate an iceberg that was picked up last night by an oceanographic monitoring outpost. Its rate of movement and predicted path, along with other data is passed along to the U.S. National Ice Center and subsequently all international shipping concerns. I might add this is a very special incident in that it is believed this particular berg is exceptionally large and rare for this time of year. It was most likely hung up in shallow water and became free to find its way here during a recent storm. Initial satellite information indicates it may be as big as 130,000 to 150,000 tons."

The Chief looked to the Irish girl and offered a nod and smile. He decided she was becoming quite impressed with his authoritative manner and command of the subject and so he poured it on. Another member of his crew sat stretched out behind the intern group, shook his head and rolled his eyes in disgust, having previously seen and growing familiar with the Senior Chief's routine and motive. He slowly raised his arm and shot the Chief a disapproving bird.

"It's often difficult for the average layman to imagine the actual size and danger that is an iceberg," continued Senior Chief Fortune. "So to give you some scientific perspective regarding its volume, try and compare this massive berg with the famous RMS Titanic."

The Chief could always count on the mention of the legendary Titanic to spark the attention of his visitors and of course to impress any special visitor within the group, especially due to the enormously successful movie that so impressed the newer generations.

"The Titanic, built by your folks in Ireland by the way, he directed to the girl with the auburn hair, was on her maiden voyage from Southampton, England, bound for New York, when Titanic collided with an iceberg just south of the tail of the Grand Banks. She sank in less than three hours. The loss of life was enormous with more than 1,500 of the 2,224 passengers and crew perishing. Titanic, the brand new ship of the White Star Line, was the largest passenger liner of her time, displacing 45,000 tons and capable of sustained speeds in excess of 22 knots. That's 45,000 tons as compared to the more than

130,000 ton berg you're about to see today. Impressive is it not? Of course most of it will be below the surface." smiled Senior Chief Fortune.

Facts and figures, always impressive, he thought. *Now to hit her with the density factor and the process of fizzing. She'll be so impressed she'll be cooking my breakfast tomorrow. Ah, you're a damn genius Fortune.*

"Very few people know that when a piece of iceberg ice melts, it makes a fizzing sound called *Bergie Seltzer*. This sound is generated when the water-ice interface reaches compressed air bubbles trapped in the ice. As this happens, each bubble bursts, making a 'popping' sound and…well… you get a snap, crackle, and pop just like a bowl of Rice Krispies."

What the Chief didn't know as he rambled on was that his cute Irish objective already knew everything he was now spewing out for their benefit, and in fact knew quite a bit more. Up to then she had sat politely attentive until she caught a glimpse of the iceberg in question through a side observation window. About that same time, the aircraft commander's voice came through the chief's com set.

"Perk up back there, crew. We have arrived. Target sits on our port side. And that is one big damn berg."

"Please alternate your time by the windows, folks," the Chief told them as he quickly turned away from his guests. Then addressing his crew of two said, "Okay, gents, time to click and roll."

The crew quickly manned their equipment, which consisted of various digital still and motion cameras as well as various laser devices. Chief Fortune ignored them being they were expert at what they did and he'd seen it all before. He was focused on the Irish girl who was now by the window, fixated on the iceberg.

"My god. It's massive," she said. "Absolutely massive. Like an island. A huge floating fantasy island. Magnificent!"

The Chief glanced out over her shoulder at the incredibly large iceberg, "Blocky, it's called a *blocky*," he informed her. "Bergs are categorized by their shape. A blocky is an iceberg with steep, vertical sides and a flat top. Or, if *you* so prefer, pretty lady," he said in a definite patronizing manner, "a floating fantasy island."

"It's wonderful," she sighed.

Chief Fortune smiled, accepting the fact that his dog and pony show had once again impressed and won over a sweet young intern - with a little help from an impressively big iceberg. She turned and looked at him, not with the endearing smile he expected but rather with an expression of curiosity. "Excuse me, but do icebergs usually have wildlife? I don't recall reading that they do."

"What do you mean?" replied the Chief.

"Chief," interrupted one of the crew, "Better take a look at this."

Senior Chief Fortune moved to the window, looked out, and was immediately struck by what he saw. Even at their present altitude above the berg his trained eye recognized the object below. He quickly crossed the aircraft, grabbed a pair of binoculars and returned to the window. "Oh shit," he exclaimed, looking through the glasses. He adjusted the mike on his com set and addressed the pilot. "Sir, you better make another pass, lower and closer. There's something portside you need to see. Just behind the big rise there at the edge of the berg."

"Roger that, Chief," replied Commander Shields as he banked the aircraft and made a wide turn. "Coming around now."

When the big four engine C-130 banked and eventually came around, both the pilot and co-pilot stretched to look out through the windshield. "Holy shit, Chief," said Commander Shields. "Is that what I think it is?"

"That's affirmative, sir," replied Senior Chief Fortune, continuing to look through the glasses. "Guess we better call it in."

"Copy that," said Commander Shields, who then hailed Coast Guard Station Newfoundland and informed them they had sighted a body amidst a large splash of blood atop an iceberg 198 miles due east… in the middle of nowhere.

CHAPTER 13 _____

CAPITOL BUILDING, WASHINGTON – JAN. 18, 2019

Janet Healy was furious. It was taking all of her discipline to keep her voice at a reasonable volume, an absolute necessity considering how the sound carries under the Capitol dome. "Are you out of your fuckin' mind!" she repeated as she continued to block the way of Senator Charles Armand's senior staffer and political advisor, Roger Klein.

He moved left, then right and just couldn't seem to get around her even though she was a good twelve inches shorter. She was like a highly motivated sheep dog corralling him until his slender six-foot-two inch frame eventually ended up bracing the wall.

"Janet, please calm down and lower your voice," Klein pleaded as he looked about, hoping she wasn't drawing attention.

At 96 feet in diameter and 180 feet high, raised voices under the Capitol dome bounced off the sandstone walls and drew attention like an air horn at a funeral. In addition, he knew there were reporters always camped out in the rotunda that were ready to pounce on anybody that appeared to be a source for any kind of news. Healy was certainly beginning to draw a little attention and to them that meant news. He also knew the TV crews sported microphones that could pick up a mouse fart at fifty yards. Most of the TV crews also had the capability to go live at the drop of a hat on 24 hour news cable channels. This was convenient if you needed to get your boss some TV face time or get a message out quickly to the public to beat the competition, or as in the case of some Representatives and Senators, to just feed your inflated ego. But such immediacy could also bring, as Klein called it, *instant death* if you were ambushed and unprepared. He thought of the news reporters as lions on a savanna, crouched and waiting to cut their prey out of the herd and tear it to pieces. At present Klein certainly wasn't prepared to deal with any media that this dark haired pit bull's antics might inadvertently draw to the fray.

"Calm down my ass," said Janet Healy. "Do you have any idea what the hell you're doing? Wasn't it good enough to get your man re-elected a few weeks ago? That alone was a fuckin' miracle. Are you so damn ambitious now that you have to throw his hat in the ring for the White House? What the hell for?" She punched him hard in the chest with a thumb to drive home her point. "The White House? Are you serious? If you want to make a public idiot out of that clown of yours that's your business, but you people push the panic button on entitlement reform and I swear to God I will personally hang you by your balls from the top of this dome."

"Jesus Christ, Janet, what the hell's gotten into you?" asked Klein as he noticed they were now attracting the attention of a few more people. "Will you just shut up long enough for me to explain?"

"Explain what? How your man is going to start a shit storm for no good reason? Or why as a political advisor you have the analytical foresight of a fuckin' bovine?"

"It didn't come from me or the staff. It didn't come from any of us," confessed Klein. "Neither the recommendation to run or the announcement strategy or the reason to run."

"What?"

"It was his decision. He just dumped it on us out of the blue. It's like somebody shot him up with a load of ambition or something. All I know is he's wired ten ways to Sunday and determined as hell and doesn't seem to be worried about the consequences or anything else."

"I checked with the DNC and the GOP," said Janet Healy. "Both parties are in the dark about this. They even think the entire idea of his running for President is comical, that maybe somebody is pulling our leg. So, if it's not you and it's not them, do you expect me to believe that out of the clear blue sky your politically penurious guy just had some kind of overly ambitious career brain fart?"

"Believe me, he's serious," said Klein, easing away from the wall where Healy had him captive. "He's serious as a damn heart attack."

"Then where's the money coming from?" asked Janet Healy. "Nobody in their right mind would throw money into his candidacy. And who the hell convinced him that he's suddenly grown a brain."

"He wouldn't tell me. Just said that the money was no problem and that we had unlimited backing and I was to pull out all the stops."

"And you believe him?" asked Healy.

"Yeah, but…"

"But what?"

"I'm not an idiot, Janet. I know he hasn't got a chance in hell of making a successful run for the Presidency no matter how much money there is. There's just no way. Hell, he wouldn't even get *my* vote."

"Don't be too sure. They elected that last silver tongued idiot…twice," replied Healy.

"Trust me. I've been with him for two terms. He's carried by his staff and managed by the party - lead by the nose. He's a windup doll," admitted Klein. "Keeping him to as few words as possible is the toughest part of my job. It's all I can do just to keep him from sticking his foot in his mouth. He's worse than Biden."

"So why the hell do you stay with him?"

Klein hesitated; seemingly embarrassed by the question, or the answer he was reluctant to give.

"Come on, Klein. You and I have been in this game far too long. I know you wouldn't stick with an idiot like Armand for more than one term, maybe not even that long. You're too smart and too good at what you do. So what's the catch?"

"Money. I've got a kid in private school plus child support and alimony," Klein admitted. "The DNC doubles my pay to stay and keep him in line. They think he's too unpredictable to steer his own boat but his vote is critical so he needs a minder. I make sure he stays the course and votes the party line."

"Doesn't look like you're doing a very good job," said a disgusted Janet Healy.

"Truth is, I don't know if I can go on with this deal much longer. Something's not right, ya know? I've started setting up the campaign with the funds for staffing and travel. A big chunk of money already came in; bundled, fifteen million. And supposedly more as needed and as much as needed. Now how the hell do you bundle that much money for a candidate who hasn't even announced yet? Especially this one? So I called in a few favors from some intel folks who traced it and..." Klein hesitated, looking about to see if anyone was listening.

"And..." said Healy.

He grew nervous when he noticed they had drawn the attention of a much familiar reporter known as Slider Abbot who worked for one of the popular internet news sites. Slider was an ambitious journalistic weasel with his eyes on a career with one of the TV networks and who would report anything just for a byline and some notoriety. Slider saw the commotion and had gradually made his way within hearing distance. Janet Healy noticed him as well and saw him pull out a small digital recorder as he approached.

"Hi there, Klein. What ya say there Healy?" greeted Slider as he moved in. "So what's all this? What do we have here? Looks like we have a little discontent in the Senate trenches going on? Wouldn't happen to be having some conflict on that energy bill would we?" smiled

Slider, extending the recorder. "Hey guys, ya know confession is good for the soul. Care to comment?"

"You want a confession? I'll give you a damn confession," blurted Healy. "This son of a bitch burned my brand new Belgium waffle iron!" She continued angrily for Slider's benefit, while forcefully poking Klein in the chest for affect. "And I just got it for Christmas from my mother. Can you imagine that? Could he be any more insensitive? Don't expect to get laid any time soon, Roger. Not until I get a new Belgium waffle iron."

"Roger Klein's eyes widened with surprise as he rubbed his chest where Healy poked it.

Slider bought Healy's act, immediately grew disappointed, and tucked away the recorder. "Sorry folks, I don't do couples counseling, You're on your own," he said, then walked away laughing to himself. "A waffle iron? You gotta be shittin' me," he mumbled.

Klein quickly led Healy away, out of the audible reach of the reporter and anyone else within view. "Oh, great, now there's going to be rumors about you and me. How will I explain that?"

"You should be so lucky," declared Healy. "But that's nothing compared to the rumors that will start if your man holds that press conference this week."

"Listen, I got some info less than an hour ago," said Klein, lowering his voice in confidence. "The money came from a multitude of places, bundles within bundles, but it all leads back to the same two sources. The Global Social Justice Organization and the World Open Society

Union. Like I said, not my cup of tea. I had enough of that shit with the last administration."

Janet Healy stared in disbelief for a long silent moment before she spoke. "Are you sure?"

"Yeah, I'm sure. Believe me, my source could trace a bad penny around the world and back again. I'm damn sure."

"Jesus Christ," said Janet Healy. "Arisztid Backos!"

CHAPTER 14 _____

IRVINGTON, VIRGINIA – JAN. 18, 2019

Vincent Stagliano sat in the round rattan chair near the window. He sat bare-chested and barefoot, his jeans on but not fastened, and nursing a hot cup of freshly brewed specially blended Arabica coffee laced with Bailey's. The early morning light bounced off the water in the cove and streamed in through the half open curtains, spreading softly across the room to capture the beautiful naked body stretched out across the bed. The powder blue of the sheets created a contrast that suspended and framed her softly lit skin and long flowing blonde hair. He felt as though he was observing some sensuous painting in the Louvre in Paris; a masterpiece that had long outlived its creator and promised to exist forever.

It was his favorite time, especially with Luka. A peaceful unthreatening time just before she and the rest of the world rose to meet the day. Until recently, after being forced to retire from the Army and his duties with the Delta Force, such times were rare. There had been too many wars and too many special ops involving post-operational long edgy nights full of fear and violence followed by cautious mornings. Now, following those times, there would be restless sleepless nights and weary mornings that were full of vicious memories. Not much had changed until he met Luka Varnas. She was like a drug for the soul, able to wipe away the memories and insanity of the rest of the world.

He sipped his coffee and reminded himself of the day they met. He had been staying in a hotel for a week while being debriefed by a team at the Pentagon regarding his final mission. This was soon after he'd been released from Walter Reed Army Medical Center and a few days before he was to be discharged by the Army due to his combat injury. Having already been accepted as a visiting professor at Georgetown, he rented a small garage apartment in Falls Church and had stopped by a local Humane Society thrift store to find and throw together a cheap collection of used kitchen appliances and cooking utensils. Stagliano was not one to worry about impressing guests, and associated his new domicile with that of his college days, temporary and functional. He also hated shopping and often found the secondhand stores a fast and easy way to avoid having to deal with the big department stores' bewildering mass of choices to be conquered in an effort to find the least important item.

He first spotted her while he was in one of those second hand stores searching for a decent used toaster. She was near a glass counter looking at some jewelry and appeared to be captivated by a used two-strand cultured pearl necklace with a glistening oval false diamond cluster at the base. He watched her for the longest time as she moved about the small shop but repeatedly returned to the glass case and the pearl necklace. On one occasion when she wondered away, he went to the case and looked at the necklace to discover it had no real value and was priced at only $14. He stepped away and soon after she returned for one more look at the necklace before departing the shop.

He watched as she crossed the street and entered a small cafe. Everything about her captured his interest, the way she moved with confidence, her neatly dressed slender and well formed body, long blonde hair, and especially her face; a face that showed she was comfortable with who she was and knowledgeable about the world in which she lived. A few minutes later he found her sitting alone in the cafe sipping a cup of hot tea and picking at a raspberry Danish. He ordered a cup of coffee at the counter, carried it over and sat at her table.

"I'm not impressed," she informed him before he could say a word.

"You mean there's absolutely nothing I can say that will impress you?" he said as he added some sweetener and cream to his coffee.

"No," she replied flatly.

"I really was hoping it would be love at first sight. At least give me a chance to impress you with my wit and wisdom," smiled Stagliano.

"No, Major. Sorry."

"Major? You know my rank?"

"Of course, it's on your uniform which also doesn't impress me," she said as she sipped her tea. "Even with that huge cluster of ribbons."

"Would you believe I'm actually a college law professor?"

"Meaning what, that you're a fake soldier?"

"No, that's real enough. For two more days at least," said Stagliano. He sipped his coffee and then suddenly his expression changed. "Jesus, this coffee taste like shit!"

Luka laughed. "That's why I only get the tea here. They have good coffee but that high school geek behind the counter hasn't got a clue as to how it should be made. You have to get the coffee when he's not working."

"I've had better coffee from an open fire kitchen in the desert," said Stagliano.

"Oh I'm sure," she replied. "And I bet you eat bugs and snakes and lizards.

"Not if I can help it," he laughed. "You've been watching too many movies."

"So, in the field you eat prime rib and asparagus?"

"No, just snakes and lizards. No bugs. Bugs are out."

She offered a cursory smile.

"Hmm… There's nothing I can do or say to impress you?" asked Stagliano. "I confess, I've never really been very good at this sort of thing you know, the catchy pick-up lines and all that. But if there's anything I can do please feel free to help me out. I'm open to suggestions."

"Sorry, you're failing big time, soldier," said Luka. She smiled, broke off a piece of her Danish and offered it to him."

"Aaah, a peace offering. Maybe I'm making progress," smiled Stagliano.

"Not really. Just thought I'd help you get that shitty coffee taste of out of your mouth."

"Okay, I give up. I surrender. You've won. You made it clear that perfectly strange, strikingly handsome, intelligent, virile men in uniform simply don't have a chance in hell of getting to know an incredibly beautiful mysterious woman such as yourself."

He thought that would have been the winning line but she simply sat silent and tossed the offered piece of Danish in her mouth.

"Okay, I get it. You're going to force me to bring out the big guns?"

"I saw you in the shop down the street. Why shouldn't I assume that you're nothing more than some perverted predator clown?"

"Because I come bearing a token of my affection...along with a promise that if I'm rejected I'll jump of the Francis Scott Key Bridge."

She thought a moment, then responded, "You know that bridge isn't really very high."

"Um, yes, but...the water's cold, very cold – especially in January."

"And the big gun?" she asked as she finished off her tea and picked up her bag to leave.

Stagliano reached into his side pocket, pulled out the pearl necklace and set it on the table. "It's not worth a lot as jewelry goes. But I've got a feeling it would look priceless on a lovely lady who truly appreciates its beauty."

Luka sat back in her seat, speechless for a long moment, then reached out and touched the necklace with great care.

"Ahh. I've struck a nerve. There's hope after all," smiled Stagliano.

"My grandmother in Lithuania had a necklace very similar to this one. She told me it wasn't very valuable but it was her favorite possession because it was given to her by my grandfather just before the Russians took him away. She never saw him again. She said it would be mine some day. I was only five years old at the time. My parents and I left the country soon after."

Way to go, Stag. You sure screwed the pooch on this one, thought Stagliano. "I'm sorry. You seemed to admire it so much that I thought..."

"That's quite alright, Major. The reason I didn't buy it was because I was afraid it would remind me of her. She was so wonderful in her letters to me for years...and in her photographs so beautiful. Her hair had turned white but she was still so beautiful. You see, when my father went back there to get her years later she was gone. No one knows what happened to her. But seeing and touching this necklace now I realize I was wrong. I *should* remember her...often."

"Well, please accept it. And I apologize for my intrusion and stupidity. Now if you don't mind, I'll go jump off that bridge."

Luka laughed. "Not so fast soldier boy. You can't dump cheap jewelry on a girl then not take her to dinner."

After that they walked together for the better part of the day, stopping to watch a kid's soccer game, getting to know each other, and ending with a casual dinner in a small Italian restaurant. He discovered she was a former employee of the National Security Agency working at its headquarters at Fort Meade, but having grown weary of the politics and bureaucracy and the anonymity of functioning with thousands of other government workers, she resigned, choosing instead to teach computer science to children in a private school. She had a master's degree in the subject with specialties in programming areas of which Stagliano had absolutely no knowledge or understanding. However, when she attempted to explain it to him he was fascinated nonetheless, not so much due to the subject but more the enthusiasm in which it was being delivered. That day more than a year ago, she produced the most winning smile he had ever seen, the same smile she often has each morning.

Vincent Stagliano never thought he would be so lucky as to find anyone like her. He rose, went to the bed and pulled the blanket over her. Although the old small water-front cottage was well heated, it was mid January and the old place had a few spaces that just didn't seem to cooperate when it came to keeping out the cold. He started from the room to the small kitchen for another cup of coffee when she stirred and without opening her eyes ask, "What time are we leaving?"

"No rush," he replied. "Just relax. How 'bout some breakfast?" He paused and looked out the window, noticing that some ice had formed along the shore of the cove and around the dock. He zipped and fastened his jeans, grabbed his University of Michigan sweatshirt lying across the back of the chair and put it on. "Gonna be a cold one."

Luka rose and put on a terry cloth robe, went to the slightly frosted window, and looked out across the still water of the small inlet. She noticed two deer had wondered to the edge of the shore opposite them and watched as they nibbled at the ground. They were soon joined by three others. Feeling a slight chill coming off the window, she pulled the top of the robe closer together under her chin and smiled. Two strong arms circled her from behind, one offering coffee.

"Mmm," she said as she accepted the warm cup. "Over there across the cove... look."

"Well lookie there," said Stagliano. "Breakfast has arrived. Quick, get me my gun."

Luka elbowed him and turned away. "You would shoot Bambi just for breakfast?"

"Well, hell yeah. Better than lizard meat. But then again, guess you're right. Not really *that* hungry this morning anyway. Besides, I've already got some bodacious French toast with strawberries in the works."

"Strawberries? Mmm… my favorite."

Stagliano discovered their hideaway cottage only a few weeks after they'd met when they decided to take a long weekend and just drive south, destination unknown, a wandering discovery ride that ultimately took them to the tidewater area of Virginia. Traveling about the Northern Neck area that lay between the Potomac and Rappahannock rivers, they came upon the tiny berg of Irvington and the Tides Inn where they decided to stay a few days. The small town and surrounding area sat in the midst of a honeycomb of small bays, creeks, coves, and inlets that fed into the Rappahannock River which eventually ran into the Chesapeake Bay.

Due to his training as well as natural instinct, the retired Delta Force Major was always aware of and always surveying his environment. Of course this place was no exception. From their room at the Tides Inn overlooking the water he could see a small secluded inlet. A few inquiries later revealed the name, *Dead and Bones Cove,* a name that intrigued him to no end. When he returned a week later in hopes of finding a special place where he and Luka could repeat their wonderful wandering weekend on a regular basis, his curiosity took him to *Dead and Bones Cove* where he discovered an old waterman's cottage that had been empty and on the market for nearly five years. He closed the deal with cash of which he had more than enough since he had been single his entire military career and mostly living, traveling, and fighting on the Army's nickel. His military pay had piled up. Even after his purchase of a new Jeep Wrangler there was more than enough left in the pot. The place was, for him, an investment in a peaceful secluded place where he could tame or purge his inner combat demons, but also and more importantly, it was for Luka. Though she never asked for anything, he impulsively wanted to give her everything. A few weeks later he and Luka were cleaning, painting, fixing, and furnishing the little place nestled on the shore of the cove. The place they affectionately came to call after researching its history, the *Old Oyster House*.

Stagliano was freshening Luka's coffee where she now sat at the kitchen table when his thoughts jumped to the flash drive he had gotten from Senator Bernhardt the day they left for their Oyster House weekend. He then remembered Luka had worked at the NSA. He set the coffee pot back in its cradle and sat across from her to attack his three slices of French toast draped in strawberries with link sausage. When he looked down, he noticed there was something wrong. "Hey, what the hell's going on?"

Luka just laughed. "What? Is something wrong?"

"Yeah, I'll say. Seems some of my strawberries have disappeared."

"Oh my. Must be that old dead oysterman's ghost again. You know, sometimes I think he's in the bathroom when I'm taking a shower."

"That guy might have been a peeping Tom but ghosts don't eat," said Stagliano, deadpan serious.

"They don't?"

"That was the last of the strawberries."

"Oh...um...sorry," said a smiling not-so-sorry Luka.

"Just for that I think I'll put you to work," he said as he took his fork and stabbed a sausage on her plate and popped it in his mouth.

"Hey, I like sausage. You took my sausage," she objected.

"Wasn't me. Must have been the ghost."

"You said work. I don't do windows or toilets," she declared. "Or oil changes or organ transplants. They're too messy."

"Don't worry, nothing physical. In fact, I'm not so sure you can even do this."

"I'll have you know I can do anything I put my mind to," she said defiantly with a seductive smile. "Just try me."

"Not what I had in mind," he smiled. "When you worked at the NSA did you break codes and encryptions and stuff like that? You know, mess with those...data thingamajigs and stuff?"

She laughed. "I'm sorry, but I can't talk about that."

"Yeah, yeah, I know. You could tell me but then you'd have to kill me. Jesus, I can't tell ya how many times I've heard that one. Even used it a few times myself," said Stagliano. "But you *are* a computer genius and all that, right?"

"I said I can't talk about what I did at the NSA but then just what do you think the NSA does? Duh."

Stagliano smiled and went to the other room, retrieved the flash drive and returned to his French toast, noticing he was again short a few more strawberries. "I have a very special powerful friend very high in the government who wants me to find out what's on this flash drive but he's not sure he can trust anybody at the CIA with the info. It's encrypted. You think you can crack it?"

"Maybe. Maybe not."

"What's that mean?"

Luka turned, very serious. "You think I'm some kind of idiot that I would do something like that for nothing?"

"What…"

"It's gonna cost ya… big time."

Stagliano looked at her. Was he seeing a side of her he had not seen before? "What do you mean?"

She stared dead serious in his eyes for the longest moment then looked down to his plate. "The rest of your strawberries. And it's not negotiable."

"Damn lady, you drive a hard bargain."

An hour and a half later after they had cleaned, dressed, and packed to leave, Luka sat at the kitchen table with her laptop computer working on the contents of Senator Bernhardt's flash drive. Suddenly she burst out laughing.

"What…what is it?" asked Stagliano.

"A joke. You did this as a joke, right?" laughed Luka.

"What?"

"Okay, you got me. Am I supposed to play it now or what?"

"Did what? What are you talking about?"

"Your mysterious encrypted flash drive."

"You cracked it?"

"Of course," she laughed. "In fact, most of my students could have cracked it. It's just a standard commercial encryption program."

"Really? So what's so funny then?" asked Stagliano as he moved to her side and looked at the display on the laptop screen.

"You really don't know?"

"Not a clue."

"Then somebody is jerking your chain."

"What do you mean?" asked Stagliano as he sat beside her.

"It's what was encrypted. It's just a kid's thing, a game. See. It's the cookie monster from Sesame Street. Catch all the cookies and you win."

"You can't be serious. I mean a man died because of this thing."

They looked at each other in disbelief.

"I mean, there has to be more."

"That's the only file on the drive. Sorry," said Luka.

Stagliano thought for a moment but kept coming up blank. Now he would have to tell the Senator that his old friend had died for nothing, for a Sesame Street Cookie Monster game. He rose and went over to the sink and stared out the window. In front of the window Luka had hung an eight-inch circular stained glass donut that reflected various colored light into the room as it turned. In the open center of the glass hung a similar smaller one and in the center of that one hung a cut crystal. Stagliano glanced at it for a moment and started to turn away. He then turned back quickly and examined it further. The thing had inspired a question. "Don't all you computer geeks know how to put stuff inside of stuff?"

"I beg your pardon," replied Luka, insulted. "Are you calling me a *geek*?"

"Well, hey. If the shoe fits...," said Stagliano, returning to the table. "But those are some damn nice legs attached to those geek shoes. And above those damn nice legs is…"

"Okay, that's enough. This is no time to talk dirty." She smiled, "The answer is yes, some of us geeks know how to put stuff inside of stuff. I assume you are talking about shadow programs or hidden files and such."

"Yeah, you know, computer stuff hidden inside other computer stuff or linked or connected to stuff. You know, like back in the old spy days when they used to put little tiny micro dots in pictures or books."

"Actually, I think they still do that," said Luka.

"Oh really? How do you know that?"

"Duh. NSA. Remember?"

"Oh, right. So it's possible isn't it? You know. Computer stuff inside of other computer stuff I mean?"

Luka was already on it, focusing intently, her fingers rapidly working the keyboard. "Wait," she said. "Wait, there is something here."

Stagliano came to the table and watched as Luka played the keys on the laptop until up on the screen popped some document folders. In the folders were files and more files of material. Over her shoulder he studied the first page of the first file, then some of the others until he froze with fear after studying a fourth.

"Open another folder," he told her.

She opened another file, the type of which Stagliano immediately recognized. He studied carefully then had her open another which contained more of the same. "Jesus Christ!" he said to himself, then looked to Luka. "Have you got a thumb drive? A flash drive?"

"Yes," she answered, pulling one out of her computer case.

"Good. Quick, copy of all that stuff on a thumb drive for me then get your things. We have to get to Washington in a hurry."

"I can use the one you gave me."

"No, that one's encrypted remember. Then I want you to send an unencrypted copy of this stuff to this email address," he said as he wrote down the address.

I can't get a connection here. We'll have to go into town, to that little café. I think they have wifi." Luka transferred the data to the flash drive as instructed, then rushed to the bedroom to collect her bag.

Stagliano turned and glared out the kitchen window. The pleasant scene outside hardly focused in his mind as it churned with fear while he formed the actions he expected to face in the near future. But first he had to warn the Senator.

CHAPTER 15 _____

WHITE HOUSE, WEST WING – JAN. 18, 2019

Senator Bernhardt stood in the hall just around the corner from the President's Oval Office in the west wing of the White House. His mind was racing through the many possibilities and problems that would arise if and when Senator Armand held his press conference the next day. He thought of how the collective efforts to right the government ship achieved by the White House and the GOP controlled Senate and House of Representatives would be shattered. He was sure that all of their work, research, and the careful preparations of the past two years would be wasted and their entire fix of the county's so-called entitlement programs, not to mention what progress had been made with the nation's massive budget problem would evolve into just another Capitol Hill fiasco of political rhetoric, partisanship, and media mayhem. He was sure it would become a circus with little attention paid to reality and the actual facts, and how few real facts, as opposed to the more colorful aspects of the players, would actually reach the public. Because of that he knew the true benefits of the changes in the entitlement programs would never see the light of day during his remaining time in Washington.

The previous administration had pretty much gone wild, bypassing congress and even the constitution by simply creating and appointing so-called Czars that acted as cabinet members, and bypassing constitutionally required procedure by signing a plethora of executive orders that imposed mountains of regulations through existing bureaucracies. And by blatantly using those same bureaucracies to destroy or fend off any individual or group, political or otherwise, that disagreed, questioned, or failed to fall in line and support their agenda, as well as those who outwardly opposed them or appeared to be a threat. Many referred to it as gangster politics or just a way to play the game, but the seasoned Senator Bernhardt knew differently. He saw and outwardly called it what it was, a subversive attack on the republic. No president in our history had used, abused, or expanded his authority more and in doing so expanded the government and government's control over its citizens, bloated the national budget and subsequently the national debt beyond belief, all the while weakening our defenses and debasing our international standing. Historically in other countries it took revolutions, violent uprisings, and sometimes the death of a great many people to overthrow the government. The former President seemed to appreciate the writings of revolutionary Saul Alinsky more than our Constitution which he swore to protect. His supporting Progressives, formerly known as communists, had infiltrated and gained control of the Democratic Party and did it by continually feeding the public misleading political propaganda and abusing their power with the constant stroke of their trusted President's pen. They used the very freedoms that were the foundation of the republic to undermine those very same freedoms. Now, a single political clown in the form of Senator Armand, under the guise of seeking the Presidency, could obstruct the progress and the difficult task of reversing the process and progress of repairing the damage created by the previous administration and Progressive mob.

Senator Bernhardt stood and began pacing the hall when he heard subtle laughter. Looking up he saw Vice President Markus Banion exiting a room, leading a group of men that included a few recognizable members of Congress and three high-ranking members of the military. Bernhardt was never very fond of VP Banion and opposed putting him on the presidential ticket during the primary election, but he was overridden by the party for what was considered strategic reasons. Banion was personable, a convincing and persuasive campaigner who was well liked on the hill among many members of both parties. Bernhardt, however, remembered when Banion first came on the scene nearly thirty years ago when first elected to the House of Representatives as a Democrat, then capriciously changed his party affiliation after losing a subsequent election. He ran again two years later as a Republican, taking advantage of redistricting and winning a seat in the House of Representatives. He then ran again a few years after that to win a seat in the Senate. It was Bernhardt's contention that tigers never change their stripes, so he has always viewed him with caution and kept his distance where Banion was concerned.

Of the military in the group exiting the VP's office, the Senator only recognized General H. Conrad Lewis, the Army Chief of Staff whom he had come across numerous times, both officially and socially. He found Lewis to be an extremely capable man but often lacking in humor. Probably the residual effect of too many years of cautious career climbing along the dangerous shores of the Potomac, thought Bernhardt.

General Lewis glanced back and seeing Senator Bernhardt he immediately grew serious, then quickly grew a genial smile and nodded recognition. Bernhardt returned the greeting with a slight nod. At that same time, a White House aide came to escort the Senator to the oval office for his meeting with President Moreno.

As the group departing along with the VP turned the corner, the General leaned in and spoke softly to the Vice President with an air of concern, gesturing in the direction of Bernhardt. The VP glanced over and then turned back to the General with a smile of reassurance to dismiss his concern. After the General and others in the group departed, Vice President Banion again glanced down the hall where Senator Bernhardt had been. Now, however, he appeared very concerned.

As Senator Bernhardt entered the Oval Office he turned off his cell phone so as not to interrupt his meeting with the President. He wasn't sure of the Oval Office occupant's reception of the facts but as far as he was concerned the subject matter they were going to discuss was too damn important for interruptions of any kind. Hence the dead phone and the one on one meet.

At that same moment in Virginia, Stagliano whipped out his cell phone and dialed. The phone rang repeatedly then switched him to voice mail. He left a message. "Senator, this is Stag. We've decrypted the item you gave me. It's...well...I can't tell you on an unsecure line. I need to see you immediately. It's extremely important. I should be in DC in a couple hours. Call me when you get this message. Urgent."

President Moreno had just hung up the desk phone and came from behind his desk to greet the Senator. His smile that came with an extended hand was short lived however because he had already been apprised of the subject of their meeting. They exchanged the usual niceties then sat opposite each other in the center of the room on the matching red white and blue striped sofas.

"As I told you on the phone Mr. President, I believe there is some serious shit about to hit the fan if Armand goes through with his press conference. I don't have to tell you what that would do to our efforts to fix the budget and entitlement and assistance programs. Not to mention the social recoil which could be, well...could be violent to say the least."

"I'm afraid it's far worse than that, Jesse," said the President. "Somehow we have to keep that man from making that announcement and spewing any unfounded campaign garbage or...as you just said, we could have the worse racial uprising since the assassination of Martin Luther King."

"As I said, I expect the response to be bad simply because…"

"No, you don't understand," interrupted the President. "Armand's bullshit press announcement will likely coincide with the news of a sweeping arrest by the Justice Department."

The President stood and shoved his hands in his pockets with a pause to collect his thoughts. Bernhardt watched the President's concern with renewed interest.

"You're aware of the investigations that are underway regarding many of the activities of the previous administration?" questioned President Moreno.

"Of course. I was on the committees that held the hearings that led to most of those investigations," replied the Senator. "But of course, due to the confidentiality of the investigation process, few of us, if any, are aware of the investigative progress. To be honest, many of my colleagues are just writing it off as posturing; not expecting much to come of it except political points."

"No, I'm afraid it's more serious than petty politics. Arrest warrants have been issued and tomorrow more than a dozen high-level members of the previous administration will be arrested for serious breaches of the law and the Constitution, a few even for treason. There will most likely be civilian arrests to follow as well when those people arrested begin to start talking to save their own asses. Then…well, I'm afraid it could get worse. We already have information that could lead to the possible prosecution of my predecessor. Christ, can you imagine? This is unprecedented to say the least. To make it worse, being he was African American; it's certainly open to interpretation as the ultimate act of racism on our part. As you know, that isn't the case. But it can't be ignored. Evidence of his abuse of power is obvious as we all know, but it has led to confirmed treasonous actions including international implications."

"My god that alone is enough to trigger a race war, not to mention how the Progressives will spin it and send things out of control. To arrest a former President...is that wise? How is that going to look in the eyes of the world?" stated the Senator. "Why not just put the case together with the testimony of the others and let the facts be revealed during their prosecution... give the country and the African American community a chance to absorb the facts and then, when necessary, prosecute your predecessor? Better yet give the SOB the opportunity to fess up on his own in public. He sure as hell isn't going anywhere. But the sight of him being carted off in hand cuffs would be..."

"Exactly. So, can you imagine what it will be like if Armand stirs everyone up by telling them they're going to lose their socialist freebies just before the news of the Department of Justice's actions and these arrests? It'll be like throwing gas on a fire," said the President. "But leaving him free and giving him time to spread his lies and rhetoric certainly would make the prosecution of the others a hell of a lot more difficult. Besides, I honestly don't think the man is capable of believing he has done anything wrong, much less committed treason. So how can we expect him to step up and admit anything?"

President Moreno walked to the window and looked out. "I'm not concerned with what the rest of the world will think. Most of the world saw him for what he was long before the average American would admit it. His arrest and prosecution will demonstrate that our justice system and our constitution works and we're putting our house in order, maybe contribute to our efforts of restoring our standing worldwide. Lord knows that's been a major task in itself. That's paramount as you know, and personally I believe the SOB needs to answer for his crimes if for no other reason than to keep history from repeating itself." The President looked to Bernhardt, as he continued and asked with serious concern, "Can we stop Armand? That's the question at hand. Somehow we have to stop him from spreading a bunch of misinformation that's going to scare the hell out of everyone and rile the dependant masses. As for my predecessor, we've already considered your concerns and have decided to delay his prosecution then let him come in on his own, just as you suggested. It's bad enough the liberal media will show him sympathy. Bad enough they'll be writing headlines comparing our actions to Hitler's Nazi Night of the Long Knives. If the former President makes a fuss of it…well, we'll just have to deal with it. Hopefully, the media will be busy enough with the prosecution of the others involved. Their testimony and prosecution should expose the acts and motives of their chosen chief executive. Hopefully the best scenario is the country will demand justice. I know, it's a sad state of affairs, but you have to agree that these people didn't just break a few rules or even violate laws. They took an oath to serve and protect the Constitution. Instead they knowingly and blatantly ignored and violated it in an effort to remake our country into a socialist state. That's treason by any definition of the word. So you see Armand could be a serious thorn in our side just now, a barrier to the justice process, to defending ourselves from an enemy of the state... *the enemy from within* who attempted to overthrow our country by convincing its citizens that is was their will to do so."

Senator Bernhardt nodded in agreement, "From what we know there's some big money behind him. Sources say its Arisztid Backos. Armand has to know he can't get elected, that he won't even survive the primary no matter how much money he spends. We can try to stop him, to reason with him, but it might require informing him of the upcoming DOJ sweep. But then if we do that there's a good chance that son of a bitch will leak that and then who the hell knows what will happen." The Senator paused, then as an afterthought, "Speaking of leaks, is there a chance there's a leak in the DOJ and that Backos, whom I'm sure is connected to all that treasonous crap, is turning Armand loose for the very purpose of heading off the arrests? He might be assuming that if that were done you will call off the dogs at the DOJ."

"I don't dictate to the DOJ or the Attorney General. But then anything is possible, I suppose," replied a concerned President. "We've got people looking into that very scenario right now, and in fact Backos is also a target in this broad conspiracy, but we're talking about only one day here before Armand's announcement. That time restriction doesn't give us many options, if any."

A tired, concerned Senator Bernhardt leaned forward, resting his elbows on his knees. President Moreno looked at him and could see how the many years of service to the country had taken its toll.

"Not so many years ago you took me, a young Senator, under your wing," he said to Bernhardt. "Do you remember what you told me when I first arrived here in Washington? You told me our country was under siege, that our government had been quietly infiltrated and invaded by the progressive movement that had taken over the Democratic Party. You told me we were at war, a war just as intense and dangerous as a conflict consisting of bombs and bullets. You couldn't have been more accurate. The DOJ is going after the enemy, going after the people who subverted our government and circumvented our constitution to force their ideology on the American people. We can't just let them skate free for appearances or political convenience, or to avoid a social uprising. In doing that we would be no better than they and only be giving them the opportunity to regroup and finish what they started. We've all taken an oath to serve and protect the Constitution. The Constitution is America, the heartbeat of our country. Now unfortunately, too few take that oath seriously."

"I know," replied Senator Bernhardt. "I know too well."

"The war you referred to didn't end by voting them out in the last two elections. In fact they've become even more dangerous. Those forces are still intact, have used our own government to amass influence and money, and now having gotten a real taste of power they are becoming more aggressive…flagrantly so. We all know how they used government agencies and entities to manipulate elections on all levels and to fend off competition, to influence the demise of varied industries, bring down the economy to gain control, but it's gone further than that, way beyond their unsavory tricks of politics."

"How do you mean?"

"The FBI has determined that the death of Senator Stephenson was murder, not natural causes as originally reported. She was poisoned. Considering the importance of her mission, I think that shows they will stop at nothing to take over this country, to continue trying to, as they like to say…'fundamentally remake America.' But they have to bring it down and create a dependant society before they can build it back their way and before they can create their so-called *new world order* full of so-called social justice. We can't allow that to happen," said the President, as he turned and looked out the window. After a brief pause he continued, "We have reason to believe that Senator Stephenson may not have been the first on their list and probably won't be the last. So, considering such a drastic and dedicated conviction on their part you have to wonder…who is next?"

"Perhaps we should hold off on the arrest until we deal with Armand?"

"I wish we could, but as I said the problem…is time." The President opened the top drawer of his desk and removed a small plaque. "You gave me some other words that are written on this plaque, remember? It's by Edmund Burke and reads, '*The only thing necessary for the triumph of evil is that good men do nothing.*' Do you remember? I've always kept this close as a reminder."

"Of course I remember. And I'm glad you remember it as well. A treasured quote also used by Lincoln and Kennedy. A truthful quote."

"We've got a number of witnesses and whistleblowers under protection, some hidden away. This became necessary because two have already died, one supposedly to have committed suicide and another supposedly was accidently electrocuted in his home. One other has gone missing altogether. So you see, they have upped the level of the game, changed the rules, thinking we'll back off. That's why I want the arrests and prosecutions process to begin as soon as possible. I'm told that even the Attorney General's family has come under threat. Because of that they are being relocated and put under protection as we speak. I know it's not the purview of the President to get involved in the DOJ process but this is different, the very DOJ is threatened."

"And the AG?"

"He's sticking to his guns, refuses to be intimidated and trusting the Secret Service for protection."

"Well, it appears we have quite a predicament," said a concerned Senator Bernhardt. "I'll get with the DNC. It's my understanding they are in the dark with this Armand thing as well. Perhaps they can dissuade him to give up this foolish stunt. Meanwhile, I'll try and reason with him, although he's not likely to listen to someone from the opposing party. Maybe we can generate enough pressure from both sides of the isle to put a muzzle on him for a while."

"That would be extremely helpful," agreed the President. "I'm eager to hear your results. Call me anytime…anytime at all and inform me of your progress. Remember we have very little time."

The two men shook hands and Bernhardt exited the Oval Office. President Moreno watched his old mentor depart; knowing he had just placed a great weight of responsibility on the man's shoulders, knowing the Senator already had enough to deal with just running the Senate. He sincerely hoped the man would succeed, and succeed quickly, because he also knew that due to the time constraints and potential for extreme civil unrest, there might only be one other option left on the table.

CHAPTER 16 _____

IRVINGTON, VIRGINIA – JAN. 18, 2019

Luka and Major Stagliano had stayed in the small café in Irvington only long enough to purchase a token cup of coffee and for her to send the email to Senator Bernhardt. They were now en route to Washington.

"So, what do you want me to tell your mother?" asked Luka.

Stagliano was lost in thought. Tightly gripping the Jeep's steering wheel with his eyes focused on the road ahead, oblivious of the reading on the speedometer that fluctuated between 85 and 90 MPH. "What? Do what?" he replied, still distracted by his own thoughts.

"I said, what do you want me to tell your mother?"

"What? My mother? Tell my mother what?"

"Yes, your mother. What do I tell her after you wrap this pretty new four door four wheel drive Jeep machine of yours around a tree and kill yourself?"

"What?"

"You're cruising at ninety. I figure when we hit a hundred on this country road then that's all she wrote. But then on the other hand maybe I'll get lucky and just have to call your mom from the police station after they lock you up for trying to fly a Jeep like it's some kind of subsonic aircraft."

"Oh, sorry. My mind was somewhere else." He slowed down to a more reasonable 70 MPH which was still 15 over the speed limit.

"It must be pretty important. That stuff on the thumb drive, I mean," she said.

"Very."

"I saw schedules and dates, mostly with start dates of just a few days from now. Others in a week or so," she continued.

"Yes. They were combat operation plans like I've seen in the War College or actual combat ops. The kind of intel and planning the military puts together before we go to war or launch a special action. It also included a list of pre-op assassinations. You know, first strike stuff, cutting the head off the snake. All that stuff."

"So it's a war game plan. So what?" replied Luka.

"No, I don't think it's a game. The objectives were all in the U.S. and...the assassination list...consisted of real people, including Senator Bernhardt."

"And you think it's real?"

"The man who gave the thumb drive to the Senator killed himself immediately after. People don't kill themselves over a game."

"So if it's real then I'm assuming nobody is supposed to know about it, correct?"

"Correct," agreed Stagliano.

"Then we just screwed the pooch as you say... big time," stated Luka.

"What...what do you mean?" asked Stagliano, taking his eyes off the road and looking to her for an explanation.

"Eyes on the road. Keep your eyes on the road, Speed Racer, and I'll explain."

Stagliano looked back to the road just in time to avoid weaving head on into a pickup truck in the other lane. The driver of the truck hit the horn and held it until he was well past. Soon after that a dark SUV passed from behind at breakneck speed nearly running them off the road.

"Wow, that guy's crazier than you. Must be something in the air around here," said Luka.

"What do you mean *we screwed up*?" repeated Stagliano.

Luka took a deep breath and slowly exhaled after the near miss, then continued, "You had me send the entire package to the Senator's email address. You just don't send confidential material via email unless it's highly encrypted and even then it's just a matter of time."

"What do you mean?"

"The NSA; I used to work there, remember? I happen to know they monitor everybody's email and it's filtered, searching for key words that generate their interest. Those are the ones that get priority and are quickly scrutinized. What we sent the Senator a half hour ago is jam packed with such words that will generate a red flag and will be read for sure...if it hasn't been already. If that stuff is what you say it is, then you better hope its being intercepted by a friendly party. And even if it's pulled by an agency friendly, NSA protocol demands it be shared with a few other higher ups. There's no telling where it will go from there."

"Email? You...I mean those guys are reading everyone's email?"

"You can't be that naïve. You were a special ops guy. You must have known where the intel comes from."

"Yeah, I had limited knowledge and assumed such things took place but that it was limited to the bad guys not everybody on the net in the U.S., and certainly not government officials like a senator."

"Like they say, you can't find a needle in a haystack unless you look at the entire haystack. Those guys scan every bit of every technical mode of communication on the planet. Why does that surprise you? How do you think the Secret Service knew enough to bust into a second grade classroom and snatch up a little kid the day after he put a message on Facebook regarding his concern for the safety of the President. All the kid said was 'the President better be careful?' They took it as a threat, swept in and hauled the kid off in handcuffs. A second grader," said Luka. "And they did it the very next day. That's what the NSA is all about. They're a space age super high-tech data collection entity with the most advanced toys on the planet. Anything else and they'd just be another version of the CIA which in itself *ain't* too shabby. As it is, when it comes to the big brother theory, comparing the CIA to the NSA is like comparing a mom and pop store to the entire Wal-Mart company. So now since 9/11, even though they won't admit it, they are mandated to share all that info with other federal intelligence offices. Or at least they're supposed to."

"So big brother really exists. I'm not sure if that's good or bad. But all lines of communications in the U.S. without a warrant? That's illegal. That's bad shit."

"More like big grandfather. Been around for a long time actually. They got around the phone tapping laws ages ago, way before cell phones and the internet, by setting up a listening facility just across the Canadian border. Operates in conjunction with the Canadians under a Canadian flag. Simple concept actually. If they're not based here and not doing it here than they're not breaking any U.S. laws here, right? It gives them full deniability. Who knows what other facilities they have around the planet...or above it?" And now, with today's advanced technology, they and other agencies can perform wonders. You know, of course, how they can track your cell phone within a few feet but did you know they can turn it on and off, use it as a microphone to listen in and even use the photo/video function to monitor and take pictures of you and watch what's going on around you. Hell, they can even run facial and voice recognition programs through it. Gives the phrase *smart-phone* an entirely new meaning doesn't it? And they've been doing this without warrants. It's a problem that's in the courts right now because law enforcement agencies are wanting and playing with this technology as well. By the way, did you know that this nice new Jeep of yours has a built in tracker and computer recorder? They can push a button and know where it's been, where it is, and even how fast it's moving, which might be good where you're concerned."

"I heard rumors. Guess I always knew it was possible but never thought it would encompass everybody on the globe," said a surprised Stagliano. "And you did that? Snooped and poked around in millions of innocent people's lives... Americans?"

"I guess you could say that. Indirectly at least," replied Luka. "But if anybody ever asks, I answered your question with a *no comprendo*. Understand? Actually, I helped design and update some of the search algorithms and decryption programs that make it possible."

"But you got out. Why?"

"One day we were testing a new decryption program on a batch of emails we lifted from an internet security service. They claimed they provided a so-called *unbreakable encryption* service to its clients and subscribers. Well, of course we broke their encryption and while testing it we discovered a series of desperate emails from a woman who was distraught because her three-year old son was dying of a very rare disease. The child needed an experimental or newly developed treatment of some kind but the doctor who developed it and was the only one authorized to do it had been called to active duty in Iraq. The military wouldn't bring him back long enough to treat the child. We followed the constant emails and monitored her computer where she kept her diary entries. We followed and observed as she suffered from having to watch her child die. She had recently lost her husband in a work accident and was now contemplating committing suicide if she lost her child." Luka paused, looking out the side window at the passing Virginia countryside.

"And…" said Stagliano.

She hesitated, then continued, "The NSA simply watched the entire situation unfold, using it as a training exercise. She was struggling with medical expenses and grieving her husband's death while watching her baby approaching death. They went into her phones, monitored her computer, her every movement and communications, predicting her actions… some even betting on whether she would follow through with suicide or not. It was like the ultimate TV reality show or soap opera. Her… child died and soon after she killed herself with an intentional drug overdose."

"If she was suicidal why didn't they help her, call somebody to help her?"

"Because then they would have had to explain how they discovered the situation in the first place and that would expose part of their precious program, generate too many questions, invite too much scrutiny. It would have been politically inconvenient. Most people think of the NSA as some kind of super intelligence think tank but the truth is it's a massive high-tech data collection and snoop machine that knows no boundaries. They can track your car, track and use your cell phone, monitor all your financial transactions and health records. They know what food you purchase and your favorite drink at happy hour. It's like a black hole sucking in data. The NSA alone is Big Brother but combine it with the CIA, FBI,

DOD, Homeland Security and the many intelligence arms of other federal entities, hell, even civilian corporations like Google and Facebook, and not just the possibilities but the realities are frightening, especially if controlled by the wrong people as demonstrated by the last administration. And they've all stepped up their efforts since 9/11 with bigger budgets and new capabilities, gathering and coordinating info, feeding a central point that feeds on itself. Think about it…just think about the possibilities if all this power falls into the wrong hands. The scandals of the last administration were only the tip of the iceberg created by neophytes. We've created a monster that can be controlled by a single man in the White House or a like administration controlled by who know who."

"You're right. The potential for misuse is frightening."

"And it doesn't stop there. Now they're hoping to get into biometrics and DNA sweeps and the science is quickly getting there if it hasn't already. They want every living soul in the country on file with DNA and bio info recorded at birth because they anticipate someday having the capability to trace, find, and follow people with satellite biosensors, kind of a biological spin off of the GPS system."

"Are you serious?" asked a truly surprised Stagliano.

"Yes I am. They've been legally collecting and storing the DNA of every newborn child since 2008 and it's not likely to stop there. And there are rumors they have been experimenting with members of the military. For all you know they could have done it with you. Well, now you know. So now what?"

Stagliano gave her a quick glance then turned his attention to the road and took his jeep back up to 90 MPH, his primary goal being to get to Senator Bernhardt as quickly as possible. "My concern right now is a present threat. About the rest, I'm not sure. But you still didn't say why you left the NSA."

Luka thought a moment then said with serious concern, "I don't want to be a part of a government like the one that took my grandparents."

The tall trees and dense forest that lined and shaded the mostly deserted two lanes of the road opened up to four lanes with a broad view of a new wider road and bridge to a gradually rising hill leading into the town of Warsaw, Virginia, just a few miles ahead. Just beyond the bridge at the top of the incline a dark SUV sat parked on the side of the road. As Stagliano's Jeep reached the bridge, a man behind the SUV raised and rested a heavy sniper rifle, targeted the Jeep's front left tire, and calmly squeezed the sensitive trigger. The Jeep's tire exploded, sending the vehicle into the bridge's guard rail, then rolling it over numerous times across to the other side of and over the side. It continued to flip in the air until it crashed and settled top down in the grassy shallow water near the bank of the small calm tidewater river. As the Jeep settled, an unmarked helicopter appeared overhead and hovered for nearly a full minute.

The shooter was on his cell phone talking with the observer in the chopper. When he finished he shoved the phone in his pocket, watched as the chopper flew off, quickly tossed his weapon into the back of the SUV, covered it and calmly slid in behind the wheel. His steely blue eyes showed no emotion of any kind as he cruised slowly to the edge of the bridge, stopped, exited his vehicle and looked down on the Jeep where he observed no sign of life. After he checked the road ahead and behind to determine there were no oncoming vehicles and no witnesses, he quickly made his way back to the SUV where he calmly slid in behind the wheel, turned on the radio, played with the dial until he found some easy listening music, and waited. In his rear view mirror he saw a car approaching. He then pulled away slowly, continuing to observe the approaching car. When it arrived at the scene and pulled over, a man and woman exited the vehicle, the woman appeared excited and shocked by the site of the wreck while the man quickly made his way off the bridge and to Stagliano's Jeep Wrangler below to provide assistance. The shooter smiled and continued on his way, turning up the radio to drown out his thoughts.

CHAPTER 17 _____

TAPPAHANNOCK, VIRGINIA – JAN. 18, 2019

The helicopter landed easily on the pad in the rear of the Riverside Tappahannock Hospital where it off-loaded Senator Jesse Bernhardt and his number one staffer Janet Healy. It then lifted off to fly to the small private airfield just a few miles away, leaving the pad free for a soon to arrive Life Flight from Washington. Senator Bernhardt and Healy were met at the entrance of the emergency room by a hospital administrator who escorted them to the ICU. There the object of their concern lay in a coma.

"Senator Bernhardt?" ask the attending physician as they approached.

The Senator nodded confirmation.

"I'm Doctor Richards, attending physician on this case. As you can see, sir, the patient is unconscious, in a coma actually. There were numerous contusions about the upper torso, a dislocated shoulder, two ribs with minor fractures, and minor fractures in his left arm."

"That doesn't sound like the type of injuries that would induce a coma," observed the Senator.

"That's correct," replied the doctor. "The coma is most likely the result of head trauma that resulted in a barely discernible hairline fracture in his skull. There is some swelling and brain bleed which may or may not increase. The Life Flight is scheduled to arrive within the hour to transfer him to Walter Reed as you've requested and the receiving medical team there has been fully briefed. X-rays and MRI results have been forwarded as well."

"What is the status of Miss Varnas?" inquired the Senator.

"We've treated Miss Varnas. She suffered some slight trauma on the head and legs, but fortunately they are only minor injuries. She's resting there if you'd like to speak with her."

The Senator looked across the ER where he saw Luka sitting up in a bed while being attended by a nurse. There were two State Police officers nearby who began to intercept them as they approached her. "Deal with those guys," Senator Bernhardt said to Healy. She quickly stepped up and produced an ID as the Senator continued to Luka's side.

"Miss Varnas. I'm Senator Jesse Bernhardt," he introduced himself. "Are you alright? Have you been seriously hurt?"

"You got Stag's voicemail?" she asked, ignoring his inquiry.

"Yes."

"We couldn't reach you. Stag said it was extremely important. About what's on that flash drive, I mean. We were rushing back to DC when we wrecked and went off a bridge. I told him to slow down but he was convinced that those plans were real."

"Plans?" asked The Senator.

Janet Healy joined them.

"On the flash drive. I decrypted it for him. It contained operational war plans."

"War plans? Do you have them?"

"I put a copy of the unencrypted data on another flash drive. Stag had them both."

The Senator turned to Healy, "Be sure and collect all of Stagliano's personal belongings. Find those flash drives."

She nodded and left to do exactly that.

"I'm having you flown to Walter Reed with Major Stagliano. Once you've had a very complete checkup and are released we'll get you home."

Healy returned with a plastic bag that contained all of Stagliano's personal affects. "No flash drives," she said.

The Senator looked puzzled and turned to Luka, "Are you sure he had them on him?"

"Yes," she replied. "I saw him place them in his jean pocket." She thought a moment. "There was a man. I couldn't see all of him because I was pinned under the Jeep. I thought he was part of the rescue squad; that he was trying to help us but he wasn't dressed like the others. I couldn't see everything but I saw him pull Stag out of the water and up in the grass. I thought he was applying medical aid but now that I think of it, it was more like he was searching his pockets. I didn't see him again when they pulled me out of the Jeep. He's the only one I can think of that might have taken them. Unless it was someone here in the hospital but I can't imagine why."

"You didn't see the man's face?"

"No. Sorry. I passed out about then. Hit my head when the Jeep rolled and like I said, I was pinned down. Lucky to have my head above the water. The man probably thought I was dead. I don't know what happened to the flash drives but then it doesn't matter anyway."

"Doesn't matter? Why not?" asked Healy.

"Because you have them already. Like I said, we couldn't get you on the phone so we emailed the data to you," said Luka. "When they brought me here I told them to call you. Well, because of the wreck... you know... the wreck, it just doesn't make sense. I mean, Stag was driving fast but he was a good driver with a new Jeep and there wasn't any traffic at all or anything on the road or that new bridge. And then there was that noise."

"Noise?" said the Senator.

"It sounded like a shot. Like a rifle shot from somewhere ahead of us."

"Check with the State Troopers," the Senator told Healy.

"Is he going to be alright? I know he's in a coma but that's all they're telling me."

"We're going to do everything we can," answered the Senator. "And Stag is a fighter. You know Stag's a fighter."

Healy returned with one of the Troopers and pulled the Senator aside.

"I was there when they pulled the Jeep up, sir. Didn't see any bullet holes anywhere. I can't rule out any mechanical problems, but then it was a new vehicle so that's unlikely. I won't swear to it at this time, sir," said the Trooper, "but, when they pulled that Jeep out of the water I saw what certainly could have been bullet damage to the left front tire. It was chewed up pretty bad. I'd say that would explain the blow-out."

"What do you mean?" asked the Senator.

"Just not likely is all I'm saying. Good road, newly constructed bridge, a new vehicle with new tires. You're boys at the FBI should be able to determine the actual cause but my money is on a man caused blow out…if you know what I mean. Tell them to look for bullet damage to the inner rim. That should be conclusive evidence."

"You seem to know a little more about these things than most troopers," observed Healy.

"Had a couple tours in the middle east. Seen my share of bullet damage to vehicles," replied the trooper. "Oh, I heard what the lady said about a man coming to their aid, that Good Samaritan and his wife at the scene of the accident; seems they left before anybody could get their statement or their names. All we have is a vague description of the two and the make of their vehicle."

Their attention was quickly drawn away when from outside there could be heard the life flight helicopter as it landed on the pad near the hospital. The medical crew immediately began to prepare the unconscious Stagliano for transport.

"Anything else I can do?" asked the trooper."

"No thanks. You've been very helpful. Appreciate it," replied Bernhardt who then turned to Healy. "As soon as that flight clears the hospital, call our chopper back. We need to get back to DC…ASAP."

CHEVY CHASE, MARYLAND – JAN 20, 2019

Senator Charles Armand was conversing on his cell phone as he entered the back of the waiting town car in front of his home in Chevy Chase. The car arrived on time as always just at the crack of dawn but the Senator was running behind, causing the driver to wait impatiently as usual. It was the drivers that always managed to save Armand's ass when it came to arriving on time for the many meetings and social events that cluttered the Senator's schedule. On this particular morning the driver who was opening the door nodded, not with a slight hint of irritation but with a smile, and the Senator paused and made note of the new face. It was the face of the new driver Roger Klein obtained that would be his chauffeur for the next two weeks while his regular driver was on vacation.

"Where we headed this morning, Senator?" asked the driver.

Armand pulled the phone away from his face, "Senate building for a few minutes then we have a meeting in Crystal City," he answered. He noted the man looked capable, clean cut, and intelligent, which lead the Senator to assume he would be adequate for the job. The only thing that concerned him was the driver's ability to demonstrate any degree of confidentiality, not for reasons involving matters of state but necessary more for matters of the Senator's frequent incidents of infidelity. Armand made a quick mental note to have a brief discussion with the new driver to make clear what he expected regarding that personal issue.

"Can you believe that?" said Armand, continuing his conversation on the phone. "Just because he's been on Capitol Hill forever he thinks he can call the shots when it comes to my career. Hell, he's not even in the same party."

Armand was on the phone with Roger Klein, discussing a conversation he had with Senator Bernhardt the previous evening.

"The arrogant bastard had the balls to tell me that I'm not capable of holding the office of President and that I didn't have a chance in hell of winning the election. Then he accuses me of intentionally trying to undermine all the hard work of the Congress and the administration. Said that I would set the entire process back years if I hang my campaign on the false premise of the demise of the social programs. I got to tell you, Klein, I'm not happy with any of this. I'm wondering how he gets his information. How the hell did he know what I was going to say at my press announcement? I want you to find out. I want you to find out who the hell leaked. It had to be one of our people. Find out fast. I can't run a campaign with an enemy sympathizer on the crew."

On the other end of the line Klein was gritting his teeth, tensing his jaw as he listened to the ranting of his boss. All the while wishing he could say what he really wanted to say; that Senator Bernhardt was correct and that Armand was a damn fool.

When Armand finally calmed down and concluded the call, Klein was more than glad to replace the phone in its cradle on his desk. Listening to the man rant each morning was part of his daily routine and he had long ago grown tired of it. The man seemed to have multiple personalities which seemed to be a characteristic held by too many politicians. For most it was intentional but with Armand it was most likely an honest case of bipolar affliction. Armand, thought Klein, was a regular Dr. Jekyll and Mr. Hyde which far too often made for a pretty shitty day for his staff that suffered perhaps the highest percentage turnover of any other member of Congress.

Klein hesitated as he slowly reached into his inside jacket pocket for the special cell phone he was given the day before. He paused, looking at the phone as though it were some instrument of evil, then entered the ten digits required to make the only call he would ever make on the device before he would later toss it into the Potomac River. On the other end it rang only three times before Klein discontinued the call. He didn't have to wait for an answer. The three rings were the message and the message was that Armand had not changed his mind about throwing his hat in the ring for the presidency; that Armand was about to start an uprising the likes of which this country has never known. Klein knew what would happen next, though he didn't know how.

The driver of the town car felt the quiet vibration of a cell phone in his inner coat pocket, reached in and casually glanced down at the brief text message that appeared on the small screen. He slid the phone back into his pocket and continued driving. When the town car was just a few miles from the senate building, the driver eased the brakes and brought it to a halt at a red light. Oddly, the traffic was light for that time of day. While waiting patiently for the light to change, he checked and rechecked his seat belt. When the light finally changed he eased the town car into the intersection. Suddenly a fully loaded cement truck came fast into the intersection and slammed into the passenger side of the vehicle, throwing Senator Armand across the back seat where he struck his head against the window. Both vehicles slid a full twenty yards across the intersection before they finally came to rest. Armand's driver released his seat belt, checked himself for injuries and finding none, quickly exited the car. He looked about in all directions, rushed to the rear door and yanked it open. Senator Armand lay across the back seat, his hands covered with blood as he tried to stop the bleeding from the gash above his left temple.

"Senator, how badly are you hurt?" asked his driver.

"My head," answered Armand. "My head and my shoulder, I think."

"Okay, sir. Sit back and hold still. Don't move. I'm going to check your head injury."

Senator Armand did as instructed, leaned back and closed his eyes. The driver placed his right hand at the back of Armand's head and cupped his chin in the other. It only took a single quick twist and in an instant the driver snapped the Senator's neck. When he let go,

Armand fell over onto the seat, dead. The driver stood and looked around, comfortable with the fact that no one witnessed anything other than his attempt to help his passenger. He looked to the cab of the cement truck and saw that its operator had fled the scene.

Senator Armand's campaign for the presidency had just been terminated.

CHAPTER 19 _____

SENATE BUILDING – JAN. 20, 2019

Roger Klein sat at his desk waiting for the call. When a call finally came, it wasn't the one he expected.

"Roger. Arlene Ferris here, New York Times. Obviously I'm calling to offer my condolences on the loss of Senator Armand."

Klein, the head of Armand's staff, had not yet been officially notified of his boss's demise, yet the New York Times already had all the facts as was explained by Ferris. She was looking for a formal statement from the Senator's office. Klein mumbled some generic words of grief from his guilt ridden hazy state, barely hearing journalist Arlene Ferris as she continued the conversation.

"I also thought you should know that we're still going to run a story on your Senators expressed motivation for wanting to enter the race for the White House"

"What?" replied Klein. "You're going to what? What are you talking about?"

"Senator Armand's statement that he was going to make at today's press conference. You know, about the cancelation of the social programs," clarified Ferris.

"Statement? We never put out a statement."

"Sure you did. I got the fax only an hour ago. Sent from your office."

Klein's heart began to race. They had silenced the Senator but what they feared most, the message, had been leaked to what he considered one of the worst possible outlets of information, the New York Times. What the Times printed, be it true or not, accurate or not, was always disseminated to most every other form of media on the planet. It would spread like an unstoppable pandemic, all the while becoming the gospel and gaining credibility through simple repetition, a very loud repetitious bell that could not be un-rung.

The New York Times had become a shining example of that most famous adage; *if you repeat a lie often enough, it will become the truth.* The Times was the source, the starting bell that all too often set off media feeding frenzies over issues and non-issues alike, and if there is one true uncomplimentary characteristic of our contemporary free press it is that it feeds on itself like an uncontrollable fire.

Klein knew this, as did most everyone else in the business of government. The problem was that most of them also knew how to use and play those very same negative characteristics to their advantage by creating and tossing out or simply feeding information to the Times that they knew would cause a media frenzy that would in turn create a smoke screen of sorts that would hide or diminish more secret or serious concerns or issues and actions that the powers that be wanted kept low key or better yet, unknown. It was an old game played by masters on both sides; the DC gang using the media and the media knowing it was being used. The irony is that both sides were always winning; a lazy corps of reporters and editors capitalizing and advancing their careers on the Capitol's constant flow of BS, and our so-called national statesmen manipulating their message for their own purpose.

"Arlene, I didn't send you that fax," said Klein. "I don't know who did and neither I nor anyone else in this office will confirm whatever information it contains."

In the back of his mind as Klein spoke, he wondered who had actually sent the fax and most importantly how they got the material in the first place. No one except Armand and Klein had seen it and likewise no one else possessed it. And, recalled Klein, just that morning not long before Armand had been killed the Senator was bitching about a leak and had ordered Klein to find it.

"Look Roger, I appreciate your not wanting to mix the news of the death of your boss and the subsequent grief with the man's politics but…well, we simply can't ignore an issue and story of this magnitude."

"Arlene please, you just don't realize the damage that story will do. Like I said, we won't confirm it. In fact we'll deny it and put out a statement that it's an erroneous fax sent by an unknown. Believe me, it must be someone trying to stir up a political hornet's nest. You're being played."

"I'm sorry, Roger," replied Arlene Ferris. "But I've already confirmed it with two other sources in your own party."

"Whoever they are, they're lying," insisted Klein. "You have to promise me that you'll hold off on the story, that you'll talk to the national committee and the minority leader first. I'm sure they'll confirm what I'm telling you."

"Okay, I promise I'll talk to them but for a follow-up piece. For now though, it's like I said; we've got confirmation and I'm sure our editors are going to run with it. You know how it goes. We aren't sure who else got the fax so we have to strike first. It's all about timing. Sorry." With that she discontinued the call.

Klein slammed down the phone, putting his face in his hands in frustration. He then picked it up, dialed and waited for an answer.

"This is Klein. We have a serious problem. We need to meet immediately," he informed the recipient of the call.

"Okay. The concession stand near the Lincoln Memorial. Fifteen minutes," replied the man on the other end of the line.

Klein replaced the phone and exited his office. As he entered the outer office he discovered the rest of the staff together talking softly. Two of the girls were in tears with others trying to console them. Klein had his coat in hand and made for the door, wondering, were they sad because the bastard was dead or because they were about to lose their jobs?

"Any instructions, Roger?" asked one of the staff.

"Sit tight," replied Klein. "No comment to any media at this time pending a formal statement." With that brief order Klein quickly exited, wondering which of the staff in the room was the leak.

The man Klein had called hung up his phone and looked about, then rose to leave his office as well.

"Going out, sir?" asked his secretary as he exited.

"Be back in forty minutes," he said curtly.

"But what about your morning meeting with the President?" she asked.

"Tell him I'll be a little late and I'll explain later," he said.

Following his departure the secretary called the President's receptionist. "Hello Joan," she said. "Would you please advise the President that the Chief of Staff will be late for the meeting today and that he will explain why when he gets there?"

As Bo Peppers, the President's Chief of Staff made his way out of the White House and away from the grounds, his mind was racing with a dozen scenarios to deal with a dozen of the day's problems. He was the solution man, the fix it man, who ran interference for the White House and the President and today, he thought... for the entire country.

CHAPTER 20 _____

LINCOLN MEMORIAL – JAN. 20, 2019

When Roger Klein arrived at the concession stand near the Lincoln Memorial it was obvious he was extremely upset. He looked about until he found Bo Peppers, sitting on a park bench sipping a cup of coffee. Each sip of the hot coffee from the tall paper cup resulted in a small puff of steam that quickly vanished into the crisp morning air. Nearby were a couple of secret service agents continuously scanning the area, paying particular attention to the few early bird tourists who were already making their way to the memorial. Klein joined him on the bench and when he sat Peppers handed him the cup of coffee he was holding in his other hand.

"Sorry, it's not the designer stuff. It's straight up, black," said Peppers. "I don't know how you take it but you sure as hell look like you need it. Got creamer and sweetener in my pocket if you want. Really hits the spot if you ask me. Pretty damn chilly out here this morning. Odd, it didn't seem this cold when I was out jogging just before dawn."

Bo Peppers was one of those down south good ol' boys, a can-do man of many talents as is often the case of President's Chiefs of Staff. He had been with the President ever since his time in the Florida Legislature, using his country charms to affirm, protect, and help manage the rising career of a good man he sincerely believed in. As the President rose through the ranks of the Republican Party to become its new golden boy, Bo Peppers was always there, watching his back, as Peppers would often say, *'for King and country.'* Where Peppers was concerned, there seemed to be a notion that he was always a step ahead of everyone by way of an accumulation of privileged knowledge and possibly, thought some, of some hidden agenda that only he was privy to.

Klein figured it was all of that and more that generated and fed the man's perpetual grin, intimidating some people, putting some off guard altogether, and putting others off balance while he messed with their minds for whatever purpose was on his agenda at the time. It was Peppers' eyes that were the true windows to his mind and motives, thought Klein. If he observed them closely enough he could see the slight alterations that gave him away in various situations or conversations, which gave away the bluff. That was one of Klein's plusses, being able to read people's eyes, measuring their sincerity like he possessed some kind of built in lie detector. Right now Klein wanted to look away, not wanting to deal with Peppers at all, to lose himself in the surrounding winter-bare trees. Instead he forced himself to maintain eye contact.

"For nothing, it was all for nothing," Klein told Peppers. "I mean, I understand the why of it all but it didn't make any difference because somebody beat us. They leaked the damn presser talking points to the New

York Times. Shit, man, the Times! And there's no way in hell we can shut them up. It's got to be those Backos people. That foreign bastard is…"

"…not your concern," interrupted Peppers.

"What the hell does that mean? Are you telling me you can deal with him? I don't think so. Nobody can deal with him. He's too damn rich and powerful and the man is a fuckin' ghost, an invisible ghost with better security than your boss. All we can do is hope that bastard dies of old age before the day is out."

"Like I said, Backos is not your concern. He's a national security problem and will be dealt with accordingly. That's all you need to know."

Klein searched Bo Peppers' eyes finding only total confidence and what should have felt like assurance of some kind. But oddly enough, this time he didn't trust his own instincts and had little faith in what he saw.

"Okay, fine. So now what?" asked Klein. "What am I supposed to do now when the Armand shit hits the fan? After the New York Times opens that can of worms nobody on the Hill is going to be able to hide. The Progressives are going to have a field day and the old-line Dems are going to hop right on their wagon and we're all going to be eaten alive."

"If you think you can't handle it then close up shop and leave town. Go back to that cozy little town in west Ohio. Spend some time with your folks. Simple enough," smiled Peppers.

"Then who will be left to deny that fax to the Times?" asked Klein. "Somebody from the wrongly claimed source of the information has to be available to refute it. Not that it'll make any damn difference. Hell, in a matter of hours it will have a life of its own and nothing anyone says or does will make any difference. Not even the President."

"You're probably correct," replied Peppers. "But like I said, your part is now limited. You can pack it up or you can take the problem on and hope for the best. My suggestion right now is that you go be with Armand's grieving family and do what you do best, hold things together, be the family spokesman. We'll be in touch."

"You'll be in touch? Why? What more can I do? I did what you asked. I thought I was doing something important, preventing an uprising, saving the country. But all I did was kill a friend. Sure, he was a jerk and pain in the ass but he had his moments and didn't deserve to die for no reason."

"I wouldn't say it was for nothing. People die for this country every day, some knowingly, others unwittingly. It's a reality of our national survival. Did you actually think the democratic system is what protects, preserves, and holds this country together? I don't think so. Hell, there are those who would say it's just the opposite. As for you, well, I don't think you're that naïve. Now go back to your job and dammit, lose that Judas self guilt shit because it doesn't apply to you. Your man brought this on himself by sleeping with the enemy and the outcome would have occurred with or without you. He left us no other choice. It's that simple."

Klein looked down to the coffee he clinched between his hands and saw it as a cup of burning betrayal.

Peppers rose, took a final sip of his coffee and tossed the half empty cup into a nearby trash receptacle. "You're not drinking your coffee, Roger. Is it that bad?" observed Peppers as he adjusted his coat.

"Coffee?" replied Klein as he stared at the cup. "This isn't coffee in my hands," he replied as he handed it to Peppers, "it's the blood of the damned."

CAPITOL BUILDING, DC – JAN. 20, 2019

Senator Bernhardt was exiting a meeting when he was intercepted by Janet Healy. "It's not there, the email that Stag and Luka sent you," she said with great concern as she walked at his side. "There's no trace of it anywhere on the net. Somehow someone intercepted or deleted it."

"You're kidding," replied Bernhardt. "They can do that? Intercept private email and make it disappear?"

"Of course. If you can think of it, there's a geek out there somewhere who can pull it off. Civilians call them geeks, hackers, whatever, but when they're paid with the taxpayer's money they're usually called analysts. Hell, our government's been doing it for years. Surely you're not surprised, especially after all the scandals of the last administration?"

"Guess not. Just never thought of it as happening to me. I mean, to go into cyberspace and pluck out a single email and make it vanish. High-tech push button shit gripes my ass," mumbled the Senator. "So what do we do now?"

"The girl, Luka. You still have the original flash drive, yes?"

"Of course," replied Senator Berhardt. "Why didn't I think of that?"

"Because you have me to do it for you," replied Healy.

"Oh yeah, I thought there was a reason I kept you around," said Bernhardt. "Get over to Walter Reed and see if she's cleared to leave the doctor's care. Bring her to the office."

"What about the other thing. Shouldn't we put out a statement?"

"What other thing?"

"Armand."

"Oh, he's not budging," said a disappointed Senator Bernhardt. "I talked to him last night. You're right though. We should be prepared to jump on things as soon as he makes his press announcement. Not that it will do any good. The possible consequences of that idiot's announcement are unimaginably horrible."

"Then you haven't heard."

"Heard what? I've been in a meeting all morning."

"Armand is dead. Killed in an auto accident this morning."

"Are you serious?"

"Very serious. And we got a call from Bo Peppers a few minutes ago. Said the President needs to see you as soon as possible."

Bernhardt walked quietly for a moment then stopped and turned to Healy, "That's very unfortunate for Armand but I have to admit it may be a fortuitous remedy to what could be a seriously explosive situation. It's certainly not a remedy I would have wished for however." He stopped and thought a moment. "Okay then, I'm on my way to the White House. You get that Luka girl to my office so she can deal with the flash drive, then we'll see where we're going from there."

"You know the press is going to come down on you like a ton of bricks if Armand's intended campaign agenda leaks," said a concerned Healy. "And I have no doubt there will be leaks or at least rumors of some kind."

"Well, let's just hope that doesn't happen. Get in touch with that guy you know…the one who works for Armand. Klein is it?"

"Yes."

"Talk to him and find out who knows what so that we can put a lid on this crap before the whole world begins to fall apart and we have a general uprising."

"Will do, sir," acknowledged Healy.

CHAPTER 22 _____

THE WHITE HOUSE – JAN. 20, 2019

Twenty minutes later Senator Bernhardt was about to enter the west wing of the White House when he was intercepted on the portico by Bo Peppers.

"Morning Senator," smiled Peppers. "I suppose you can guess why we asked you here?"

"Not really. The President and I met yesterday and I updated him last night over the phone. So what's so urgent that I need to see him now? Especially since our problem seems to have met with an unfortunate accident."

"Unfortunate in more ways than one," said Peppers.

"Meaning what exactly?"

"Meaning the messenger is dead but not the message."

"You're telling me his announcement got out?"

"As best we know, yes it did. Apparently we didn't quite deal with the problem soon enough," replied Peppers. "It seems someone was ahead of us and forwarded the message to the New York Times."

"So we counter it. Refute it. Why should that be so difficult? It's the truth and the truth is we're not killing the entitlement programs, just dropping the deadwood and reworking the critical ones and making them viable again. Fortunately we won't have Armand on the campaign trail shouting and repeating all that misinformation ten times a day."

"You don't get it, Senator. Whoever is behind this is way ahead of us. They anticipated Armand's death and will most likely anticipate and counter everything else we can come up with, including any form of truth."

"Wait a minute. What do you mean *everything else* and you said '*not soon enough?*' What the…" Bernhardt stared in disbelief. "Are you telling me that Armand's death was no accident? Are you saying his death was sanctioned by the President?"

"I didn't say that."

"Of course you didn't. You wouldn't would you?"

"You're jumping to conclusions, Senator."

"Jumping to conclusions? Bullshit. The man's body isn't even cold yet and you're talking about him as though he were a pawn on a chess board that you just sacrificed. That's a conclusion easily come by. Don't you think for a minute I'm going to let you slide on this."

"You're only concern should be damage control, Senator. You should be more worried about the effect and not the cause. What's happening with the programs and the blowback from the leak to the press is all going to come back on you and subsequently the President. But you will take the brunt of the flack, certainly enough to ruin your career if mismanaged. We can't allow it to fall on the administration."

The Senator steamed, reached out and jammed a finger into Peppers' chest. "I'm going to see the President in a minute and I'm going to ask him outright if he had anything to do with this. If he tells me he had no knowledge I'll be left with the assumption it was you… and I swear to God I'll have your head on a chopping block before I'm through. This President is a good man and will likely prove to be one of the best this country has ever had. He inherited one hell of a mess, has done all the right things to fix it, and I'll be god damned if I'm going to let you ruin his Presidency and hard work. I'll not see him destroyed because of the blind, misguided, or demented dedication and self perceived importance of some half ass self-serving staffer."

"Now wait a minute there, Senator. Staffer? Just who the hell do you think you're talking to?"

"I know I'm not talking to the President so shove that little pecker of yours back in your pants and crawl back under the rock you came out from son. And don't you ever begin to think you can dump your bullshit on me. I've seen people like you come and go in this town; ambitious political leaches who think their shit don't stink just because they work under this roof. I've also seen the likes of them ruin the careers of good well meaning statesmen but I know that damn game so don't you think for a minute I can't get your slick ambitious ass shipped back to the stump jumpin' boonies you came from."

Peppers grew angry, locking his jaw while wanting to lash back at the powerful senator. Over the past two years in the White House he had grown accustomed to being catered to and treated like royalty simply because he had the ear, trust, and total access to the President; enjoying all the perks because he was the President's Chief of Staff. A good Chief of Staff was a necessity for any sitting President. However, it was also a position that could consume a person with self-admiration and a belief they were the critical linchpin and moving force of the administration, the President behind the President, untouchable, invincible. Unfortunately, some Chief Executives became so dependent on the services of their Chief of Staff they were blind to the personal transition taking place right in front of them in which their Chief of Staff was turning from a loyal dedicated aide and servant into a regular Rasmussen who began to take things into their own hands. This were rare but one of the curses of power. Having spent many decades in Washington, Senator Bernhardt had seen it all with the various administrations and members of Congress, and as a result had little difficulty differentiating between those orders and directives that actually sourced with a President and those orders and requests that manifested from a staffer backed with an assumed or perceived presidential blessing.

"You have to know the President can't be implicated in something like this. He shouldn't even be questioned on the subject," said Peppers.

"Then you tell me," said Bernhardt. "Answer me truthfully and I won't even raise the subject with him. Was there an executive order to kill Armand?"

Peppers paused, his eyes showing a rare glint of doubt as he weighed the consequences of his answer, knowing that if he said yes, the President would lose all support and respect of the Majority Leader of the U.S. Senate, something absolutely critical to the success of the administration. He also knew that if he answered no, the Senator would most likely ruin his life professionally or quite possibly result in his being incarcerated. And then there was the possibility that regardless of which answer he gave, it could lead to Senator Bernhardt discovering the real truth of which could be catastrophic for all concerned. Peppers decided that for lack of any other alternative he would not answer the question at all and chose to simply turn and walk away, leaving Senator Bernhardt to his own conclusions.

Would the Senator be so bold wondered Peppers.

CHAPTER 23 _____

VALDOSTA, GEORGIA – JAN. 21, 2019

They drifted into the city in one's and two's by private vehicles, all checking into the same hotel and all for the publicly expressed purpose of holding an Air Force pilots' reunion. In appearance it was a simple get together of good old flyboys out for a weekend of booze and bullshit. In reality they were a group of highly qualified A-10 pilots on a mission with all their arrangements made by Colonel Floyd Mayfield. This accounted for the purpose of the numerous cash advances and instructions he received by personal currier over the past eight months. All delivered in person to avoid monitoring by government intelligence agencies.

The group of pilots consisted of former U.S. Air Force flyers along with American civilians and a few foreign mercenary types. Some were there just for the money and others for a cause, an ideologically motivated cause that would have them commit the ultimate form of treason.

Now what the hotel staff thought were closed door private lunches and parties were in fact briefing sessions conducted by Mayfield and a few others; detailed sessions that if they were discovered prior to implementation would most likely result in a prosecution that would cost the participants their lives.

Across town, Big D and Keen were sitting on the top row of the Valdosta Wildcat's football stadium. It was a repeat of their weekly ritual where they would sit and look down on the field and remember the events of their last game except now that the season was over they would sometimes repeat the process to review their most impressive victories and worse defeats even though there were none of the latter. They would read the field like it was a huge map, pointing to the lined green gridiron, analyzing and evaluating the details of each of their plays, talking about what they did right, what they did wrong, and what they should have done. They had developed this ritual as freshmen, making this a method of honest open shared criticism to help propel them ahead of the pack. It involved reviewing everything while feeling the expanse of the field and stadium, a kind of virtual flashback to benefit their future performances. As far as they were concerned it was a successful exercise which kept them focused and was sending them to the bigger venue at Georgia Tech. And so now they sat there in the chill of January of their senior year, continuing the exercise in the off-season to keep their mind and perspective in anticipation of their future on the national stage.

On this day however Big D was moody and reserved, his mind seeming to be on something other than football.

"You know you blew it, right?" said Keen. "I mean, it was a simple timing pattern and you should have been there. I threw a perfect ball and you were supposed to go ten and in. What were you thinkin', man? You went ten, cut in then headed for the post. Made me look pretty damn stupid."

Big D just nodded agreement as he stared down on the field. He wasn't thinking about the game. He was thinking about the future and if it would even include any football at all.

"Okay, I give up," said Keen. "Your brain's been everywhere except on this planet all friggin' day. I mean, it's not like we lost the game or anything. We kicked their asses. I can dig it when you usually got your mind on somethin' and that's all you want to talk about, but man, I ain't never seen you not even want to talk about *anything* before. Not since you were eight years old and that hornet flew in your mouth and stung your tongue and it was all puffed up and shit. I mean, man, you gotta be sick or somethin'. You ain't said a damn thing all day."

Big D continued to sit silent as he leaned back and shoved his hands in his jacket pockets. He wanted to talk, to just blurt out everything on his mind, but knew he couldn't because the cost would be too great. All he could do was remember the shocking conversation he had with his father, Col. Mayfield, the night before, a conversation that somehow brought back and clarified the numerous subtle comments his father had made over the years. He always thought them to be a joke or just a fleeting expression of racial frustration implanted in his father's character by generations past. He never took them seriously, never thought his father capable of what he was told the previous evening. He couldn't imagine anyone in his family being capable of what he was told was about to happen. Now he knew why his father insisted on the lifetime of martial arts training and weapons training and of course why, over the years, his father would take those long weekend trips alone to places unknown.

Sitting there now, he realized by any definition other than biological that Keen was his brother and never could he have asked for one better. Had there ever been a need or desire to confide in a brother it certainly was now, thought Big D, but if there was ever a brother he couldn't confide in now it was also Keen, because Keen…was white. Big D was torn both emotionally and philosophically and had been struggling, wondering all day whether to trust his own judgment or to be obedient to his father.

He looked at Keen for a long silent moment, their eyes locked, leaving Keen confused while seeing Big D's eyes pleading for answers. Then Big D abruptly rose and ran off, leaving Keen sitting alone in the stands staring at the field affectionately known by the city as *Death Valley*.

WALTER REED MEDICAL CENTER – JAN. 21, 2019

The Walter Reed National Military Medical Center campus was a massive complex, the result of years of moves, mergers, and expansions by the government to accommodate the needs of each branch of service. Here in this large facility Luka had just left the private room where they had rolled in Major Stagliano after another MRI; this one performed because the swelling in his brain had diminished and Stag had come out of his coma. He was woozy to say the least, due to the medications he was given to ease the extensive pain of the previous combat injury that resurfaced due to the accident. In addition, he was somewhat disoriented even though he had been told where he was and why. When he was told that he had been transferred to Walter Reed by order of Senator Bernhardt, something in his memory was triggered, something important. But he wasn't quite sure what. Only that he felt he had to see the Senator and it was urgent. There were other things he couldn't remember as well. He was told his memory loss was most likely temporary and would gradually return. A result of the trauma, they told him. Stag didn't give a damn what the explanation was, he was just plain angry and frustrated that he was even partially mentally incapacitated. To Major Vincent Stagliano, memory was control and control meant survival. To him, not having control was simply not instinctive, not characteristic in the least and just plain unacceptable.

Later that morning when he'd become more lucid, Stagliano asked about Luka and was told she had been discharged and picked up by someone from Senator Bernhardt's office. He was relieved to know she was well, but continued to agonize over the memories he could not pull together; the various pieces of important information somehow tied to the Senator. *Urgent! It was urgent but...what the hell was it?*

"I'm glad to see you're feeling better," said a nurse as she entered the room. 'Now I won't have to worry about you when I leave on my vacation."

She was a pleasant middle aged woman who performed her duties with caring, confidence, and authority. When Stag tried to sit up she gently pushed him back down.

"I said *feeling better*. Didn't say anything about being fully recovered. You just cool it and lie back and relax," she ordered as she punched the power control and raised the head of his bed a bit then adjusted his pillow to accommodate his desire to sit up. "There, how's that?"

"Better," replied Stagliano.

"Good, now let me check your vitals. My name is Gracie by the way. The first time I introduced myself you were a near comatose zombie so I won't hold it against you for not remembering," she said as she checked his pulse.

"You're right, I don't remember. In fact, there's a lot I don't remember. How long have I been here by the way?"

"Would you believe me if I said you've been in a coma for seven years?"

"Hell no."

"Good, because you haven't. You got here yesterday. New kid on the block and fortunate to still have your faculties. It's not a very good idea to try and fly a Jeep off a bridge these days. What with gravity and all that."

"Vacation? You're going on a vacation?" asked Stagliano.

"Yep, first vacation in five years. I mean I've taken vacation time before but never went anywhere because my husband and I could never coordinate the time off together. This time the old man and I are taking a cruise, a week in the Caribbean. That's why it's important for you to get better. I don't want to have to worry about you. Time is critical. I'm counting down – six hours thirty-two minutes until I punch out. My guess is you're still going to be here when I get back so I'll tell you what... how bout I bring you a souvenir, one of those coconuts carved into a pirate head or something like that? A must have item for every man of means like yourself, right?"

"How did I ever get along without one," smiled Stagliano.

"Damn right, soldier," laughed Gracie as she recorded her findings, took his temperature, checked his IV, then turned to leave the room. "Don't forget...if you gotta take a leak you use that urinal cup thing right there. If that's too complicated then just push the button for some help and I'm sure some cute young thing will be glad to come in and hold it for you or maybe that big hairy guy from Philly. He's not a nurse but he looks good in scrubs."

Stag chuckled. "I think I can manage."

"Oh yeah, I almost forgot. That Senator friend of yours said to let you know he'll be here to visit as soon as he can get free. Also, I ordered you a sandwich, coffee, and juice. Don't forget, you have an old back injury and a few minor fractures so take it slow but get better. I'll check in before I leave." She looked at her watch. "Countdown, six hours twenty seven minutes and I'm off to Margaritaville."

Stag laughed to himself as she left the room, then his mind clicked as a few of the things she said gave him an insight to memories lost. *Countdown*, she said. *Time critical* and the *Senator*. Somehow they went together. *What the hell was it that he couldn't remember? Why was it so important? Damn, why couldn't he remember?*

CHAPTER 25 _____

NEW ORLEANS, LOUISIANA – JAN. 21, 2019

Farin Dupré sat comfortably in front of his personal computer in the dimly lit room that he often referred to as his *Chamber of Inspiration.* In reality it was a climate controlled rented storage unit where he kept a cache of weapons and operational computer equipment more than adequate for his purposes. The walls were plastered with racial posters from around the world. Pictures of the late Martin Luther King, Nelson Mandela, and enlarged photographs of black people being beaten, hung, and burned. The photos were taken in foreign countries but he didn't care. To him it was all the same, it was all America and he used those photos as propaganda all the while claiming it was taking place in the US. This was a place and method whereby, *so he thought*, his efforts on the internet couldn't be traced to his home.

Usually he would do the bulk of his work offline on his computer at home, then bring the material via disk to his so called secret chamber and upload it and post it as quickly as possible before getting offline. He was computer savvy enough to do that but not smart enough to know that his covert efforts were useless simply because, as he wrongfully thought, he would not be traced in a way that phone calls have traditionally been traced. However, computers leave digital trails that are rarely hidden from entities with the talent and extremely advanced resources such as those possessed by the government. So of course he had raised a few flags and this resulted in continuous monitoring by the government. Fortunately for him they considered his work as just another hate site protected under the First Amendment of the Constitution, one of a great many such sites on the internet. Their only concern was the false name under which he operated it. Their investigations turned up nothing because to date there was no physical activity or known existence to trace, only a computer that piggy-backed on the wifi access of a coffee shop nearby.

It was there on his internet website he could express himself in a manner unencumbered, a manner showing the true hateful radical person he actually was. There he could hate anyone and any system he chose without repercussion or blowback and without endangering his better known image, an image that generated his main source of income. And it was where he could hate all white people for any reason, true or false, that he deemed legitimate or necessary or conveniently persuasive to his readers and cause. There in his hideaway and on the internet, under the name Abdur Rezzaque, he created the radical website titled *A Horizon of War*. The pseudonym he used he chose from a list of Hadith scholars, perhaps expecting the name to give him creditability and, of course, to hide his real identity.

He created the website for the sole purpose of generating fear and unrest among African Americans; the contents of which is largely based on his personal anger and paranoid perception of racial persecution. For the most part the website contained works of fiction as well as a few cherry picked actual accounts and testimonials of atrocious acts of discrimination and cruelty against people of the black race around the world. Such examples weren't difficult to find because the world had no shortage of such things among all races, even though many were committed by people of the same race, a fact he often left out of his reported accounts when he wasn't claiming they were backed or financed by some unknown white faction. And of course they were supported with actual but dated historical acts by people that no longer existed, acts of racial abuse dating back a hundred or more years. He possessed a real talent for spin and the ability to interpret words and actions of politicians and others in such a way as to not even closely resemble the truth, but at the same time be most effective.

His website warned of a worldwide genocidal conspiracy by whites and white western cultures to eliminate the black race. Because of this he encouraged the taking up of arms and the preparation for a global war. He informed his readers that in America the call for black social justice and the fight was near. He supported this rhetoric by citing signs and predictions by fictitious racial savants, some of which he himself invented simply by attributing literary works he also created out of thin air. A few of them he self-published to add credibility. Most of these fictitious authors had conveniently passed away, but, of course they all possessed impeccable degrees and a litany of credibility or a glowing personal history. It always amazed him how quickly and easily all this fantasy was accepted. Some of his books by imaginary sources even becoming profitable items that he sold direct from the internet. To him these were not lies simply because he claimed they were true. They were *his* truth, which many minorities wanted to and were eager to hear and believe. And because they believed the rhetoric often it became even more relevant.

His rhetoric was especially tailored for those of his race in the United States, tailored with hate driven accounts of government and corporate agendas that targeted black people for discrimination through programs of exclusion or total elimination. He created fictitious accounts of secret scientific programs, the object of which were to create, in the guise of a disease, a way to curtail and eventually eliminate the ability of blacks to reproduce, in essence to sterilize a race of people. These fictions, both historic and current in nature, were received much like the acceptance of the African American holiday Quanza that in reality is just another fantasy invented back in the sixties by a radical Black Panther. Quanza wasn't a true or traditional African holiday but the black community accepted it as such because they wanted it to be and thought it should be. They wanted to claim their own holiday like the Jewish Hanukkah and *white* Christian Christmas. They wanted it so badly they never questioned its source and so now it is their recognized exclusive traditional holiday.

Farin Dupré had long ago learned one of the first rules of deceit by observing politicians and race mongers like

Jamison Johnson. The lesson learned being; the bigger and more ridiculous the lie and the more it is repeated, the more likely it will be believed and accepted. Knowing this, he created multiple layers of big lies and relentlessly fed them to his followers. His books penned in his real name as well as his speeches had effectively generated a great deal of interest by like minded African Americans and all of them included references or tidbits to steer the readers and listeners to the web site and the fictitious Abdur Rezzaque, which in turn became his tool for donations and the recruitment of his reserve army, an army that at last count numbered roughly in the many thousands, an army that came to be known to its members as the American Socialist Union, an army waiting for just the right time to strike.

Now, thanks to Jamison Johnson and Arisztid Backos, Farin Dupré was beginning to think that the time had finally come, time to call up his followers for the great fight, time to cash in. However Farin Dupré had his own agenda in spite of Johnson and Backos. What he didn't know was that each of those men had separate agendas as well. All three were using each other for personal gain or purpose, all turning wheels within wheels that may or may not take them on the same journey.

SENATE BUILDING – JAN. 21, 2019

Janet Healy and Luka Varnas had just arrived at Senator Bearnhardt's office and went immediately to retrieve the flash drive. After opening the safe Healy stared in disbelief, "Oh my God. It's gone," she said, her eyes looking everywhere and nowhere, wondering and trying to figure out how, why, and where it could have gone. And most importantly...*who the hell took it?* Was it an agent and if so were they civilian or government? How did they gain access to the office and safe? Or was it possibly a staffer? One of their very own? Who? But most importantly...why? She had watched the Senator put the flash drive in the safe the day before and the only other person who knew the combination was her. It wasn't even known to any of the other staffers.

"It's gone?" asked Luka.

"Yes," replied Healy. "Whatever is on that thing must be awfully damn important for someone to come in here and steal it. And it was a pretty damn slick job, too."

"Stag certainly thought so," said Luka. "Being important, I mean. He damn near went into a panic after seeing it."

When young Jimmy Britton suggested they put security cameras in their offices they had all laughed it off and the Senator had flatly refused just as he had years earlier when the building security wanted to do the same. "There's nothing secure about security cameras," said the Senator. "Just more damn people sticking their noses where they don't belong." For the first time Janet Healy wondered if maybe they were wrong, if maybe had they installed a camera it could tell her who breached their office and safe.

"I'm going to have to call and inform the Senator. Meanwhile we're going to need you to park your pretty ass at that desk and start writing down what you saw in the files of that flash drive after you decrypted it. And hopefully you have one hell of a good memory because whatever it is it's drastic enough to cause a good man to kill himself and nearly cost you and Major Stagliano's lives."

"But I emailed the decrypted contents to the Senator," said Luka.

"Yeah we know. But some damn cyber geek snatched it up and made it go poof before we ever received it. Disappeared just like the flash drive. Can you believe that?"

"Sure I can," replied Luka. "The right geek with the right toys can do just about anything. Even I can do it. In fact, I can probably find it. Nothing ever disappears in cyberspace. It's just a great black hole full of gazillions of bits of crap. It's just a matter of knowing how to find it."

"You can do that?"

"Sure. But not here in this office with these clunky average Model-T PC's of yours."

"Okay, if not here, then where?"

"NSA. But I don't work there anymore. Haven't worked there for over two years. I doubt they'll let me just stroll in and use their stuff. The security protocols are incredible. It's not like they're a public library or anything. Besides, who's to say they're not the ones who pilfered the email in the first place?"

"That's not speaking too kindly of your former employer."

"What can I say? These days it seems there aren't too many government agencies worth speaking kindly of at all. Sure I worked there and I have friends there but like the song says, '...friends in low places'."

"Is there an alternative to the NSA that you can use?"

"My first thought was my own notebook computer. But I'm told it ended up somewhere in the river after the jeep wrecked. Knowing what I know now, I'm beginning to think there's something fishy about that story as well. I should have been able to call up the email I sent you guys, but when I went to my email accounts on a computer at the hospital in an effort to let a few friends know I was okay, it seems all that stuff I had in the so-called cloud has blown away. Guess it was gotten by the mystery geeks. Somebody out there really doesn't like you folks."

"So it's the NSA or nothing?"

"Well, there are a number of major corporations with that capability, but the problem is time and getting their cooperation and getting through their many layers of corporate stratus. It would be worse than a root canal at the dentist. And, of course, there's the fact I don't think you would want them to know what that hot email is all about anyway."

"So it's the NSA or nothing," repeated Healy, smiling.

"Pretty much, yes... if you want the most immediate results, and especially if they're the culprits behind all this. A smoking gun would be more easily found in the bad guys own closet, wouldn't you say?"

"I certainly would. But my many years in Washington would lead me to think that if the NSA is involved, it's probably through some sort of outside influence and probably limited to only a few individuals who would be pulling the strings of a few lower level geek geniuses who are oblivious as to the whys and what-for's; possibly under some bullshit false security pretense requiring departmentalization. And, of course, there's always that good old edict of what you don't know can't hurt you. *Plausible deniability* is a much overused concept in this damn town. And it's a phrase that sounds a hell of a lot more palatable than what it actually means, being, *cover your ass*."

"Do you actually think it could be the NSA?"

"If like you say it takes their kind of talent and resources, then well... if the damn shoe fits. But first things first. Let me contact the Senator. I think he can remedy the access problem although I don't think we'll be able to get in there until tomorrow. By the way, as of right now you are officially one of Senator Bernhardt's staffers," smiled Janet Healy. "That's step one. Step two is getting you inside the NSA and that trick is up to the Senator."

WALTER REED MEDICAL CENTER – JAN. 21, 2019

Vincent Stagliano lay in his hospital bed at Walter Reed still straining to discover the lost memory of what he somehow knew was some form of important or possibly even urgent information regarding Senator Bernhardt. Searching his memory he discovered instead a maze of confusing information and thoughts that would flash by like a child playing with the remote control of a television set, sending people and pictures past his eyes faster than he could place them. One second Stagliano was seeing flashes of childhood memories and the next there were flashes of combat. He tried to control the process, to slow it down and expand on a memory of choice, but he failed, the result being a sharp pain of frustration. With his head throbbing and his brain rebooting itself on its own terms, he surrendered to a more patient process of waiting for nature to takes its course and hopefully put his gray matter in order.

He laid further back into his pillow, took up the TV remote attached to his bed and touched the ON button. The TV, mounted high up on the wall in the corner of the room came to life. Even having the sound muted, he instantly saw that what was on the screen was an infomercial pushing another miracle pill guaranteed to make your sex life improve. Of course the small print at the bottom of the screen read that the results stated in the advertisement are not to be expected by all consumers. *Now there's a life lesson, no guarantees...ever,* thought Stagliano. *A real reality show.*

He hit the channel button repeatedly until he came upon the FOX News Channel, paused on that station, and watched with little interest. He kept the TV on MUTE, not wanting the sound to contribute to his slight but constant headache. Across the screen he saw scenes of destruction in Syria from the most recent conflict between the radical Muslim extremist ISIS, and just about everyone else. Then a news story change brought the images of convoys of Russian separatists still fighting in Ukraine. Still he kept the sound off as he viewed the latest fighting and strife in Iraq. *The more things change the more they stay the same*, he thought as he continued to view the latest atrocities being committed by the wide spreading ISIS in Europe, the new and strongest radical Muslim terrorist organization to date involved in their caliphate. He laid watching but paying little attention until just as he was about to doze off he noticed the information crawler at the bottom of the screen with a news update on the death of Senator Jean Stephenson that stated the FBI had determined she had not died of natural causes as first suspected but was in fact poisoned, leading to the conclusion she was assassinated.

Poisoned, thought Stagliano. *Poisoned means murdered. A United States Senator murdered. No, she was not murdered...assassinated. A senator assassinated! That's it! Yes, that's what I've been trying to remember!*

He sat up quickly, trying his best to hold on to that thought, to focus and bring back the complete memory that he knew was incredibly important. There came a sudden pain and he winced, dropping the TV remote and bringing his hands to his head. "No!" he said to himself. "No damn way you're going to pass out, Stag. Not now! Not..."

He fought the constant pain and throbbing in his head and began to get out of the bed but soon lost the fight when a sudden stronger burst of pain struck him like a baseball bat and all went black as he fell to the floor. When he finally returned to consciousness he found himself surrounded by nurses and a doctor who eventually put him back in his bed. Then to be tended to by a nurse and orderly. After a moment of regaining his bearing and realization of his situation he began reassembling his thoughts. *The senator*, he thought. I *have to get to Senator Bernhardt. But why?* Once again the memory had vanished, leaving Stagliano feeling as though he was grasping at smoke.

CHAPTER 28 _____

GREAT FALLS, VIRGINIA – JAN. 21, 2019

As the sun dipped below the horizon and the shadows of the many trees on his six acre estate in Great Falls began to merge with the darkness, General H. Conrad Lewis drove slowly up the long winding driveway to his home. He was awash with thought, occupied with concerns for all the possibilities of failure within the massive operation known only to him and a handful of others as *Operation New Dawn*. So deep in thought that he failed to notice the lights that were on in the house. Not that it usually should have been something of concern. On this occasion however, there should not have been anyone home. The General had sent his family out of the country, telling them he would join them soon for a long overdue vacation. The fact the lights were on in the house didn't faze him until he entered from the garage to the kitchen and quickly noticed the smell of freshly brewed coffee and the presence of a tall ominous looking man with penetrating blue eyes who just smiled and nodded a silent greeting. The man had just poured himself a cup of coffee and after taking a sip, directed the General to the living room by simply pointing a thumb in that direction. He then looked to his cup with displeasure, noting silently his disapproval of the General's choice of only stocking decaf. He poured another cup and handed it to the General, "You're going to need this," he said with slight concern.

General Lewis declined the coffee and moved on to the living room where he discovered Arisztid Backos comfortably sitting on the sofa with his two bodyguards positioned strategically about the room.

"Good evening, General," smiled Backos. "I hope you don't mind our letting ourselves in. You see, no one was home and I didn't want my occupied limo and escort vehicle waiting in the driveway to draw any undesired attention. As you can see I sent the vehicles away and will have them return when we complete our little chat. I know it doesn't seem fitting to meet at your home, but then I knew you'd sent your family to France and, well... it seemed more convenient. After all, we certainly could not meet at the Pentagon now could we?"

"I don't mind at all," replied the General as he removed his uniform trench coat and tossed it over a chair, "But did you have to bring him? After all, this is my home."

"Oh, honestly, General," laughed Backos, "After all these years and especially these recent weeks. You're not getting squeamish on me now are you? Mr. Robinson is actually quite a pleasant man when you take the time to know him. And of course, he's exceptionally proficient in his duties. Don't you agree?"

"Pleasant? That's a matter of opinion. But then I wouldn't know anyway because I haven't taken the time to socialize with our lethal specialist. As far as proficient… yes, he is most proficient. By my count he's eliminated at least a dozen little problems for us in a very complete and expedient way. With the exception of his most recent assignment regarding Major Stagliano, that is."

"Oh, I disagree," replied Backos. "Considering the short notice we gave him, I think the results were somewhat satisfactory. All the flash drives have been obtained and Mr. Robinson assures me that any unfinished business regarding Major Stagliano and associates will soon be remedied. And even if that turns out not to be the case there is simply not enough time for anyone to obstruct our little operation."

"Little? Are you serious?"

Arisztid Backos laughed as he rose, crossed the room and placed a hand on the General's shoulder. "I understand, General. This adventure certainly may not seem so inconsequential to you. Of course not; being so widespread and complicated as it is, years in the planning and all that. But you see where I'm concerned it is a small part of something with much more meaning to me, something so much bigger. It has been a major part of my entire life and will affect so many people. And without a doubt you are the most important factor in all of this. Not for those petty reasons you were led to believe in your younger more susceptible years by the Reverend Johnson. Certainly not that parade of straw men and separatism rhetoric. No, this is far more important and it requires you to bring it to fruition." Backos turned and glanced around the room for a long silent moment then turned back to the

General. "I honestly feel I haven't enough time left on this earth to see it through but I'm confident that you and good men like you will succeed and bring order after the chaos. A true... *new world order*."

"Divide and conquer is a simple concept in a battle plan or even a nation," replied the General. "But on a global scale... in a world unhinged... it may evolve into a mere theory contrived of empty words, circumvented by ambitious opportunistic power mongers. The basic human element is not so easily altered. The history of mankind has proven that time and time again."

"Yes, so it would seem and how well I know," said Backos. "But we have the power to try haven't we? And if we succeed perhaps we will give mankind a thousand years without dissention...without strife."

"By offering a cure that may be worse than the disease?" asked the General.

"You're having doubts?" asked a surprised Backos.

"No," replied the General, "only an honest moment of reality."

"Yes, my friend. And that's your forte... why I've chosen you above the others. You possess no illusions, no grand ambitions, or if you will, to put it in your uniquely American vernacular – no proclivity for *bullshit*."

General Lewis didn't reply to the words that should have inspired him. Instead they seemed to add weight to his already massive burden, though he dare not show it because he knew that Ben Robinson had not come along for the ride or just to make coffee. He was there to quickly eliminate any dissent or irreversible wavering regarding upcoming events. General Lewis knew, as did Backos, that for the most part his work was done, merely waiting only a go or no go order, and for all he knew someone else may have been prepared to replace him and deal with the outcome, to pick up the pieces and create the Arisztid Backos utopia. It made sense. *It was what he would do,* thought the General. Certainly it will take the efforts of a great many people but it will take the coordination derived from a true military mind to see it through; not a ruling dictator over the people but certainly an authoritative dictator with the correct priorities and missions; someone who was determined and ruthless enough to see things through but patient and understanding as well. He wondered if he was truly that man, if he could actually rise to achieve those goals. Ironically, he was asking himself if he could rise to the level of the founding fathers of the very country he was about to destroy.

"Now, shall we take a little time to review our plans and timetables?" said Backos.

"Sure," replied the General as he took a seat.

Backos sat across from him and smiled, showing nothing but confidence in his man. As he did, he looked to the doorway that led to the kitchen where stood Ben Robinson, one hand casually tipping a cup of coffee to his lips and the other behind his back gripping a pistol with a silencer. Backos nodded slightly, showing Robinson that all was well and his services, his special services, would not be required; at least not on this night. With that signal from Backos, Robinson eased his grip on the pistol.

"Anybody want fresh coffee?" He asked with a smile. No one replied. He backed away and returned to the kitchen to freshen his own. He knew his services would not be needed and so looked forward to a night on the town as soon as his employer was through here. Still he kept his mind on business, formulating a plan to accomplish what he was going to do in the morning to derail yet another hiccup in Backos's master plan. "At least a dozen." he said under his breath, repeating General Lewis's comment. "Hah. A dozen? If you only knew General. If you only knew," he laughed.

CHAPTER 29 _____

BERHARDT ESTATE – JAN. 22, 2019

Senator Jesse Bernhardt sat heavily in his old brown leather chair behind the desk of his home study. He simply sat there amid the walnut paneled walls and bookcase ridden dimly lit room, staring ahead at nothing, occasionally glancing through the wood sash window at the light snow that had begun to fall only minutes before. Gradually the sun dipped below the horizon to eventually leave him sitting alone in the dark, alone with his dark troubling thoughts. As the sun sank entirely in the distance so did his spirits while he pondered and struggled with the possibility that the President had lied to him. Senator Armand had been murdered. Of that he was certain. As to whether the President actually knew or even ordered this was the question. And if he did, if it was in fact an action dictated or approved by President Moreno, regardless of how essential or justified such an action might be, should it be condoned or…or what? The President had seemed honestly surprised at Senator Bernhardt's suggestion that Senator Armand might have been murdered. That reaction along with the rest of their conversation seemed convincing enough but as the Senator well knew, in Washington and the world of politics in general, lies and deception can often be as subtle as the flutter of a butterfly's wings.

The elder Senator leaned forward on his desk and put his face in his hands, knowing that regardless of his position and opinion of the matter there was little or nothing he could do where the President was concerned. There would, of course, be no possible way this could be tied to the President even if he were in fact guilty. Someone in the administration would have made sure of that. And considering everything that was at stake, was guilt even the right word to be applied to this case. And then there were the consequences of going public, of the incredible harm and effect such an accusation would have on the nation and the institution of the Presidency, especially coming from the leader of the U.S. Senate and even more following the previous administration which turned out to be the most corrupt in the nation's history. The Senator was torn. Just as President Moreno had reminded him of what he himself had said long ago; *they were at war, not a war of guns but a war of ideology, a war to save the soul of the republic.*

There was also the real possibility that the President had no knowledge of the action at all. And this, Senator Bernhardt had concluded, was the more reasonable and likely conclusion. It was the conversation he had with Bo Peppers prior to his meeting with the President that was convincing him there was something anomalous taking place. Certainly Peppers wasn't beyond taking things into his own hands by using his position and the perceived power of the President, but to commit murder was beyond comprehension...or was it? Such things were rumored in regards to previous Presidents and administrations, but to prove such a rumor would take a platoon of investigators with talents exceeding those of the fictitious Sherlock Holmes. Senator Bernhardt refused to believe that President Moreno had been directly involved in Armand's murder and so the real question was why Bo Peppers would ignore all possible avenues of reasoning with Armand and opt directly for the most extreme solution? Yet another question heavy on the Senator's mind was who could he trust enough to find out just what motivations or influences actually drove Bo Peppers to do such a thing?

His first thought was to assign Major Stagliano. Stag's loyalty was unquestionable and he certainly had the wherewithal and connections to conduct such an undertaking. But Stagliano was laid up in the hospital, himself a victim of whatever was going on. Was there anyone else he could trust as much as Stag, he thought, and this being Washington, was there actually any way in hell an official investigation could be kept quiet and confidential? He ran the possibilities through his mind and settled on only one name, that of the daughter of an old friend. A young lady he had known since birth and who he had helped get a foot in the door of the FBI. In doing so she had not disappointed him by climbing through the ranks and eventually landing on the White House Secret Service detail. *No better way to get the inside scoop on Bo Peppers than getting it from someone who was already on the inside,* he thought. He picked up the phone to make the call, then paused and decided to make the request in person.

FALLS CHURCH, VIRGINIA – JAN. 22, 2019

Senator Bernhardt knocked on the second floor apartment door and waited. As he waited he looked around and noted that the apartment complex and surrounding neighborhood was exceptionally quiet except for the rhythmic music coming from behind the door. Full grown trees now seasonally naked of their leaves surrounded the small Falls Church apartment complex and a slight rain that followed the earlier snowfall left the bark of the bare trees glistening with ice and the reflection of the lights of the nearby parking lot and walkway. The late night scene and the throbbing music somehow came together in odd harmony where somehow something soft and seasonal would have sufficed.

When no one answered he knocked again, louder, and it was then he heard the volume of the progressive jazz music coming from within the apartment diminish. When Lindsey Ford opened the door Senator Bernhardt immediately noticed her overwhelming beauty and exceptional body, even though she was wearing worn and faded old FBI sweat pants with a hole in one knee and a faded sleeveless t-shirt sporting a Margaretaville logo. Her long dark hair was shoved up under a Washington Redskins ball cap that she wore backwards. She was sweating profusely which caused the shirt to cling to her form from her waist to her shoulders in a most revealing manner. So much so that even the elderly Senator did a double take before he took mental pause to remind himself of his age and their relationship.

He had not seen her very often during her early years with the FBI and during recent years he had only seen her occasionally with the Secret Service as she performed her duties on the President's security detail. At those times, even though her required business suit showed she was now a grown woman, it failed to reveal just how well grown she had become. On those occasions the two of them usually exchanged only a smile or a wink of recognition, respecting the fact she was on the job and he was most often present in some sort of official capacity. Protocol and prudence didn't allow for their unofficial uncle to niece relationship. Senator Bernhardt's usual source of information regarding her life came during the rare times that he and her parents came together for one of the intimate dinners that were occasionally arranged by the Senator's wife. It was some time ago during one of those dinners that Lindsey's mother, his wife's college roommate, asked the Senator to put a bug in the ear of the FBI recruiters to snatch their girl up as soon as she graduated from law school. Her mother's reasoning was that the young girl was so headstrong and impulsive that the restrictive environment of the FBI would serve her well. The girl had a natural taste and drive for extreme adventure and her parents were sincerely concerned, having no idea where she would wind up if left to her own desires. She had once mentioned the FBI as a possible option to her future but later dismissed the idea and was then thinking of a future as a fighter pilot in the Marine Corps, so they decided to give her a nudge in the direction of their preference, the FBI. Little did they know the FBI and eventually the Secret Service were just the ticket as far as Lindsey was concerned, and she accepted the challenge with complete dedication.

"Oh my God! Uncle Jesse!" she exclaimed as she jumped at the surprised Senator, giving him a big hug. "I'm so glad to see you," she said as she suddenly realized what she was doing. "Oh, I'm so sorry. I'm all sweaty and…"

"Hah," laughed Senator Bernhardt, "No problem, kiddo. This old suit's been through worse."

She pulled him into her apartment, snatching up a towel along the way and while wiping away the perspiration she led him to the living room of the small apartment that doubled as her personal gym. The room was a mix of tasteful furniture, a treadmill, and dumbbells on an exercise pad. She led the Senator around the treadmill to the sofa then snatched a remote control off an end table and hit a button that turned off the music she had been listening to during her workout. "Please sit," she insisted. "I'll fix you a drink. Anything special? I know you're a scotch guy but afraid I haven't got any. How 'bout a beer?"

"Nothing for me, thanks."

She flipped the towel around her neck and grabbed him by the arm. "Well come on then, sit with me," she insisted as she pulled him down to sit on the sofa.

"Don't they have exercise facilities for you folks in the Secret Service?" asked the Senator.

"Oh sure. But I have my own routine that I like to do here, a kind of mix of dance and workout. Here I can push it without having to put up with the prying eyes and sexual innuendoes of the male agents. Not that I really give a damn. Doesn't bother me as much as it does those oversexed Neanderthals, but I have to be careful."

"Oh, and why is that?" asked the Senator.

"Well, one of them got a little too rude and crude one day and tried to get all touchy feely so I put him in the hospital," she replied. "He deserved it though because the asshole was married. But I, um... well I can have a bit of a temper at times. So I decided it best to just avoid those situations altogether. In spite of what you might hear, it's still a boys club."

"Hah," laughed the Senator. "Good for you."

"So tell me, were you just in the neighborhood and decided to stop in and check on your favorite unrelated niece or did you get a craving for my bodacious cinnamon rolls?"

"Cinnamon rolls? Oh, that's right. You used to make those when you were a kid," laughed the Senator. "Yeah, they were pretty damn good weren't they? You mean you still make them?"

"Sure. Why the hell do you think I need to work out so much," she laughed. "You know I actually made those for the first lady once. POTUS was off somewhere on Air Force One and the good ol' boy boss thought I would be better company for her than any of those ass kissing stiffs on his roster. So while they had to endure some boring speech at a rubber chicken affair where they had to smell the food they didn't get to eat somewhere on the other side of the country, the first lady and I made cinnamon buns and watched Survivor on TV. I've got to say I thought I would be shit canned after that but the first lady swore herself to secrecy and has honorably kept that oath ever since."

The Senator chuckled then grew serious and thought carefully for a moment, almost deciding to dismiss his reason for the visit and just leave, not wanting to put her and her job in jeopardy. The job of which he knew she was completely dedicated. He then dismissed his doubts and concerns, knowing she was more than capable of handling such an assignment and remembering how important it was that he finds out the truth of the situation in the administration.

"Lindsey, I, came here, well to... This may sound corny but the country needs your help in a most unique way, and unfortunately if you decide to do this it could put you and your career with the Secret Service in jeopardy."

Her smile turned to concern and suddenly the Senator could see he was no longer looking into the eyes of the young adventuresome girl whose career he had jump started, but was now seeing a strong experienced capable woman who could understand the importance of the task he hoped she was about to accept.

"It involves the investigation of certain individuals at the highest level in the administration," he continued.

"Individuals who may have been responsible for a very serious crime. And one person in particular."

She sat silent for a moment, contemplating the seriousness of his words and seeing his obvious concern. She knew him well and weighing the hazards of the request against the dedication and integrity of the man she had known and loved as family all of her life, she had no problem reaching a very quick decision. In addition, her professional instincts told her that whatever the mission involved, the risk was necessary. Not because of her fondness for the Senator but because it was extremely important. This she concluded simply from the fact he was making the request. And so through her faith in the man and her still existent youthful sense of adventure, she smiled and accepted the job. "You let me worry about my ass and my career, Uncle Jesse. I'm all yours. Now, what's the deal?"

CHAPTER 31 _____

NATIONAL SECRUTY AGENCY – JAN. 23, 2019

"You're kidding, right?" said a very irritated Janet Healy to the head of security in the NSA. She turned to Luka with the expression of a pissed off babysitter dealing with an unruly child. "Can you believe this? I think these people are so damn paranoid they don't even talk to their mothers." She turned back to the man from security, "Listen, dumbass. Like I said, we are staffers here on behalf of Senator Jesse Bernhardt and we've been cleared by your boss, the Director, to do this assessment…right now…today. Not tomorrow, not after lunch, but now, this morning, today. So forget your goddamn computerized appointment file, strap on a pair of brass cojones and give the man a call for confirmation. Real simple, right? It'll just take a minute and I'll bet my favorite pair of sneakers you won't get fired for doing it."

"And why are you here again?" asked the tall intimidating man as he glared suspiciously at the two women.

"That's above your pay grade and none of your fuckin' business," declared Healy.

"Don't I know you?" he asked, looking at Luka.

"You've probably seen me around if you've been here a while. I used to work here," she replied.

"Oh yeah, you worked over in…"

"Just make the damn call, will ya? We don't have all day," interrupted Healy.

The call was made and the intrepid ladies were on their way into the workings of one of the largest information gathering facilities on the planet. They were there under the guise of doing a budget assessment regarding various functions of the agency as requested by the Senator who insisted they meet with various department heads directly. His request was approved by the head of the agency without hesitation due to their long time friendship. He had no reason to believe the request was for anything other than what the Senator stated. Security was instructed to give the ladies the run of the house but the suspicious security head insisted on them being accompanied by a minder; a suggestion that was short lived when Healy stepped up and objected by saying, "Again, listen dumbass. We've been given the run of the house. Do you know what that means? And don't worry, we won't get lost. My colleague is quite familiar with this mystery palace. So take a hike, okay?"

The security head was about to object even further when he was cut off not by Healy but by Luka.

"Do we have to make another call?"

He stared in a way that demonstrated he was not going to give in until Luka again spoke up with, "By the way, are you still porking that redhead in section B7. Isn't she married?"

The man was taken aback and the ladies turned and walked away. Luka turned back to the security head with a final comment.

"She's not really a red head you know. Oh wait. I guess you *would* know that wouldn't you?" she laughed as they walked away, leaving the man frustrated as he watched.

Healy chuckled. "That was a good one."

"Yeah, the worst kept secret in the place," laughed Luka.

"Okay, here we go," said Healy. "Um, by the way, where *do* we go?"

"Just stick with me. I know very solitary rooms with very limited clearing which means fewer than four people have access. It has the means necessary for us to access the main program," said Luka. She then instructed Healy to stop in the broad hallway next to an electronically locked door.

"This place looks more anticeptic than a hospital," observed Healy.

"Yeah, doesn't actually inspire a mom and butter-nut muffins, does it?" replied Luka.

"If it's that secure then how the hell are we supposed to get in and when we do then what?"

"Simple. I used to be one of those four people, but first we have to get through this door."

"But you're not one of them now. Obviously you've been written out of the security system."

"Not anymore, correct. I'm not. But… well, have you ever heard that old urban tale that if there were a nuclear holocaust the only things that would survive for thousands of years would be roaches and Twinkies?"

"I heard about the roaches but not the Twinkies. So what's that got to do with anything?"

"Just watch and learn," said Luka.

About that time the electronically controlled door opened and a young man unfamiliar to Luka and deep in thought hurriedly exited. Luka quickly slid in through the door, grabbed Healy's arm and yanked her through just before it closed. They turned to discover a large atrium leading to a huge climate-controlled room with a monster of a computer processor that towered over two floors high in the center. The entire room was surrounded by thick heavy glass.

"Wow, what the hell is that?" asked Healy.

"That's Big Moe," said Luka. "You should feel privileged. You are now one of less than only 15 people on the planet who have ever seen it."

"No shit," replied Healy. "What does it do?"

"You know my answer to that don't you?"

"Oh, yeah, you could tell me but then you'd have to kill me."

"Well yes, there's that, but actually if I told you, you wouldn't understand any of it and probably have a brain freeze trying. Just settle for the explanation that Big Moe hears all, sees all, can decrypt and analyze any code ever created, and probably any that have yet to be created. And Big Moe never sleeps."

She led Healy around Big Moe and up the stairs to a large room encased by glass walls in which there sat in the center a single curved desk with two computer consoles. Sitting in front of one of the consoles was an

Asian-American man in his thirties with premature graying hair that stood out against his original dark black. He wore a faded New Kids on the Block concert t-shirt below his thick horn rimmed glasses which gave the impression he could be just as happy and comfortable working in his mother's basement game room as here at the NSA.

Luka tapped on the electronically locked glass door and when he looked up he quickly grew a smile so wide it nearly changed every feature of his face.

"I hope it's warmer in that room than it is out here. I'm freezing," said Healy.

"It's Big Moe's cooling system. Brings the big room down into the 50s."

Though he was obviously happy to see Luka, instead of hitting the electronic lock to let them in, the man behind the console raised his hands as if to say what are you doing here? Luka smiled and pointed to her purse and then raised two fingers. The young man put his hands to his head in a joyous way that was almost childish, then quickly reached across the desk and hit the control that unlocked the heavy glass door. As Luka entered he jumped from his desk chair and rushed to give her a big hug.

"Luki girl! You're back!" he exclaimed.

"No, sorry, Zigs. Just here for a quick visit. Been assigned to run a decrypt on Big Moe. Didn't they tell you?"

"Oh hell, Luki girl. You know how this place is. Nobody tells anybody anything. That way nobody can be blamed for anything. Typical, right?"

Luka turned to Healy, "Janet Healy this is my good old friend Ziggy Chang. There are only two things in the entire world that Zig cares about. One is a challenging computer encryption and the other..." She paused and smiled as she reached into her purse. "...the other is Twinkies," she said as she withdrew the pack of Twinkies and handed them to Zig.

Zig grew a broad smile as he accepted the package of the two Twinkies like they were manna from heaven.

"You haven't lost your touch Luki girl," he said with a gracious smile. He looked to Healy, "You see, we're not allowed any consumables in this damn high-tech cathedral but my girl Luki here could always find a way to bring in the goods." He cradled the Twinkies as though they were made of the finest delicate crystal and then set them on the desk. "All in good time," he said to himself then turned to Luka. "Now what's this big important decrypt you got stuck with?"

"It's no big deal. Just take a minute to run on Big Moe. You won't even have to shut down your current runs."

"Well, let's have it then Luki girl," he said with his hand out."

"Oh, you don't think I would make it that simple do you?" she smiled. "I have to find it first. It's out there in cyberspace and the only key to recapturing it is that it was originally sent from my laptop. So step aside and let me do my magic while you dive into those Twinkies and finish them off before Carlyle comes around."

"No problem. That slave driver Carlyle is off today. Gone to some conference somewhere. All the department heads went. Just us chickens in the hen house today."

"Seems a little odd that all the department heads in the NSA would be gone at the same time," observed Healy. "Wonder whose bright idea that was um… Luki?"

"Word was the directive came down from the Presidents Chief of Staff. Said we were restricted to one off-site conference a year now because of budget cuts and because of some bozos in some other agencies turning their conferences into parties at vacation destinations. And we only had one month to do it. So they threw it together quick. Down in Myrtle Beach is what I heard, and they all went. That is all but the big cheese Director," added Zig. "We were instructed to call him if anything serious comes up. Yeah, sure, like anybody is really going to call the Director every time there's a screw up or a glitch or a burnout or something. Duh. What's the point? I mean he gets a direct feed into his office regarding anything serious anyway. Everything from broken water fountains to national threats. He's got more tentacles than an octopus. I actually saw him this morning as I arrived; him and the Chairman of the Joint Chiefs strutting down the hall with their Starbucks in hand. Only thing that would make me give him a call is if Big Moe there lost his cool and screwed the pooch. I mean, let's face it; Big Moe is the decrypt monster of all monsters, the heart of the system, the original God machine.

Without him, we're pretty much blind. But then you know all that, right. I mean, Big Moe has never failed and probably never will."

"Yep, that's why we're here," replied Luka as she sat behind his computer console. "Now enjoy your Twinkies while I fly through cyberspace to find that missing data."

"Gotcha," said Zig as he plopped into the only other chair at the desk and reverently retrieved and opened his sweet treat. "And you know what? One conference a year means us low levels don't get one, and our next one was supposed to be in Orlando with free tickets to Universal. Sucks doesn't it?"

"Sure does," said Healy. "You know, that Big Moe sure is a monster," continued Healy to keep Zig distracted. "Climate controlled is it?"

Zig filled Healy in on the climate system between bites of his Twinkies while Luka did her magic on the keyboard. She hadn't chosen his console as a whim. She noticed he was already signed on and was monitoring the process of a decryption program being run by Big Moe. If she had gone to the other console she would have had to sign on which of course she would have been unable to do. It only took her a little over two minutes to scan, locate and retrieve the missing email using the fast and powerful NSA system. The only thing to do now was to forward it to a safe location where it wouldn't be intercepted and dislocated again. She decided to send it to the school where she worked so they could run by there and print it out as soon as they left the NSA. She knew that getting though security and leaving the building with a flash drive was impossible. She immediately exported the decrypted files then called Healy over to look at the data. Zig being Zig also stretched over to take a look.

"So, what's so damn important that they have to bring my gorgeous Twinkie smuggler and our countries top algorithm mama back into the fold?" he said as he licked his fingers.

Luka was slowly scrolling and reviewing the data in some of the files when Zig casually offered an explanation.

"Seen those before," he said. "When I worked for the DOD."

"You have? What is it?" asked Healy.

"Oh, that's part of a war plan. The other files are probably the rest of it. Yep, that's what it is alright. I know 'cause I helped put some of those things together. They're always doing those for war games, training and such. And, of course, the real things like the Middle East war and such. Judging from the size, this one is pretty big. Looks like it involves the entire damn country. See there; listed are targets and times for their destruction. Bet some dudes over in the Pentagon hated working on this booger though. Whoever did it has some real serious imagination I'd say. Look at all those U.S. Heads of State that are supposed to get zapped at the outset. It's a cut off the head of the snake kind of deal. Talk about creating a ship with no crew. Boy oh boy, taking out that bunch would sure do the trick. I'd say this thing is really complicated. Probably done up by Homeland Security or the CIA along with the DOD since it all seems to be originating in-country. A major terrorist thing, ya know? Worst case scenario, widespread, not your usual invasion kind of stuff. See there," he said, pointing at the screen. "You got to have a shitpot full of info regarding our defense systems and the status and locations of our military to pull off this thing. Yep, you'd have to have full and total access to every bit of our defense make-up to pull this off. Impossible. Could never happen if you ask me. But it's good to be prepared."

"My god," said Luka. "That's why Stag and the Senator were so concerned. This thing is real." Knowing the urgency of the situation, Luka decided to also send the files directly to the Senator's office immediately and then take the chance of copying it to a flash drive. If one or both got intercepted there would always be the backup at the school.

"We have to get this to the Senator right away. Let's go," insisted Healy.

"Already finished. Just sent it," replied Luka as she stood and snatched up her purse. "Hope it gets there."

"Oh, hey there Luki girl. Leaving so soon?" asked a disappointed Zig. "You know I really miss your company here. That guy they replaced you with…well, he's about as personable as a zombie on Methaqualone. Zero people skills. Know what I mean? I mean his hobby is putting together jigsaw puzzles and watching reality shows on TV. I'm in co-worker hell here girl."

"Sorry, Zig baby. But don't worry, I'll catch you next time," she said as she gave him a quick kiss on the forehead. "Now buzz us out will you. And thanks for the use of your system. By the way, there's another surprise for you behind your console."

Zig quickly rolled his chair over to his console, reached around and pulled out another package of Twinkies then looked to Luka with a big smile. "You're a true angel Luki girl. I'll love and miss ya. Thanks."

A few minutes later the two women were approaching the security check at the exit when they spotted the security head coming their way.

"Oh shit. Here we go again," mumbled Healy as they retrieved their cell phones.

As he intercepted them, and before he could say a word, Healy went on the offensive. The two women didn't want to answer any questions and they especially didn't want to have to explain the flash drive if it was discovered.

"Well thanks a lot, dumbass," she said, pointing at the tall imposing man as she and Luka continued walking. "You know you could have told us that all the department heads were out of town. But no, you decided to just let us waist our time wondering from office to office for no reason. Was that some sort of a joke? Do you think that was funny? Maybe we should call your Director again and see how he feels about that. I'm sure he wouldn't appreciate his security head playing games with his guests. Jesus Christ, where do they find you people anyway? Now get the hell out of the way and don't waste any more of our time."

CHAPTER 32 _____

WALTER REED MEDICAL CENTER – JAN. 23, 2019

Stagliano's efforts to regain his full memory seemed almost torturous. As various memories would begin to return they would just as quickly disappear. They were bits and pieces, flashes of places and things, some very old and others very recent. The one thing he knew for sure was that the most recent memories were somehow extremely important. He decided he needed to talk to someone, someone who could push the correct buttons and put his brain back in gear. A nurse had arrived in his room just an hour before with a plastic bag, telling him it was his personal affects that had been sent from the hospital in Tappahannock. She placed them in the small closet after showing him that in the closet hung his clothes which had been washed and placed there by her while he was still in a coma.

My phone, thought Stag, wondering if his cell phone was in the bag with his other belongings. He pulled off the oxygen tube that wrapped around his head to his nose then disconnected the IV line from his arm. This time he made it a point to get out of the bed more slowly, avoiding the blood rush that would cause another black out. Once finding and steadying himself on his feet, he went to the closet and withdrew the bag that contained his personal effects, wallet, and, at the bottom his cell phone.

He tossed the bag on a chair and immediately hit the speed dial and was soon connected with Luka.

Luka and Healy were walking through the large NSA parking lot to their car when Luka's phone rang. She could see on the phone's screen that it was Stagliano.

"Stag," she answered, relieved to hear from him. "You're awake. Are you feeling better? Are you up and about?"

"Yes," he answered. "I'm in Walter Reed and..."

"Yes I know," she said, cutting him off and then began filling him in on recent events including the mysterious disappearance of the flash drives that had been in their possession and disappeared after his Jeep ran off the bridge, and how the original flash drive had disappeared as well from the Senator's office. She told him of the mysterious loss of the email they had sent to the Senator, and why she and Healy were now at the NSA and what they had done there. At first none of that clicked in his mind until she told him they were on their way to meet Senator Bernhardt and inform him of the contents of the war plans files and show him what was on the flash drive they snuck out of the NSA. The mention of files and the relationship to the Senator finally clicked in his mind and an extreme sense of urgency along with the memories of what he had seen in the files when they were first opened rushed through his mind. The *Senator,* he remembered. *My god, they're going to kill the Senator!*

"Luka, listen to me," said Stagliano desperately. "The Senator! You have to warn the Senator and..."

In mid sentence his phone died; the uncharged battery having depleted over the past few days while he was laid up.

"Stag? Stag, can you hear me? Are you there?" said Luka as she and Healy approached the car. "I've lost the signal," she said with concern to Healy.

"Just keep trying," said Healy. "Should get through sooner or later after we drive out of here. Either way, after we meet with the Senator you can head over to Walter Reed and see him."

"I'm so glad and relieved he's getting better," said Luka as she slid into the passenger side of the car and closed the door.

"I understand he's a pretty tough bird. I'm sure the Senator will be relieved as well. But right now we have far more important things to deal with, especially if the shit in these files is for real," said Healy as she started the car and drove from the parking lot.

"Do you really think someone is actually planning a massive attack on the country like it says in those files? In those plans?" asked Luka. "I mean, according to the small amount of files we looked at it was all so... big. Nationwide. It just seems near impossible."

"Well, the real question is can we afford not to? It's my understanding this thing caused a very important man to commit suicide," replied Healy as she turned on to the main road. Not to mention the attempted demise of you and Major Stagliano.

A few miles down the road a loud horn from a large truck sounded as the truck sped by and cut in front of them, forcing Healy to swerve and run off the road. She slammed on the brakes and the car came to a sliding halt just short of striking a light pole.

"Jesus, what the hell was that idiot doing!" Healy exclaimed as they watched the truck speed away.

Once realizing they and their vehicle was still intact, the two women relaxed and Healy turned the car to re-enter the road when suddenly the vehicle erupted in a massive explosion and fireball. The fire engulfed the vehicle completely and a secondary explosion finished the job when the gas tank erupted.

A quarter mile behind them another vehicle, a black SUV, had pulled over to the side of the road. Behind the wheel sat Arisztid Backos's blue eyed assassin Ben Robinson. In his glove covered hand was a remote control, the same remote he had just used to blow up Healy's car. He casually pressed the button of the electric window and when it slid all the way open he tossed the remote out onto the road where it was summarily smashed by a passing car. He then waited for a brake in the traffic, re-entered the road, and drove past the smoldering wreckage. He drove slowly and carefully through the jumble of people and cars that had stopped or pulled over at the scene of the disastrous explosion. Looking through the smoke and flames he could see two charred bodies in the front of the vehicle. He showed little or no emotion as he confirmed to himself that this latest chore was completed.

At the Walter Reed Medical Center Major Stagliano had pulled the rest of his belongings from the bag and was getting dressed when a nurse entered and asked what he was doing.

"Checking out," he said.

"You haven't been discharged yet. You're not well enough. You could relapse. Maybe slip back into a coma and who knows for how long. Wait and let me get the doctor."

"Sorry lady, but I don't have time for that shit. I'm out of here," he said as he exited the room.

CHAPTER 33 _____

The department heads along with the Assistant Secretaries of the NSA were all seated at a large assortment of round tables in the ballroom of the Island Vista Resort Hotel on Myrtle Beach, South Carolina. They were about to partake of a prime rib dinner when Assistant Director Justin Howard approached the podium to speak. The sound of low volume voices and clinking glasses subsided as he adjusted the microphone and cleared his throat to begin his brief address.

"I can see by your eyes that a great many of you took it upon yourselves to have an independent meeting this bright sunny morning. Correct me if I'm wrong but I believe most of you attended the meeting held in the hotel bar just off the lobby."

The comment resulted in a subtle uncomfortable chuckle, being they weren't certain if that was a joke or a reprimand.

"Personally I prefer the stock in the room fridge. A little expensive but no tips involved and well... what the hell, its Uncle Sam's nickel right? Besides, I'm on a different per diem than most of you and I don't have to pay alimony like the rest of you."

The laughter grew a little louder when everyone realized they were not being chastised for filling the earlier part of the day with a liquid breakfast in the bar.

"And since our work doesn't begin until tomorrow I won't hold it against the group from B Section for playing miniature golf through the first half of the day. I'm only disappointed that I wasn't invited to join your exercise program and had to instead settle for steak and eggs and a Bloody Mary for breakfast and a quiet morning in my room."

The laughter grew more boisterous and glasses were raised in approval to what was said.

"I have to say this beach town must have more miniature golf courses than the IRS has agents, and if you ask me, it's too damn cold to be putting a little white ball around dinosaurs and pirate ships."

The laughter grew and everyone relaxed.

"Now," continued AD Howard, "Regarding the upcoming agenda which begins first thing in the morning. At each of your table settings there is a folder inclusive of your individual and group training schedules and, of course, the criteria of review. I suggest you be sure and read these thoroughly, fill out the required forms, and make sure you keep note of your results of each session in which you participate. You will not be tested, but yes, you will be evaluated. And I wish to emphasize, *you will* participate as required in each session according to your schedule."

Except for a very few groans of disappointment the room fell silent with the knowledge and anticipation of being evaluated. Most considered this outing as a bonus or reward and an opportunity for a few days of fun and games - a reward at the taxpayers' expense.

"The head of each section will evaluate your cooperation, input, and obvious knowledge of the subject, and... are instructed to give extra credit to winners of the miniature golf games that will obviously take place during our four days here. That means to get through this event you must either know your job or be damn good at cold weather miniature golf."

The laughter returned.

"Especially the winner of the bunch who will be participating in the Great NSA Put Put Open. So prepare yourselves folks because this event will be gruesome. Sorry, but the World Tour Golf Links is off limits. There's no time for it unless you choose to stay the weekend after this conference has ended... *on your time and dime.* And if you're lucky enough to have a warm day or two. So until then, no one plays the pro eighteen holes during the conference... except me. Oh, and yes folks, this will be an actual working week because do to budget restrictions we are now restricted to only one such training event per fiscal year. Now as you enjoy your meal, training director Sara Portis will quickly review the locations of your sessions and the facilities we will be utilizing. And I'll leave to her to apologize for not scheduling this conference in a warmer climate," concluded AD Howard before stepping down from the podium and taking his seat.

He sat, smiled, and reached for his drink just as a very deep muffled thump shook through the building, followed shortly by another that rocked the entire structure. Then there came another and then a series of small explosions that caused the entire building to shake violently, sending tableware to the floor. Waiters dropped their trays and fell into nearby tables. Within moments the walls and ceiling began to crack and shatter. Before anyone could leave their seats the entire hotel collapsed, killing all the attending members of the NSA and nearly all of the hotel staff and guests.

Jonathan Lamorna, the Director of the NSA, was sitting turned to the window behind his desk at NSA Headquarters when his private phone rang.

"It's done," said the voice on the phone. "A hundred percent successful."

The Director said nothing in reply, turned off his phone and stared out the window, knowing for all practical purposes, his agency had just been emasculated.

NEW ORLEANS - JAN. 23, 2019

Farin Dupré had just finished delivering a moving sermon as a guest minister at a local AME church that was holding a week long revival. He was now perched next to the resident minister at the doors of the building, greeting church members as they departed when one of them put a folded note in his hand. The man was one of Dupré's many internet soldiers, a principal aide who accompanied him many times on his activities and who had, among his other duties, the primary mission of monitoring the media.

"I'll be in the car," the man said softly.

Dupré opened the short note which read, *It started! In the news now!* He then shoved it in his side pocket. He impatiently remained until the last church member passed through the door, then turned to the minister, "I'm so sorry, Reverend, but I'm afraid something has come up and I won't be able to have lunch with you today." He could hardly contain himself, hoping his eagerness to depart in order to jump into the upcoming national fray was not obvious.

"Oh really? I hope it's nothing serious. Is it something I can help you with my brother?" asked the Reverend.

"Well, we'll soon see, Reverend. We will soon see. I think it may be time for all of our people to step up and help themselves." With that said he skipped down the steps, leaving the Reverend watching, confused, as he went quickly to his idling car and slid into the passenger seat.

"Are you sure?" he asked of his driver and aid while they drove away.

"Yeah man. It's all over the news. Pretty much the only story running on all media right now. TV, radio, internet, print. I was getting text feeds all during your sermon. Your mystery money man sure did his job alright. There's no way in hell anybody is gonna put that rabbit back in the hat."

"So that's why you left the church while I was speaking, to make calls," said Dupré. "I didn't think it would happen so soon. Can we put everything together by tomorrow?"

"No problem. But actually, I think it might even be better to give it a day to fester, you know? Monday, a full weekday news cycle and all that crap. Let the masses chew on it for a day. Let the fear of losing their benefits sink in and piss'em off. Then we can start with a small group to catch some media attention. Use the media and that event to call the people out. Do a couple TV interviews and let'em tease and feed the masses, just as you planned. Matter fact I got two set up for you today already. Second team weekend reporters eager for a national feed, you know... sound bites to put a feather in their cap sort of thing. Ambitious bastards are hungry for sound bites and just about anything else right now...know what I'm sayin'? You can blame all the white men on the planet and get away with it because they're so hungry for air time that they'll all go for the drama instead of the facts."

"Good. Sounds good," agreed Dupré. "Gives me a chance to plant the seed of displeasure among the dependant masses…our brothers and sisters."

"Hah, seeds of displeasure, right. And be sure to plug the planned protest rally."

"How much time until the first interview? And how the hell did you do this so soon?" asked Dupré.

"The story actually broke last night in the late edition of the New York Times. I waited until the wire services started to spread the message then I started making the calls. Your first interview is in about an hour and a half with the local NBC affiliate at their station. Soon after that is a shot with CNN. An outside street shot which is where we can do a little magic. They're all hungry to put a face and a sound bite or two with the headline. Makes them look like they actually did some work on the story. Truth is you could shovel shit all day today and the bleedin' heart liberal media will eat it up. I say liberal because that's the nature of the beast. Shameful right? And those stupid bastards actually think they're on our side."

"Shameful yeah. And shamefully convenient for us. Well, all except FOX News and the Wall Street Journal," laughed Dupré. "Those motherfuckers think they're supposed to deal in facts and tell the truth." Dupré paused for a thoughtful moment, his mind churning excitedly as he strategized. "Yeah, that's all good…the outside thing. But I also want some protesters at those locations. Maybe just a busload. Those damn media people love good wallpaper. I'm sure they'll love the outside thing after they see protesters. Makes the interview look like an event. Makes it look bigger and more important than it actually is because that's how those dumbasses always shoot it."

"No problem."

"I also want the shooter team a few blocks away. I want them to open up on cue, soon after my arrival and interview are nearly finished and when the camera is rolling. Just enough gunshots and noise to imply there are angry people in the streets all around the city."

"Got it."

"After the last interview I want a meet with all the team leaders, all of them. Then we conference call and coordinate with the other cities coast to coast. That's important because once the shit hits the fan there might not be any communications for a while. No time to waist. Time to activate the real deal, my man…and there ain't gonna be no turnin' back."

"Okay, but what about the Reverend? All this jumps his own conference call and undercuts his plan of action."

"Yeah, well, fuck the Reverend Johnson. That two-faced bastard had half a century to make something happen and all he did was talk separatist shit and line his pockets. And to think that mealy mouthed son of a bitch actually ran for president once. Hah, what a joke."

"He might be able to make things difficult."

"No," replied Dupré with a sly smile. "Trust me. I got that covered."

An hour later Dupré entered his apartment to discover his ex-wife, Shinella, puttering around in the kitchen making tea. He said nothing and just stood and stared until she turned with the cup of tea in hand.

"What the hell are you doing here?"

"I used to live here, remember? Still got a key."

"Yeah, so what. Get out. I got work to do."

"Yes, I know. In fact I know everything."

"You don't know shit and you ain't gettin' no money. So get the hell out."

"You think I'm here about money? I don't give a shit about your money. I don't need it and I don't like where your money comes from anyway." She crossed into the living room and sat on the sofa, placing her tea cup on the coffee table. "Like I said, I know everything. And I know that if you succeed no one's money will be worth the paper it's printed on."

Shinella Dupré was a former Miss New Orleans from ten years prior. She was a beautiful mix of French Cajun, African American, and Gypsy, and possessed the wit and wisdom of all three. She had latched onto Dupré when he was a favorite son and rising star destined for political success. When he ruined his stellar future and went to prison, she stayed with him until a year ago when she discovered his secretive radical activities. She left and he cared very little, believing she had become a distraction and thinking his newly chosen future would provide him with all the beautiful women he desired.

"And I know you're about to begin your fucked up scheme that will destroy a lot of lives," she continued.

"Is that right? If you know so much then why don't you join me? Why don't you want to share what promises to be a very lucrative future?"

He grabbed a bottle of beer from the fridge, twisted off the top and strolled from the kitchen to face her in the living room but when he arrived she met him, not with her tea cup and a smile, but with a 9mm pistol. "What the hell are you doing?" asked Dupré.

"I'm putting an end to your screwed up program. I'm putting an end to you before you destroy the world we all live in."

Dupré stood in shock for a long silent moment. Surprised she had the courage to even consider doing what she claimed she was going to do.

"You're insane," she continued. "You're just plain stupid and selfish and... and your ambitions are beyond ridiculous."

"And so you're going to do what with that fuckin' gun?"

"I'm going to stop you the only way I can."

"Okay, then don't sit there and talk about it. Pull the fuckin' trigger. DO IT BITCH! PULL THE TRIGGER! DO IT!" he yelled.

Shinella slowly tightened her finger on the trigger, staring him dead in the eyes but his sudden burst caused her to flinch and delay just long enough to allow him to jump her, push away the gun and strike her on the temple with the bottle of beer. She screamed and scratched his face just as he snatched the gun away then stuck her upside her head with it, knocking her unconscious. He stepped away, stood and stared, contemplating what remedies were available to deal with what he now considered to be a crazy woman who could ruin everything he had planned and worked for. He sat on the coffee table, gulped down the remainder of the beer and pondered the situation until he decided there was only one solution. With Shinella still unconscious, he picked up a throw pillow and put it over her head, shoved the gun into it to muffle the sound of the shot and pulled the trigger.

CHAPTER 35 _____

SENATE BUILDING – JAN. 23, 2019

Stagliano exited the cab in front of the Senate Building and began to move quickly toward the entrance when he found it necessary to pause and let his head clear of an unexpected dizziness. He turned and leaned on the vehicle for temporary support.

"Hey man. You okay there?" asked the cab driver.

Stagliano stood away from the vehicle, nodded yes, and waved the cabbie on. He then turned and entered the building, to make his way to Senator Bernhardt's office. Though he wanted to run to the top floor office he knew he wasn't in any condition to do so. He carefully walked to and entered the elevator. Arriving on the top floor, he again paused and leaned against the wall to allow the light-headedness to subside. As he did he peered down the hall and saw two of the Senator's aids rushing in, one in tears.

No, he thought. *Damnit, no! I'm too late.!*

Stagliano pushed himself from the wall and sprinted to the office. When he entered he found the Senator's staff milling about, some sitting in tears, others standing in quiet disbelief. Stag looked about desperately for Senator Bernhardt, and then rushed to Bernhardt's office to discover it empty.

"Where is he?" He shouted. "Is he…"

"On his way to the NSA,' replied one of the staffers.

"What... what the hell's going on? Is he okay?"

"Yes."

"Then what are you people upset about? What happened?"

"It's Healy," answered one.

"And that Luka girl," said James Britton.

"What? What... are they in trouble?" asked Stagliano.

James took a deep breath, knowing that Stagliano had a relationship with Luka. The others watched in anticipation of his words while some turned away. "Um, I'm sorry. They're dead," stated James. "Some kind of auto wreck or explosion or something. They were over at the NSA. We're not completely sure. Um... but the Senator is on his way there to sort it out."

Stagliano's head started to spin and he fell back into a nearby chair. "Are you sure?" he asked. "Are you sure they're dead?"

"Um... yes sir. That much we know for sure."

Major Stagliano rose and started for the door when all of a sudden his head began to ring louder and louder until he passed out and fell to the floor.

A short time later he awoke on the sofa in the Senator's office. Tending him was one of Bernhardt's secretaries. "No, no," she ordered politely as he began to sit up. "You lay back and take it easy."

"I have to find the Senator... now! It's important... now!" he argued.

"Senator Bernhardt has just arrived and is on his way up. He instructed us to keep you here and also to not call for any medical assistance unless it's absolutely necessary. So you tell me Major, is it necessary?"

Stagliano lay back on the sofa to wait for Bernhardt. As he did he recalled the painful news of Luka's death, somehow knowing it wasn't an accident. His eyes were closed when Senator Bernhardt entered the room.

WHITE HOUSE – JAN. 23, 2019

Lindsey Ford entered Bo Peppers office after a quick tap on the door.

"Whatcha need?" grunted Peppers, his eyes buried in a file on his desk.

"Just checking in to let you know I've been added to your detail, sir."

Peppers glanced up then went back to his file. "Thought you were assigned to the President," he replied. "What the hell happened? You fuck up and get demoted or something?"

"No sir. My boss thought it would be good to shift a few assignments is all. Even Secret Service agents deserve a break every once in a while."

"Is that what you call me, a break?"

"No sir. From what I've seen here over the years, I'd call you a prick."

Peppers paused from his work and looked up to Lindsey, "Listen kid. I know who you are just like I know the rest of the agents. I run this place, remember? And I know you're some kind of a bad ass who doesn't take any shit from anybody which baffles me and leads me to wonder how the hell you managed to stay in the Secret Service to begin with. I'm assuming it's because you're the token bitch on the roster and also happen to be the

First Lady's favorite. But that shit don't cut no ice with me so you just steer clear while I'm working and we'll get along just fine. A fuckin' fly on the wall. Got it? You understand what I'm sayin'?"

"Oh, yes sir. A fly on the wall. Yes sir, I understand completely. And I'm relieved to know that my long time impression of you is correct."

"And just what would that be?"

"That you're a complete prick. Possibly even a complete asshole, so here's the deal. The Secret Service has discovered a threat to your life, for whatever its worth. And unfortunately I have been told to stick to you like glue to possibly prevent that threat from fulfillment... to protect your ass at all cost. That means wherever you go, I go, except when you are taking a shit. It's not an assignment I would prefer, sir, but I assure you I will perform my duty to the very best of my ability which is pretty damn good. Even if it means putting up with your bullshit. However, sir, I should let you know that I am not a fetch and get it house servant nor do I sweep, clean, make coffee, or pick up your damn laundry. So, as you said, you do your job and I'll do mine and we should be just fine."

"Just who the fuck do you think you're talking to?"

Lindsey straitened up and locked eyes with Peppers. "I'm the agent who was assigned to your ass by the President. The agent who might have to take a bullet for you. So would you like me to go back to the President and tell him that you are not pleased with his choice?"

"I thought you said the senior agent put you on this detail?"

"Yes I did."

"Why?"

"Why what, sir?"

"Why did you lie about that?"

"I didn't lie. I just left out the President part. I was trying to keep it short and simple. Trying not to interrupt your work. But apparently that doesn't work with assholes," replied Lindsey, all the while remaining stern faced and appearing disinterested.

Peppers stared her straight in the eyes for a long silent moment until he burst into laughter. "Hot damn!" cried Peppers. "You're one tough fuckin' nut. That's my kind of agent. Need more like that, I'd say. Yep, you and I are gonna get along just fine. Hell of a lot better than those other agents who are all mute and stand around like frozen pork pies." Peppers glanced back to his file, failing to look up as he said, "In house security huh. Just how long you gonna be here anyway?"

"That's not my call, sir. As long as necessary I suppose."

"A serious threat or some kind of damn prank?"

"No sir. Serious. Very serious."

"Yeah well, I'll be sure and let the President know I'm pleased with his choice of protection. Although why the hell anybody would want to harm my country white ass is beyond me." He flipped a page then continued, "Just stick close and stay quiet and we'll be just fine."

"Yes sir."

Just then the desk phone rang and by the second ring Lindsey had pushed the button in the palm of her hand which started the small digital recorder in her pocket. It was simple enough being that all the agents had ear jacks with talking devices attached to the same type of switch so there was nothing to draw any suspicion. In this case the device was a hyper sensitive recorder that could pick up the slightest sound in the room, including phone conversations.

"Yes," said Peppers into the phone. "All of them?" he paused and listened carefully for a moment. "Okay," he continued. "Got it. Eight o'clock."

Lindsey stood as though she were not interested and not hearing any of Bo Pepper's phone call, all the while knowing she would hear both parties on the line after she analyzed the recording that night. It was the first of numerous calls and conversations she would soon witness including one where Peppers would be complaining to an unidentified individual about Senator Bernhardt.

She was led to target Bo Peppers through conversations among fellow Secret Service members who unknowingly put together the Chief of Staff's recent activities that painted a suspicious picture. To get to Peppers she actually created the threat to his life and then got the assignment by the President via a suggested nudge by the First Lady. Once gathering and deciphering what she would see and hear she would immediately take the results to the Senator where they could both contemplate the intentions of the participants and further set a plan of action to eventually decide whether to approach the

President or the Justice Department... or both. The calls would prove to be interesting and justify Senator Bernhardt's suspicions.

The only drawback to Lindsey's actions, successful or not, was that she would likely never again be trusted by anyone in the service or in the administration and most likely be relegated to the dark depths of the FBI where career advancement was nonexistent. In other words, she would be shit canned and pressured out of a job.

CHAPTER 37 _____

BERNHARDT ESTATE – JAN. 24, 2019

Following the niceties and greetings from the Senator's wife, Lindsey Ford was escorted to meet Senator Bernhardt in his home study. She found him slumped into his large leather desk chair, his head down, his hands clasped in his lap.

"Hello Unc," said Lindsey. "I heard about your staffer Healy. I'm so sorry. I know she was with you for a very long time and I don't want to interrupt you at this time but… what I have here seems like some critical info."

The Senator looked up slowly with a forced smile, "You're not interrupting anything Lindsey. I was just wondering why my friends and operatives have started to…"

"…die?" said Lindsey. "I think I may have an answer to that,"

"Really?"

"Yes sir. Um… as much as I hate to say it, I think there's a fox in the hen house."

"A fox? No, I'm afraid it's more than just one fox, Lindsey. A hell of a lot more than one."

"I don't catch your meaning, sir."

"When did you leave the White House?" asked the Senator.

"Got off duty hours ago. Went home to change and listen to these recordings then came here. Except for a quick stop in a drive through for a fish sandwich, that is. Why'd you ask, sir?"

"Then you don't know."

"Know what, sir."

"About the NSA... In Myrtle Beach. The entire management of the NSA died in a building collapse... or should I say mass murder?"

"Oh my lord! All of them?"

"Yes, and it couldn't have been an accident. I'm sure of it."

"That explains why my phone has been ringing a hole in my pocket. The White House must be on lockdown and they're calling in all the agents. I took a three day weekend and told them I'd be out of touch," said Lindsey. "So I could help you." She paused a moment, remembering what she had on her recording of Peppers. "I... I'm afraid you might be right. It was no accident. Neither was the death of Healy and that other girl."

"What do you mean?" asked the Senator.

"Well, I've got Peppers on a number of calls. He was a little cryptic but it's not that hard to make sense of the conversations when you hear both sides. He mentioned something about finding the body of a Captain Qualin, you know, that female officer who they said died in a chopper crash, except they said she was found on an iceberg somewhere and not at a crash site in the Blue Ridge Mountains. He also made reference to both the car explosion and the NSA incident. Now that I think of it, considering the time factor of the calls, the security protocols should have kicked in before I left for the day but they didn't. That means Peppers knew about Myrtle Beach but failed to inform the President, leaving him and the Secret Service to get the report later from some other source. I didn't decipher the conversations until I got home. This means that Chief of Staff Peppers is…"

"…a traitor. A goddamn traitor who's going to experience a shortened life span if I have anything to do with it."

"And the President? Why? Why the hell would he be a part of something like this?"

"He wouldn't. But that self-serving piece of country shit Chief of Staff sure as hell would," replied the Senator.

"But a coup d'état eliminating the NSA's capability doesn't make sense. It weakens the country. And there's what happened to Healy and…"

"And Senator Stephenson and Luka and Stag and Senator Armand and… myself."

"Yourself. What the hell are you saying?"

"Yes, and who the hell knows who else is on the hit list. I was warned by Major Stagliano who right now is resting in my guest room recovering from an attempt on his life. The intelligence is based on information gleaned from a flash drive we came by that included the plans for this overthrow. It's not a coup, Lindsey, it a damn overthrow, a revolution."

"But who…"

"It's not the who I'm worried about right now. It's the how and why and… how big."

Senator Bernhardt picked up his phone, punched in a few numbers and waited for an answer. Without hesitation he began speaking as soon as the call was taken. "This is Senator Bernhardt. I want to speak with the Chairman of the Joint Chiefs." He listened as he was told the Admiral could not be found. "Then give me General Lewis immediately. That means now, right now!" He waited a moment until the voice returned and informed him the General was not available. "Well where the hell is he? This is an emergency!"

"I'm sorry, Senator. He left no messages and no way to contact him, and I don't have his private line so I'm not sure how to contact him. I'm just sitting in temporarily to replace Captain Qualin. If you will wait I will find someone who can help but it seems most everyone has gone for the weekend. I'm not sure but I did hear him say something about going to the White House before retiring for the weekend."

"Yes, yes. Do whatever you have to do. Find someone. Hell, find the General. Have him call me as soon as possible. Even sooner. As I said, this is an emergency, very critical."

"Yes sir, I'll…"

"Wait," interrupted the Senator. "Did you say Qualin? Captain Qualin?"

"Yes, sir. Captain Beverly Qualin."

"What's her job?"

"She is... um, was the General's special assistant. She died recently in a helicopter crash."

"Yes, well, okay. Just find the General... or any other members of the Joint Chiefs. Fast!" repeated the Senator. He replaced the phone and looked up to Lindsey. "Didn't you say something about a Captain Qualin?"

"Yes, sir."

"Christ. Jesus Christ, they're even in the Pentagon." He quickly snatched up the phone and hit the speed dial to the White House.

"White House. How may I direct you call?"

"This is Senator Bernhardt. Connect me to the President immediately."

"I'm sorry sir. We are in lockdown and have been ordered to route all calls for the President to the Chief of Staff. Should I connect you with him?"

"What? What the hell do you mean, 'the Chief of Staff?' I don't need the Chief of Staff. I want to talk to the fuckin' President. Now damn it!"

"Sir, I'm sorry but the White House is on lockdown and the President is unavailable. I can only connect you to the Chief of Staff."

"Is General Lewis there? Is he in the White House? Let me talk to him."

"I'm sorry Senator. I can only connect you to the Chief of Staff."

"Fine damnit, then let me talk to that little rat bastard."

"Um... yes, sir, transferring your call now."

A moment later the ring on the other end was taken by Bo Peppers. "Peppers here."

"This is Bernhardt. Now you listen to me you little sack of shit. Call it off. Shut it down or I'll run over your ass with the entire US Armed Forces."

"Oh, it's my friend Jesse. So glad to hear from you, Senator. Still making threats I see. But please don't threaten me, or should I say *us*, with a military you no longer control."

"You bastard! What the hell have you done? What the hell are you doing? What have you done with the President?"

"Oh, we're just having a little party down here in the Presidents big safe room. You know, the situation room? And you know the best thing about it is that self righteous son of a bitch doesn't have a clue about what's going on outside. And I'm betting you don't either, do you? Tried to call Joint Chiefs Chairman did ya? Sorry, he won't be taking any more calls... for a long, long time. And General Lewis too did ya? Well, let's just say he's a little busy right now running a revolution and won't be taking your calls either." Peppers paused for effect before continuing. "You know I really should have had a wet bar installed in here. Oh well, don't assume we'll be here that long anyway. There should be plenty of booze to go around when we celebrate our victory over you old farts on the Hill. The entertainment here is good though, what with all those fake feeds on the monitors and all. Yeah, it's keeping POTUS occupied. Oops, I'm being summoned by his nibs right now. Hate to cut this fun conversation short, but gotta go now ol' boy. And Senator, can I make a suggestion? Don't try to call the

President's private line. It's out of commission as yours will be soon."

"You son of a bitch," growled Senator Bernhardt. "Who the hell are you working for? What the hell do you people want?"

"The people, Senator. We the people, remember? A little revolution is good for the soul, as our beloved ol' Tommy Jefferson once mused. Welp, 'nuff said for now ol' man." Peppers paused and smiled into the phone and said softly, "You know you should consider spending your last days with your family."

The phone went dead and the Senator fell back in his chair.

"Are you alright, sir?" asked Lindsey.

He cleared his head then rose from the chair. "Get me to the Capitol."

"Yes sir. But shouldn't you go to the Pentagon?"

"No. I think that option is closed. Can you get me to the Capitol?"

"Oh, hell yes, sir. I've got a hot car with a flashing light and a cool siren. I can get you anywhere you want to go… fast. But…"

"But what?"

"Maybe you shouldn't… I mean, you said that Major Stagliano warned you, that you were in danger."

"I'm not going to hide, Lindsey. I have to stop this madness."

NEW ORLEANS – JAN. 25, 2019

Farin Dupré was sitting back in his recliner watching the news on television. It was a mix of the two major stories being the incident in Myrtle Beach which was still being reported as an accident with the cause speculated to be everything from an underground gas explosion to an earthquake, to a terrorist attack, and, of course, there was the continuous political hot item of the day that claimed the government was going to deny social assistance to poor minorities. In that news item Dupré himself was injected with a brief sound bite complete with the sound of firearms in the background. The story had been running for two days. He smiled as he was evaluating the coverage and anticipating the outcome of the news when his assistant Yondel interrupted.

"Time to go, boss. Got a date with live TV in twenty minutes."

"Yeah," replied Dupré. "Time for the show to begin. We've got a date with the world, Yondel. With the whole fuckin' world," he said as he tossed the TV remote on the sofa near the blood stain created when he shot his ex-wife. He rose, snatched up his sports coat and headed for the door. Prior to donning his jacket he checked to see that the shoulder strap holding his Beretta was secure and he smiled.

Twenty minutes later Dupré appeared at the scene of a restless crowd of activists who were protesting the fast spreading news that they were going to be denied their government assistance. He looked about approvingly, pleased with the location which was the front of city hall, and the time, nearly 3:00pm. The right time for this event to not only make the 24 hour news outlets but the standard broadcast networks and major newspapers as well. He was especially pleased to see in attendance were cameras and reporters from every news agency as well as some known wire service stringers.

There were hundreds of protesters, a full melting pot of dissatisfied dependant minority citizens who knew very little as to why they were there other than someone was going to take away their lifetime of free food, money, and medical coverage and that the white man was going to screw them once again. At least that was the rumor supplied and supported by what they heard on the news and social media. There were members of each group, Black Lives Matter, the Urban League, the NAACP, AME church members and ministers, and some groups he'd never even heard of. Also included in the crowd were those he had bussed in just to increase the numbers and raise hell. *What would he tell all these people?* he wondered. *He would tell them not what they wanted to hear but what he wanted them to hear,* he thought. *And he would win them over in a way they couldn't begin to imagine.*

He glanced around the perimeter of the crowd and saw a number of the city's police officers prepared to hopefully keep the peace with only a show of possible force. He searched for a few familiar faces among their ranks and not finding them he turned to Yondel and asked softly, "Are we set? I don't see our men."

"Yeah," replied Yondel. "One is mixed in the ranks of the cops, some are in the crowd and the other..." he didn't finish the sentence. Instead he led Dupré with his eyes to glance to the rooftop of a nearby building where he could see what appeared to be a uniformed police sniper who, like the one stationed among the ranks of the officers on the ground, was a Dupré fraud.

"And the crowd?" asked Dupré.

"Two more. Locked and loaded."

"Well, shit then, what say we start this party," replied Dupré as they made their way through the crowd.

Dupré was spotted by a TV reporter who quickly headed him off as he climbed the front steps of the City Hall. The other TV camera crews and reporters quickly followed surrounding him and shouting out questions in an effort to get an interview.

"Please, please, all of your questions will soon be answered I'm sure," said Dupré as he held up his hands in protest. Just then he spotted exiting the building, Russell Broussard, Mayor of New Orleans, and Charles Languet, Governor of Louisiana, along with the city Superintendent of Police and chief commander of the force, Casey LeBlanc. He quickly pointed to them saying to the media, "There are the men who should answer your questions. Tell us Mayor Broussard," yelled Dupré, "Tell all these people gathered here why they're going to lose their sustenance while you and your kind live large on tax payer money," shouted Dupré. The crowd rallied at the sound of his words. He continued, "Tell us why our children should go to bed hungry so you can build new roads and bridges that go to those new luxury gated golf club communities, and spend money to expand airports to serve privileged passengers and private jets. Tell us how you would rather hand money out to the unions instead of building low income housing that puts a roof over the heads of poor minority families."

The Mayor was caught off guard. He had planned to make a showing where he could spew political jargon and double talk and become a hero by calming and appeasing the crowd. To tell a few lies and make a few promises on TV, and, of course, all the while taking a step closer to the State House. Or so he thought. But instead he was met head on by a leading dissident with an agenda, a dissident demanding answers to questions the Mayor didn't want to deal with, especially in front of the media and a crowd of what he considered to be a bunch of ignorant freeloaders.

"How about you Governor?" shouted Dupré. "Perhaps you can give these people some answers and tell them why the state and the federal government are taking away what is rightfully theirs?"

The cameras and reporters squeezed in closer to the Mayor and Governor in anticipation of a response but before they could say a word Dupré stepped up and began his show.

"They can't answer because they have no answers. They can't answer because they have no conscience and because they have no sense of morals. All these people and all the white mayors and politicians in America, have is an extreme case of greed. Greed for power, greed for money, and the kind of greed that makes it necessary to beat down the black man, the brown man, the Asian, the Hispanic, and all the minorities of America."

With those words the crowd became even more intense and began chanting, "White greed! White greed! White greed! WHITE GREED!" until those chanting began to become physical and they turned on the police officers with verbal abuse and threats. From within the crowd there materialized someone with a bullhorn who began yelling "Take 'em down! Take 'em down! Kill them motherfuckers! Kill them fuckin' white redneck bastards!" With each calling from the bullhorn the crowd became more agitated, more threatening, and potentially more violent.

Eventually the bullhorn ended up in Dupré's hands and his show, as he put it, went primetime as he moved to stand next to the Mayor. "There you see it!" he called to the crowd. "All around you, do you see them? They are the strong arm of white America here to coral and control us minorities! To keep us down! To oppress us even further! TO PUT US BACK IN CHAINS! The chains of social discrimination! The chains of belittlement, of restriction, of separation, of elimination! To not stop until they wipe us off the face of the earth! To not stop until they've altered our biology and our children's' children are unable to reproduce!"

Strangely the crowd became so fascinated with his diatribe that they settled down to listen. Dupré took pause to notice their silence, realizing he had reached them and possibly the mass of people in America who would see this broadcast repeatedly on national television. He turned and walked to the Governor, grabbed his arm and raised it. The Gobernor stood dumbstruck.

"This is the source of your grief and anger," shouted Dupré. "This is your enemy!" He then took up the arm of the Mayor.

The Mayor looked to the New Orleans Superintendent of Police for protection, expecting him to give an order that would bring all this to an end. The Chief of Police looked to him with only a deadpan glare until he finally smiled. Suddenly a shot rang out from the crowd felling one of the officers surrounding them. The other law enforcement officers quickly raised their weapons, trained them on the crowd and took cover, waiting, as they had been instructed by their Mayor, for the authority to return fire, but the order failed to come.

A young rookie officer sighted one of the people in the crowd with what he thought was a gun and without hesitation he yelled "GUN!" and took it upon himself to fire. An innocent woman in the crowd fell to the ground. The shot achieved what Dupré had planned, for that young rookie was actually his man. The rookie's shot was followed by another and the crowd went into a panic.

Then two men among the demonstrators drew automatic pistols; one targeted a member of a camera crew hitting him fatally in the head and the other, strangely, shot two people within the crowd to further feed the panic. As the crowd rushed the surrounding police officers to escape the riot, the officers opened fire and people began falling to the ground in a bloody mess. Then suddenly a shot rang out from the rooftop, a shot that expertly targeted and struck the mayor who toppled dead on the steps. Another shot from the rooftop took down the Governor and a third a police sergeant.

Arisztid Bakos had just gotten his uprising, thought Dupré. The uprising Bakos thought would be just a little bit of conflict to denigrate the US and enhance his efforts to create a new world society, a new world order. Dupré knew that was now an obsolete program. He knew even before it began because Dupré had much grander plans.

The Police Chief rushed to the side of the fallen Mayor and pretended to show some concern, but in reality the black New Orleans boss cop felt nothing at all, except for an affection and affiliation with Farin Dupré. He was Dupré's close lifelong friend and a comrade from the Katrina disaster days who had never been caught. And he was a conspirator in Dupré's plan of revolt. The top cop reached to his radio mic attached to his left epaulet, pressed the speak button, and gave the order for his police force to close in on the crowd using any and all force necessary. With the death of one of their own the police officers were in no mood to follow crowd control and management protocol. To further enhance their anger,

Dupré's sniper picked off another one of their detail. What followed was nothing short of a massacre the likes of which has not taken place on US territory in living memory.

The media coverage of the event and aftermath would show not only a dead Mayor and Governor but dead civilians including a child and policemen, a news cameraman and a reporter; a scene that signaled others like Dupré across the country to begin their rampage. The scene would trigger similar riots and events nationwide. Almost all of America watched in shock not wanting to believe what they were seeing as urban America came to a full boil and erupted, resulting in uncontrollable death and destruction.

WASHINGTON – JAN. 24, 2019

The rumbles of revolt grew louder and louder still as the story, and especially the video of events in New Orleans, was shown all over the news media and picked up and run continuously on social media on the internet. When Faren Dupré's circus act was broadcast all over the country blacks and other minorities began to flood the streets. The angry crowds turned into a disorganized battle force that charged blindly through the cities destroying anything and anyone in their path, or anything remotely associated with the object of their anger and hate. Cities burned and people died and law enforcement was quickly overwhelmed becoming all but helpless. The National Guard proved to be too little too late. Many of the guardsmen refused to fight their own people and others deserted, choosing instead to go and secure their homes and protect or gather and evacuate their families to safety. Many began to choose sides which caused a breakdown in command and began to dissolve the National Guard altogether. Their weapons and equipment were quickly confiscated by the rioters who turned them on those they now considered to be the enemy.

Due to its large population of African Americans, the streets of Washington were no different, if not worse than other cities. The riots were spreading across the town and starting to advance towards the Capitol in force. When Lindsey's car slid to a stop in front of the Capitol to deliver the Senator they were quickly surrounded by armed guards. Lindsey hit the window button and as soon as it opened she whipped out her badge and yelled "SECRET SERVICE. I have Senator Bernhardt here. We need to get in."

The guards checked both their IDs and then escorted them into the building. "Sorry, sir," said a young Lieutenant, "but as you can see we've had a few problems here and it doesn't seem as though it's going to get any better any time soon."

As they entered the building the Senator and Lindsey saw what the young officer was referring to. There were at least five bodies lying about and they were told there were others at other entrances.

"It's getting pretty damn serious, sir. One of those bastards was loaded with explosives. Fortunately it didn't go off. We overwhelmed them with firepower this time but I'm sure they'll reinforce and return. It's crazy, sir. They're crazy.

"I quite agree," replied the Senator.

"We will be transporting all of you to a more secure location soon. One of the safety centers. Choppers are due here within the hour."

"Do you have any news of the President?" asked the Senator.

"Only that he's in the White House, sir. But then we're having communication problems and have been a little too busy to keep up. I'm sure he's safe and should be evacuated soon. Haven't seen Marine One or observed any other choppers lifting off from the White House though."

"I understand. Thank you," said Senator Bernhardt as he and Lindsey made their way into the Capitol.

As they did the Capitol Guard redirected them, "Those that are here are collected in the house side. All Congress members have been directed there to wait for transport."

"Is this building secure?" asked Lindsey.

"Yes ma'am," replied the guard. "As much as possible. Our resources are spread out pretty thin right now because of the short notice and we're waiting for reinforcement. There are a lot of priority locations in this town to be secured but I assure you this one is high on the list and we're well armed."

"What about the White House?"

"As I understand, at this time it's well secured. But like I said, I don't know the status of the President other then he was in residence when all this started."

"Where will they be taking these people that are here now?" asked the Senator.

"I'm not certain, sir. Some Congressmen flew out earlier. Don't know where to but I believe the next lift is destined for the FEMA bunker in Olney, Maryland."

"Hell of a mess," Lindsey said to no one in particular.

"Yep, you sure got that shit right," replied the guard.

"Need to get to my office in this building before I leave. Is it secure up there?" asked the Senator. "And what about my staff at my office in the Senate Building?"

"Yes sir. This building is completely secure. But as far as I know, the other federal buildings and facilities that have been secured were evacuated. Although, as I understand it, some folks are hunkered down inside a few. I don't know which. It's gotten pretty nasty all over the city. But just how bad, I'm simply not sure, sir. We lost all communications with command and the outside about an hour ago. Only coms we got are close range headsets. You know… old walky-talky kind of stuff."

"Okay, but don't you know there's an emergency communications center is this building? And what about sat phones? Have you tried satellite phones?"

"Like I said, sir, everything is out of service. All down or shut down… gone. I don't know who's running this revolt but whoever it is; they sure as hell know their shit."

Senator Bernhardt lowered his head in disbelief and troubled thought. He then looked to Lindsey, "Let's get to the office. My medications are there." He then turned to the young Lieutenant, "Just do the best you can, son. That's all any of us can do right now. I'm sure you will be getting help soon."

"Yes sir."

CHAPTER 40 _____

VALDOSTA, GEORGIA – JAN. 25, 2019

It was predawn when Colonel Floyd Mayfield strolled into his office at Moody Field. He was tense, and though he wasn't showing it, he was extremely nervous. He had already been to two of the base armories, unlocked and disbursed small weapons to his confederates, and was now about to send out a number of confusing orders throughout Moody Field regarding the deployment of nearly every A10 Warthog on the base. After calling in, rounding up, and locking up loyal U.S. pilots he released all the aircraft in the hands of his rogue pilots who had been given entry to the base in the dead of night by the Colonel's men posted at the main gate

The sound of the A10's lifting off caused the base to come alive and assigned personnel began to rise and question what was happening. Other groups, now armed, poured through the base capturing or killing the remaining loyalist.

With the departure of the final A10 Colonel Mayfield sounded the base alarm and as the airmen rushed to their stations they were cut down by gunfire. While the sound of the weapons bled into Colonel Mayfield's office he parked himself behind his desk, closed his eyes and white knuckled the arms of his desk chair. He knew he had crossed the Rubicon and there was no turning back. And for the first time he seriously considered the cost of his actions to his family. He thought of his children and Damarius and what this would do to him as a man, as a human being.

Mayfield's A10's had grouped then dispersed in flights of three to previously designated locations where they would orbit until certain targets presented themselves. The majority of those locations included military bases where it was estimated that the rebellious forces in the early stage of the operation would be unable to control or overrun a facility. One such Army base was Fort Benning in Georgia. There Mayfield's pilots were joined by an F16 from the Air Force joint base in Charleston. The A10's orbited the base while the F16 began to strafe and pound strategic targets then orbit above them to provide cover. The troops on the base had been called up to assist at various city riot areas and had begun to load and deploy in both trucks, busses, and by Chinook helicopters. The rouge aircraft were there to both take out the on base capabilities and manpower, to hold them back until adequate forces were formed to overrun the troops that remained. They would then be joined by other rebels in the Army already on the base.

One A10 covered the airstrip, taking out the choppers which were loaded to capacity with troops. Another enjoyed a turkey shoot as the convoys tried to depart the base. The Warthog proved its worth as it wiped out nearly every vehicle with ease. On the base and in the convoys American soldiers watched in total disbelief as they were torn to shreds by their own aircraft. Base commanders calling for assistance received none and were soon wiped out in the confusion when preplaced military turncoats ran through the base destroying everything they could to weaken the defense.

This scene played out at military bases throughout the United States and though some bases fought back and survived they soon discovered that what they were experiencing was just the beginning of a long destructive conflict.

In the streets of Valdosta, Georgia, citizens were collecting in areas they thought would be safest. Some were in the mall, some in hotels; other families with children were held up in the new high school while rioters in pickup trucks full of screaming black men shooting weapons into the air were driving by, honking horns, yelling threats, and taking occasional pot shots at the building. Keenan's mother and Diddy were helping some of the older folks and children when his father tapped him on the shoulder. When he turned his father stared him in the eye and, saying nothing, handed him a rifle. As Keenan accepted the weapon and its responsibility his father just nodded saying, "Come on."

Keenan followed as his father led him to the roof of the school building where a number of men were already positioned. They all just looked and nodded approval as Keenan and his father took their position on the front side above the rotunda. His father extended a supply of ammunition and instructed him saying, "It's a hell of a day, son. Don't know what the fuck is going on here but you better damn well believe we are going to protect our family. All of our families. So you best set your mind to the idea it ain't gonna be pretty and be ready to do whatever it takes. You got that?"

"Yes sir," replied Keenan as he loaded the Winchester 3030. "I got it."

"Those niggers got military weapons," said one of the men on the roof.

"Yeah," joined in another. "They took Moody Field. No telling what the hell they got out there. We got any help coming or what?"

"Who can say? All the lines are dead. Hell even the cell phones are out. Whatever the hell is going on is... well, who the hell knows. No TV, no radio, no nothing. All we know is they ain't foreigners. So who the hell knows?"

The residents of the cities and suburbs soon discovered there would be no help and began organizing and fighting back against a faceless enemy who was destroying their world. Confusion and violence reigned and it would be days before the country would learnt what was happening and why. The well planned assault on the nation was thorough to say the least. Like minded military leaders arranged for the satellite systems to be shut down and jammed all wireless communications. It took days before the rioters took control of many of the broadcast facilities and began sending out their own message; a message that was sourced from New Orleans. A message from Farin Dupré.

BERNHARDT ESTATE − JAN. 25, 2019

Major Stagliano was awakened gently by the Senator's wife, Margaret Bernhardt. He slowly opened his eyes to find her standing above him with a small tray from which he could detect the scent of freshly brewed coffee.

"How are you feeling Major?" she inquired as she placed the tray on the nightstand next to the bed.

"Um, better. Thank you," he replied as he scrutinized the room to gain his bearing. It was a large bedroom with furniture and décor being the obvious choice of woman but also with a few touches of a long residing male.

"You've been unconscious for a full day. You should be in the hospital, you know," she declared. "I understand you've been through quite an ordeal. But Jesse said you probably wouldn't go there so he brought you here."

Stagliano sat up against the headboard of the king size bed and eyed the coffee. "Oh, I've been through worse," he replied. "But thanks for your concern."

"Coffee?" she asked.

"Sounds good. Yes ma'am, please, and smells wonderful."

She smiled with his compliment. "I've lived in a family of kick-ass sailors all of my adult life Major. Among the many things I've learned is how to make a damn good cup of coffee."

"Yes ma'am, I'm sure."

She poured his cup and handed it to him. "And it's the least I can do for the man who saved my husband's life."

"Oh, you know about that do you?"

"Of course. You didn't think us military wives are only good for packing and unpacking and getting laid did you? We see all and know all, Major. Who the hell do you think runs our military? Not the Generals that's for sure. It's us Sergeant Moms," she laughed. "Now, there are some mild pain pills on the tray should you decide you need them. Are you hungry?"

"Um, no ma'am. But I would like to see the Senator. Is he available?"

"Oh no, sorry Major. Lindsey has taken him to Washington, to the Capitol. She's Secret Service and our niece. While you were asleep a great many things have happened. There are riots and..."

"What?" interrupted Stagliano. "The Capitol! He can't go there. Not now. What day is this? What date?"

"Um, the 25th. Why?"

"Mrs. Bernhardt I have to speak to him immediately. A phone?" asked Stagliano as he sat up to get out of the bed. "I need to tell him..."

"I'm sorry, Major, but it seems all the phones are down. Landlines and cell service both. I've tried to call him a few times myself, but there's just no service. Last call I got was a man telling me to prepare to be evacuated."

"Mrs. Bernhardt do you have a car?"

"Yes, of course."

"I need it. I have to get to the Senator immediately. It's very important."

"You really shouldn't be driving. Remember you injured your head and…"

"Ma'am, I can't argue with you and I can't explain why but I'm taking your car," he said as he threw on his clothes. "And you have to stay here. Do you understand? Stay here until someone comes to get you or be with you."

"But…"

"Trust me, ma'am. I can't tell you why now, but trust me and do what I say, please."

She nodded agreement then said, "I'll get you the car keys. But you take a couple pills and some coffee before you leave. That's an order soldier."

"Yes, ma'am," replied Stagliano with a slight smile, realizing he was indeed dealing with a military wife.

Thirty minutes later Stagliano was barreling along route 50 at 85MPH in the Bernhardt SUV and about to hit the Washington Beltway. When he came to the overpass he found it jammed with traffic fighting to get both on and off the big multi-lane road. He hit the horn, weaved through the traffic, and stayed on route 50 to get to the center of the city. Minutes later he found himself in what could only be described as nothing less than a war zone. As Route 50 became New York Avenue he found burning buildings where firefighters were pinned down behind their trucks, avoiding gunfire. They were surrounded by various burning vehicles, a wrecked and burning police cruiser, and bodies in the streets including a firefighter and two policemen.

Stagliano hit the gas and sped through the mayhem and gunfire. Bullets from an assault rifle ripped through the side windows as he passed a group of black men crashing into a pawn shop. The attached convenience store was in flames and two young boys jumped out of the broken window with arms full of cartons of cigarettes and beer. A block further along the street and through the smoke-filled torn and ravaged city there were gangs of black men and women running from building to building, dragging out people and looting their homes. As he sped quickly along, an elderly black man stepped out into the middle of the street and pointed a shotgun directly at him. Stagliano ducked and mashed the accelerator to the floor. As the vehicle leapt forward, he heard the hard thud when it hit the man and then felt the bump and thump as it ran over him.

At this point Stagliano wasn't sure he would be able to get through this part of the city to reach Senator Bernhardt at the Capitol. It was then he spotted a body spread across the curb and next to it laid an assault rifle. He slammed on the brakes, jumped from the SUV and snatched up the weapon. It was a beat up Vietnam War souvenir AK47 with a full banana clip. Not the Major's first choice, but then at this time he had no choice. When he rushed back behind the wheel a very heavy set wild eyed woman came running at him screaming and swinging a baseball bat. He slammed the door closed just as she swung the bat and smashed in the driver side window.

"Holy shit, lady! Are you crazy?" yelled Stagliano as he put the vehicle in gear. She let out an insane scream as she slammed the bat into the windshield. Stagliano covered his face, turning his head away from the flying glass. He quickly shook it off and punched the accelerator. The woman's baseball bat stuck in the windshield as she fell to the ground. When he pulled away he looked in the side view mirror and saw the woman sit up in the street waiving her arms frantically and screaming. Her hands went to her head and two small children darted from a nearby building to assist her. She looked back at him and waived her fist.

Stagliano had wanted to turn left at N. Capitol Street but could see gangs fighting in the streets. Instead soon after, he found himself cruising carefully into the business district down 7th Street which oddly seemed almost deserted. Yes, he thought, it would take him to the National Mall and Capitol Hill with minimal danger. It was an eerie scene as he drove slowly, carefully, his weapon at hand. Occasionally the sound of shooting would echo through the empty streets. When he passed H Street he saw on the corner a police cruiser parked, blocking a large 1970s Buick that had been forced up onto the sidewalk and run into a building. Behind it was a military humvee. The trunk on the Buick was open and the police officers were unloading numerous weapons and spreading them on the ground. On the sidewalk three black men lay face down, held in check by four soldiers with weapons at the ready. They glanced up as he passed but showed no concern.

Eventually Stagliano could see the mall in the distance and knew he was almost there. He decided to turn onto Pennsylvania Avenue for a straight shot to the Capitol when suddenly he was surrounded by a military unit. Armed soldiers entered the street and held their assault rifles cocked and ready as he brought the SUV to a halt. He cut the engine and raised his hands. Then he heard the rumble of a big engine behind him and turned to discover an army humvee. It stopped and a soldier in the top turret lowered and aimed its mounted .50 caliber at his vehicle.

A young but obviously serious Sergeant cautiously gripping his Beretta M9 pistol with two hands strolled over to the driver's side window,. "You out for a joy ride there, Chief?" he addressed Stagliano.

Stagliano sat with his hands up, not knowing just how wired this particular young band of soldiers were and which one would be nervous enough to inappropriately pop off a few rounds and ruin his day... or life. "I'm Major Vincent Stagliano, Army retired... kind of."

"Kind of? No shit. What the hell's that supposed to mean?"

"It means..."

"Yeah yeah. Glad to meetcha Major, and I'm Sergeant Elvis Presley," interrupted and laughed the Sergeant. "Now what say you slowly and carefully get your ass outa that vehicle?"

Stagliano did as instructed and immediately after exiting the vehicle was slammed to the side of it by the

Sergeant. While he was being frisked other soldiers were rummaging through the SUV searching for weapons and explosives. Out came the AK47 assault rifle.

Observing the weapon with interest the Sergeant pulled the baseball bat from the windshield and played with it as he questioned his detainee, then pushed the end of the bat into the small of Stagliano's back. The act triggered the pain from Stag's combat injury but he gritted his teeth and took the pain, not willing to let it be shown to these young troops.

"Tell me, what do retired Army Majors do these days while they ride around in a riot area with an assault rifle? Oh, and a baseball bat that I assume wasn't yours?"

"Oh, you know," replied Stagliano. "The usual type of shit, a little work for the CIA, some stuff for the Majority Leader of the US Senate... and every once in a while I get to kick the fuckin' shit out of assholes like you."

The smartass answer inflamed the Sergeant who quickly got into Stagliano's face using the baseball bat as a serious prop to emphasize his warning. "You apparently ain't quite aware of your situation here are ya... Major? I mean we could just leave your ass dead in the street and nobody would know a damn thing, and, well, actually nobody would give a shit."

"I would know," came a voice of authority from the other side of the SUV. "But I think it's more you who isn't quite aware of his situation, Sergeant Bates. Because that man there could clean your clock and shove that bat up your black ass before you could say your own name. Isn't that right, Major?"

Stagliano looked up to discover the familiar face of Lamont Cory, one of his former Lieutenants, now a Captain. Stagliano smiled and eased away from the vehicle.

"How the hell are ya, Major?"

"Oh, you know. Same ol', same ol'. The big boys dumped me for medical reasons. So here I am in the limbo of the swamp."

"I heard. Sorry," replied Captain Cory as he walked around and joined them, took the bat from the Sergeant and handed it to Stagliano. "Sergeant, this man here is one of the baddest motherfuckin' Deltas you will ever meet and you should be extremely lucky that I was here to save your fuckin' life. Got that?"

A hesitant, "Yes, sir," rolled from the Sergeant's mouth as he backed away.

The Captain took Stagliano's arm and led him away from the detail of soldiers. "You know that Sergeant has a really bad bedside manner. Don't like that sum'bitch much. Expect I'll be kickin' his ass before the day is over. But he did ask the right question, Stag. What the hell are you doing runnin' around in this crap and with that pig shit of a weapon? Thing looks like it wouldn't shoot water."

"Didn't have much choice," replied Stagliano. "I had to get through the city. It's important as hell that I get to the Capitol building and find Senator Bernhardt. We're in the midst of a government overthrow beginning with a series of assignations and he's among the top of the list. I have to warn him, protect him. It's critical."

"Hmm, overthrow. I thought it was something like that, but we weren't actually that thoroughly briefed. My gang is here to augment the White House security down the street there. Perimeter patrol shit. You know. Tell ya the truth Stag, this whole damn thing felt a little squirrely from the get go."

"I don't know what's going on in the White House. All I know is I have to get to the Capitol."

"Tell ya what Stag. I can't pull my full crew away from this area but I'll give you a little help. Gonna send one of my humvees along to give you cover. It's mostly open area and safer if you stay on 7th street here. Don't try Pennsylvania Avenue. There's a check point there and they shoot first and ask questions later. Know what I mean? Lot of nervous young soldiers around here."

Stagliano nodded his head, indicating he understood.

"I'd suggest you cut across the mall and beat ass up the hill. Our coms are down so I can't tell them you're coming and I don't know what kind of flack you might run into as you approach that big ass Alamo up there so I figure the presence of the humvee might help. Give them some sort of official look. Aside from that, all I can say is good luck."

"Yeah, from what I know we're all going to need some luck. The entire damn country," said Stagliano.

They shook hands and Stagliano headed back to the SUV. Captain Cory called one of his soldiers over to the vehicle, "Give this man your weapon and ammo," he said. "…better'n that pig shit thing you picked up back there," he said, turning to Stagliano.

As the Major accepted the soldier's M4 carbine weapon, the Captain went to the humvee and quietly gave them their instructions, then turned back to Stagliano with a salute, saying, "All yours, Major!"

Stagliano drove away. Glancing back through his rear view mirror he saw the Captain approach the Sergeant and throw his arm around his shoulder as they laughed and watched him drive away. To Stagliano the scene seemed awfully chummy for two men who weren't supposed to like each other. Then his paranoia kicked in and he began to piece together what he had been seeing. The riots were being performed by primarily black civilians. Captain Cory, the Sergeant and most all of his detail were black save for one young trooper who appeared Hispanic; the crew of the humvee was three black soldiers as well. Stagliano wasn't a racist but nor was he a fool and had no problem putting together the pieces.

When the street crossed Madison Drive and reached the edge of the broad grassy mall, Stagliano punched the accelerator and jumped the curb then swung a left to make a straight beeline run to the Capitol. The move temporarily caught the humvee crew off guard and they hesitated to follow. When they did, Stagliano could see the soldier manning the top turret gun grasp it, cock it, and aim, but not at any threatening rioters. The gun was aimed directly at him and opened fire. It ripped the rear of the SUV forcing the Major to swerve and avoid the shots. The chase continued until they were a mere three hundred yards from Capitol Hill. It was then the humvee pulled to the side of him and the rounds of the heavy weapon tore through the vehicle killing its engine.

Stagliano snatched up the M4 and crawled out of the side of the SUV just as the humvee closed in, firing continuously. The heavy weapon seemed to be ripping the vehicle to shreds as the Major took shelter behind it and hugged the ground. When the firing finally ceased the humvee came to a halt. He heard a voice come from inside, "Give me confirmation. Hear me up there, Corky?"

"Can't see to confirm. You're gonna have to get out and check him."

"Oh hell, man, I dun wanna look at dat shit. You killed him, you check him out."

"You lazy ass nigger. Get out da the fuckin' ride and take a look," replied the topside gunner.

"Mothafucker, you gonna owe me fo dis shit," answered the driver as he exited the Humvee. "Makin' me look at dat bloody shit and all."

"Ain't owe'n you nothin', nigga. Jus do yo fuckin' job, man."

The driver raised his weapon and walked to the side of the SUV expecting to see a bloody mess behind the wheel. Instead he found only an empty seat. When he turned to look about he found himself face to face with Major Stagliano and his M4. Stag opened fire and took off the better part of his head. He then quickly turned his weapon to the top of the Humvee and took out the gunner. That left only one man inside who was now scrambling to exit on the opposite side. He escaped from the humvee and began running for the cover of the nearby oak trees when Stagliano took a bead and put him down with two rounds. He leaned back against the military vehicle and took a breath while surveying the area around him. Determining he was now safe, he quickly gathered the weapons of the dead soldiers and tossed them into the Humvee. After he dragged the body of the top gunner out, he got behind the wheel of the humvee and drove off for the Capitol.

He decided to approach from the eastern front of the building. Passing the Capitol Reflection Pool. Circling slowly around the building he could see he was being observed by members of a military security detail. Captain Cory was correct, thought Stagliano. The humvee was the ticket that afforded him safe passage, even though the Captain had no intention of letting him get that far. Strategic gun placements were set around and on the Capitol building consisting of various teams with M60 machine guns. They watched him intensely, all the while targeting his every move and all the while he wondered just who the hell they were there for... the same side as Captain Cory or the U.S. Government?

Just then voices from the Capitol Security force started coming over the humvee's short range com system. "Six, we got a humvee approaching," he heard them say. "Appears to be working its way around toward you. Over."

"Affirmative, we will intercept. Six, over."

CHAPTER 42 _____

In the chaos of the New Orleans riots Farin Dupré and his now active staff confiscated the offices of the late Mayor Broussard. Dupré was strutting about the room barking out orders when in walked the Reverend Jamison Johnson.

"Just what the hell you think you're doin'?" yelled Johnson. "Who the hell told you to blanket the broadcast outlets with all that radical shit you been spewin'?"

Dupré and his staff stopped what they were doing and stared at Johnson. No one said a word, all waiting for Dupré to respond. Dupré simply stood and listened.

Jamison Johnson came across the room, angrily moved face to face with Dupré and continued, "You sum'bitchin piece'a shit. You 'spose to be part of the program, part of the plan. Nobody gave you a green light to turn this shit into the Farin Dupré show. This is a national deal and you ain't the face of it. Nobody said anything about you ownin' all that radical nigger leader shit. You did your part. Now you're the big fish in your little pond. Got it? Ain't nobody made you the big dog. That's my deal, You got that?"

Dupré remained silent, standing steady eye to eye with Johnson.

"Now you're gonna fix this crap. You hear me? I brought you into this damn thing and you gonna tow the line or get out. Now you're gonna get on the TV and radio and tell all the bothers in the country whatever it takes to fix it, turn it around, and start pushing the Reverend Jamison Johnson as the new dog in charge. Got that? Now fix it!"

Dupré smiled, nodding his head in agreement. "Got it," he replied. And with that he drew his pistol, shoved it in Johnson's chest and pulled the trigger. "There, I fixed it. Problem solved," he laughed, then turned away saying, "Somebody get this sack of shit out of my office. We got work to do."

The Reverend Jamison Johnson certainly had good reason to be angry but not because of Farin Dupré, although Dupré's actions were a surprise to many. What the Reverend didn't know was that he too was on the hit list because Arisztid Bakos' plan was designed to not succeed in the way he was led to believe in that it would set him up as the new President of the United States. Bakos' plan was to weaken, even crack America in half. To remove it as the world power and in doing so devalue the U.S. dollar, eliminating it as the world's prominent currency. In this way, having all of his financial moves in place, he alone would become a world power simply by being the world's banker, by controlling whatever currencies rose to prominence and whatever currency became the world standard. But like the Reverend, Bakos' was caught off guard and surprised if not disappointed at what was taking place all around the country. Bakos revolution was to just be a glitch in the republic, just enough to eliminate the powers that be and replace them with his chosen few. What he was seeing instead was uncontainable all out revolution fueled by hate and misguided anger. Bakos had lost control and was now on his private aircraft fleeing the country.

CHAPTER 43 _____

VALDOSTA, GEORGIA – JAN. 25, 2019

The evening was rolling in, cool, clear and windless; that part of the day often referred to as the golden hour when things began to slow and settle and the subtle light and hues of nature seemed to deepen, enriched, hovering for a long moment of peace and balance over all things. Most all creatures large and small, enjoyed their final period of recess before hiding in the quiet night. That is all creatures save one. Through the millennia of time mankind has learned to beat the dark and make it something to fear and on this day in Valdosta, Georgia, there was more reason to fear the night than any previous time.

Many of the men, women, boys, and girls who had taken refuge in Valdosta High School at the edge of town were uncomfortably stationed on the roof armed, watching and waiting for the next shoe to drop. Keenan Ashley leaned against the edge of the roof hugging his 30-30 Winchester and looking up into the sky for the first glimpse of a star, all the while hoping he wouldn't be required to use his weapon. No matter how he ran all the recent events through his mind he could not reason them out enough to make any sense. He then remembered the recent evening with his friend Big D. Big D was different, troubled and in some way desired to tell him something. *He knew*, concluded Keenan. *Big D knew this was going to happen and he wanted to warn me, to warn the family, but couldn't. Did he want to do this, be a part of this? Was Big D out there with them?* wondered Keenan. *Was he out there killing people?*

At that moment the sound of a muffled explosion came from the town and Keenan perked up, turned and faced out over the rooftop. "What was that?" he asked his father.

"Over there," answered his father. "Downtown. From the looks of the smoke I'd say they just blew up the Court House."

"Look," said an exited Keenan. "To the right. I can see high flames and smoke."

"Yep," replied his father. "Appears they're burning the old antebellum mansions."

"Why? Why the hell would they do that? I mean they're just great old houses. Why?"

"It's history, son. Their history and they want to wipe it out as though that might make it actually go away. Those places were built back in the slave days. Probably built by slaves and then worked and maintained by slaves."

"Those people are all gone. What good is it to destroy a house? To destroy us?"

"It's a newfound anger." Came a voice from next to Keenan's father. It was one of Keenan's teachers. The *Rev* the kids called him because he was also a preacher at the Central Church of Christ. "For decades now there have been separatist who have been instilling hate and stirring up dissention to counter the wellbeing and progress of African Americans. They did it with politics, with the media, and most unfortunately in their churches and they did it for profit and status but what they may finally get might be only a wrecked country with a lost population... a land weak and full of misery. No better than the days centuries ago when they were in chains."

"Look," exclaimed Keenan. "It looks like the streets are on fire."

His father watched for a long moment then concluded, "No, the streets aren't on fire. That's people marching with torches. People with torches like some damn eighteenth century mob."

"Like the people who burned down their homes and farms in the eighteenth century. They're getting even and they don't even know why," said the Rev. "They can't accept that those days are gone and none of us had anything to do with it."

Keenan watched and the parade of torches marched down the street until he finally realized they were coming to the high school. "Oh god, they're coming here," he said softly.

"It's time to lock and load, son," said his father. "Remember, your mother, sister, and a host of women, children and old folks are in this building and we're here to protect them. Ain't no time for second thoughts now."

"Yes, sir," replied Keenan. "I'm... I'm ready."

The parade of rioters and rebels came around the corner and spread down the road in front of the school. For the longest moment they stood silent, torches high and ready. Then suddenly a single voice rang out, "FREE AND INDEPENDENT BLACK POWER!"

With that declaration the mob began walking toward the school. Behind them was a line of men with automatic assault rifles that had been seized at the Moody Field Armories and from law enforcement facilities. Keenan rose and laid his Winchester over the edge of the roof and took aim but held his fire waiting for a signal from the older men. He watched closely, looking into the faces of angry people of all ages bent on destruction and murder. As he scanned the crowd a familiar face struck him and his heart seemed to seize up with anguish. It was Big D, his friend and brother. A torch held high, an assault rifle slung over his shoulder, and anger on his face as he yelled repeatedly, "BLACK POWER!"

The mob kept coming and finally the shots rang out from all across the roof of the school. Then shots were instantly returned by the men supporting the mob. Torch carriers fell to the ground bleeding and crying in pain. Bullets ripped across the top of the roof felling some of the men and through it all Keenan kept his eye on Big D, hoping, in some odd way that he wouldn't be shot. By now half the rioters were put down and the firing was becoming even more intense as the armed black men on the ground began approaching the school. Of the maybe 40 torch carriers more than half had been shot and lay across the ground bleeding and dying in front of the school, the others approaching under fire. They began to run for the school, waiving their torches and yelling madly, "BLACK POWER, BLACK POWER!"

In front of them all came Big D, bobbing and weaving, the shots from the roof were kicking up dirt and asphalt all around him but he was too fast and cut too quickly to be taken down. Keenan watched with torn emotion, wanting Big D to succeed but also wanting him to get taken down. The shooting from the street increased and continued and more and more of the torch carriers fell until the only one left was Big D. No one could get him and he grew dangerously close. Then suddenly Keenan's father fell back, shot clean in the head and dead. Keenan went to him, saw he was dead and stared for only brief moments that seemed like hours. The sound of the firing continued but now seemed to muffle and get lost in the moment. When Keenan looked up he saw yet another of the men on the roof fall back. They had killed his father and are coming to kill his family thought Keenan and his blood began to boil with anger. He snatched up his Winchester and went to the wall and there was Big D about to breach the school and set it aflame when Keenan took aim and yelled as loud as he could, "DAMARIUS MAYFIELD!"

Below Big D stopped and looked up at his friend Keenan, and for some reason he smiled. Keenan stood, raised his weapon and pulled the trigger. Big D fell to the ground dead. Just as he did a shot tore into Keenan's chest. He fell across the body of his father and moments later died.

THE WHITE HOUSE – JAN. 25, 2019

In the White House bunker Situation Room, President Moreno paced impatiently, occasionally looking up at the TV monitors which were now showing actual aerial shots from various cities around the country. He occasionally paused and stood staring at the monitors. "Somebody please tell me our communications are back up," he growled. "Damn it. It's been almost two days. What the hell is going on?"

"No coms yet Mr. President," was the answer.

When he turned away and looked at his staff his eyes settled on General Lewis. After a moment he questioned, "My god General, how the hell could this have happened... in this country... in this day and age? Where did we fuck up? And for Christ's sake where the hell are the joint chiefs?"

Just then the General's com set rang and he snatched it up. "Lewis here," he responded quickly.

All in the room turned and watched him, eager for any word from the outside. The General listened intently, his interests growing more intense with each moment. He finally spoke into the line, "In the air? Do we have his position?" There was a brief delay as he listened to the answer. "Alright then, take him out," he ordered. At the end of the call he slowly replaced the com set and looked to the President.

"What is it, Conrad? What's happening out there?"

The General cleared his throat then began to speak. The riots have quickly evolved into paramilitary and military assaults and operations and nearly destroyed most of our larger cities. They are being armed and supplied by likeminded members of our own military. Nearly half of our military bases have been overrun and the others are engaged with... enemy radicals. The Air Force bases were the first to go and most of our fighter aircraft are now being deployed and piloted by what are being called *revolutionary pilots*." With that information the General paused.

"But what about the Navy, we have Navy fighter planes, Navy resources to fight back, right? And can't we call back our troops from overseas?" asked one of the staffers.

A light chuckle came from across the room. The General glanced over to find it came from Bo Peppers who sat sprawled comfortably in a chair, smiling. "Oh hell, General. Cut the fuckin' dramatics and let's get to it. I want some fresh air." With that Bo Peppers stood, pulled a small automatic pistol from inside his jacket and aimed it at the President. The two Secret Service agents quickly went for their weapons but before they could act, from within the thick walls of the bunker a shot rang out that was deafening. Bo Peppers dropped his weapon and fell to the floor, dead. The shot was expertly aimed at and entered his heart.

Across the room the General stood next to the Secretary of Defense, the pistol in the General's hand still aimed at the dead Chief of Staff, Bo Peppers. Without looking away, he continued speaking. "Hostile countries and our not so friendly allies, China, Russia, Iran, Cuba, North Korea, have decided to take advantage of our domestic military situation and engage our Navy fleets at sea. My guess is to eliminate them so they can have a clear path to grab whatever part of the planet they want. One of our carriers, the Ronald Reagan, was sunk by what they thought was their own friendly aircraft. Those ships still in port have been destroyed by... opposition aircraft. A nationwide Pearl Harbor you might say. Our intelligence apparatus, the NSA and CIA, FBI and all the rest, has been decimated. Our international units are stranded. If they try and fly home it's likely they will be engaged; shot down because our offensive military capabilities are in the hands of radicals. Aircraft, missiles, even some ships. My guess is those troops will either be protected by the host country or assaulted, depending on... well, who the hell knows. Hell, they may even begin fighting each other." The General paused as he sank into obvious despair, then he finally spoke softly, "At this moment, Mr. President, we are blind and losing our country and..."

"...and? And what? How the hell do you know all this?" inquired the President.

"Because... I made it possible... I made it happen. It's all my fault. I'm sorry. I'm so sorry." With that, the regretful General Lewis put the gun to his head and pulled the trigger.

Everyone stared in amazement as they stepped away from the blood and brains spread across the room. The President stared at the General in shock, then at Bo Peppers. After a long moment he finally spoke. "I don't know what's going on but I do know we need to get the hell out of here," he said as he turned to a staffer. "We need to talk to somebody outside. Check that thing the General was talking in and check the phones again."

"Still dead, Mr. President," came the reply. "And this thing that the General was talking on... well, I've never seen anything like it. I think it only takes calls. Can't make any calls out because it's coded."

"Well how the hell are we getting these TV feeds?"

"That was arranged by Bo," said the President's secretary.

"I'm thinking all that stuff we were watching was fake," commented the Secretary of Defense. "That is until those juicy shots of burning cities were available."

"We have to get this bunker open. We have to talk to the Secret Service. Tell them to open up."

"Can we trust them?" came a voice from the staff.

"Do we have a choice?" replied President Moreno. "Use the door com and if nobody answers then just bang on the damn thing until somebody does."

As he spoke the Secretary of Defense eyed Bo Peppers briefcase and lifted and placed it on the table. When he opened it and looked in he gasps, stating, "Holy shit. That son of a bitch brought in a fuckin' bomb!"

"It was his last resort option," came a small voice from the back of the room. It was Bo Peppers secretary.

Every one turned and stared.

"It... it was... I mean, I didn't think he was serious about all this stuff. He was always joking around, you know? I really didn't think he was serious. I mean, he would say this kind of stuff to freak me out and laugh, you know? He was kind of goofy like that. But he was the Chief of Staff, you know? He even joked about how easy it would be to blow up the Capitol."

President Moreno stared in disbelief. "The Capitol? Christ, we have to get the hell out of here," he responded. Then he came around with a suggestion. "Is that damn door blast proof?"

"Yes," replied a Secret Service agent. "But..."

"But what?" asked the President.

"Well, um, I'm not sure Mr. President, but it may not be blast proof from the inside."

"That's good enough for me. Inside or out, it doesn't matter. Okay, all you killer types get your heads together and rig that damn bomb to the door. We're getting the hell out of here before this whole damn country goes down the tubes."

CHAPTER 45 _____

THE CAPITOL – JAN. 25, 2019

Stagliano slowed the humvee to a halt on the lawn between the visitor's center and the Capitol entrance. He then very carefully exited the vehicle with his hands in the air. He left his weapon inside but had it close enough that he could snatch it up if needed. He was quickly surrounded by uniformed military guards, all with their weapons trained at his torso. Two others approached the vehicle from the other side, weapons ready, only to discover it had no other occupants.

"Who, what, and why, my friend?" asked the young Lieutenant as he approached the circle of armed soldiers.

"Who the hell's asking," replied Stagliano. Soon after he spoke he realized that he probably would have done better to keep his mouth shut. Immediately a soldier from behind grabbed and threw him face down to the ground and pinned him by pressing a knee on his neck. The barrel of a weapon was pressed to his temple.

"We'll be the ones asking the questions here, smartass. Stand him up," said the Lieutenant. He continued as Stagliano was yanked up to his feet. "Now, before we blow your head off I'll give you one more chance to answer my questions like a gentlemen. Now who the hell are you and what are you doing here?"

The trooper behind slapped him upside the head before he could speak. Stagliano nearly gave in to his many years of training to immediately retaliate but remembering his purpose and also fighting the returning pain in his head that had laid him up in the hospital, he chose not to. "Stagliano. Vincent Stagliano, Major, Army Delta, retired. I'm sure you Ranger pukes have heard of the Delta Force. We're the ones who kick your asses six ways to Sunday."

The soldier behind him came to his ear and replied softly, "You wanna be a dead Delta, you just keep on smart mouthin', asswipe."

"I'm here to find and assist Senator Jesse Bernhardt. It's critical. His life is in danger," said Stagliano, ignoring the soldier's threat.

"Yeah, well the way things are going today umm… Major… all our lives are in danger. So what's so special about your man?"

"I know he's here dammit, so take me to him or turn me lose so I can find him."

The trooper started to slap him again but was halted by the Lieutenant. "Your man is inside with a woman from the Secret Service. So what's so critical about you getting to him?"

"He's on a hit list along with the President, Joint Chiefs, and other higher ups of the government. In case you haven't noticed there's a bit of a rebellion going on. Or does the Army still keep its personnel in the dark about mostly everything? I guess some things never change."

"Bring him inside," ordered the Lieutenant. He then grabbed one of his troopers and told him to go into the Capitol and find the Senator. "When you find him, ask him if he knows this Major Stagliano character. Keep your headset hot and let me know as soon as you get something."

Stagliano was taken into the rotunda and plopped into a chair, his wrist bound. He was guarded by two men, weapons ready.

"Hey, what the hell is this? I told you why I'm here. Get this shit off my wrist," demanded Stagliano.

"I'm sure you'd like that, Major. But if what you're saying is true then how do I know that you're not the one here to take out our Majority Leader Bernhardt?"

"How do you know that you and I don't have the same mother, dumbass?" replied Stagliano.

The Lieutenant stared angrily at Stagliano for a long moment, then replied, "You don't have a lot of friends do you?"

"On this day that might be a good thing," smiled Stagliano.

"And why would you say that?"

"Because today you can't trust anybody," said Stagliano. "And that includes you."

"You better hope…"

The soldier sent to find the Senator appeared on the upper level of the rotunda, looked over to see Stagliano and his guards and called out, "Got them LT!" He then directed the Senator and Lindsey to approach and join him.

"Senator!" called Stagliano looking up from his seat. His voice echoing throughout the rotunda dome.

"Stag," replied Senator Bernhardt. "What are you doing here? Is Margaret okay? Why... Just hold on. I'm coming down."

"Yeah well, doesn't look like I'm going anywhere just now," replied Stagliano.

The Lieutenant saw the exchange and waived Stagliano's guards away, ordering them to return to their post. "Looks like you're the real deal, Major," he said to Stagliano.

"Figured that out all by yourself, did ya?" replied Stagliano. "Now get this shit off my wrist, son, I've got work to do." As he spoke he looked up to where he had seen the Senator and Lindsey as they moved to descend to the lower level. Behind them Stagliano caught a glimpse of a figure moving among the shadows. He watched carefully to determine if the person was a threat or if he appeared to belong there. "Lieutenant, are there any people in this building other than those you control? Say maybe up there with them?"

"No, sir," replied the Lieutenant as he cut the tie from Stagliano's wrist. "Got some Congressmen in the chamber waiting for a chopper and my man and your Senator and lady up there. Other than that the entire building has been evacuated. Just the Capitol police and my security force down here."

"Just you chickens, eh? What about up there."

"Yeah, that's about it and there shouldn't be anybody up there except those three."

"Then who the hell is that," asked Stagliano, pointing to the upper level. Just as he did the man looked down and drew out an AK47. He let loose with a burst of fire at Stagliano and the Lieutenant who was hit and thrown against the wall. Stagliano dove across the floor and snatched the Army Officer's M4 and quickly returned fire. The soldier with the Senator turned to confront the intruder but was immediately zippered with bullets and cut down.

The young Lieutenant rolled over in pain, holding his wound. "I suggest you play dead or you'll be dead soon Lieutenant. And keep your boys out or he'll mow them down as they come through the door. Stay tight. I'll get this bastard."

The Senator and Lindsey had just entered the elevator when the shooting began. Lindsey pulled her pistol and kept it at the ready. As the doors slid open on the lower level, they immediately caught view of Stagliano as he was running across the rotunda. He signaled them to hold up. A blast of automatic fire trailed behind him, the sound of the shots deafening as they echoed throughout the Capitol dome. Stagliano blindly threw a burst of fire towards the upper level to cover his movement. Then all went silent until there came the sound of a helicopter outside. When Stagliano turned his ear to the sound he heard yet another chopper. He could tell by the sound that they were big, probably Chinooks that were capable of carrying groups of people, or in this case, the large group of politicians that were waiting in the chamber.

When Stagliano reached the elevator he instructed Senator Bernhardt and Lindsey to escape to the choppers on his signal. They slowly and carefully slid from the elevator along the wall under the rotunda overhang. Stagliano then entered the elevator pushed the up button and jumped back out. The doors closed and up it went. He silently directed the Senator and Lindsey to the door then backed out to the center of the rotunda and raised his weapon. "The troops are on their way up," he yelled to the would-be assassin. "The building is secure. You can't get out! Give it up or you're a dead man!"

On the upper level, Ben Robinson smiled, then laughed as he responded. "Is that you, Major? Hell, I thought I got you the first time when I shot out that nice new jeep of yours. But what the hell, we all get to fuck up once in a while don't we." As he spoke he positioned himself against the wall and focused on the elevator. "Guess I kind of made up for it when I took out your woman. Shame though, you know? I mean she was a hot one. Guess that must have really ruined your day, huh? Or maybe your entire life," he laughed. "What's left of it that is."

Just then the elevator doors opened and Ben Robinson ripped its interior with an entire clip of ammo. When he saw it was empty he grew angry, quickly reloaded, and stepped to the rail looking down at Stagliano. "You're a damn dead man, Major!" he cried as he lifted the weapon and aimed. Before he could pull the trigger Stagliano let loose with a burst of shots. Robinson fell back and to the floor. Leaving Stagliano relieved he had avenged the death of his precious Luka and so many others.

Stagliano went to the Lieutenant, checked his wound and then helped him up. They exited the building among the many members of Congress who were coming out and heading for the choppers. A medic quickly took charge of the young officer and Stagliano was greeted by Senator Bernhardt and Lindsey.

"Come on, Stag. Let's get back home and pick up Margaret. There's nothing I can do here."

"She's okay, Senator. She's been picked up and waiting for you."

"Then we need to get you back to the hospital. You're not looking to good son," said Bernhardt.

Stagliano offered an approving smile. "Yeah, kind of having a bad day," said Stagliano. "No, you get your ass on that chopper. Leave the rest to us dirty dogs. We'll get it fixed. See there," he said as he looked to the sky when catching sight of two F35 aircraft. They swooped in low over the Capitol then flew a wide circle over the city. "See there," continued Stagliano. "Nothing to worry about. That's your escort all the way to Olney."

As the aircraft came around again they rocked their wings in a friendly gesture then... let loose with two rockets each that completely destroyed the Chinook helicopters along with their crew and cargo of the members of the U.S. Congress. The explosion threw the Senator, Stagliano, and Lindsey to the steps of the building. After gaining their senses they rose and rushed back into the Capitol building for cover. When entering they suddenly came face to face with a blood covered Ben Robinson who quickly fired a burst from his AK47 that ripped through Stagliano and wounded the Senator. As Vincent Stagliano fell dead Lindsey pulled her sidearm and expertly put a round in Robinson's head. Ben Robinson's mission for Arisztid Bakos was over.

The tired, wounded old Senator fell heavily to his knees next to Stagliano's body. His head in hands he questioned, "How can we fix this and how many good boys' lives will it cost?"

Lindsey placed her hand on his shoulder saying nothing, then turning her attention to the sky outside where she heard the prop engines of a heavy military aircraft. She thought she knew what the sound was but had very little time to remember because at that moment the plane had dropped three 500 pound bombs that crashed through the Capitol dome with a massive explosion. The remains of the Senator, Lindsey, Stagliano, and Robinson would never be found.

CHAPTER 46

THE WHITE HOUSE – JAN. 25, 2019

A Secret Service agent and the Secretary of Defense combined their talents to set Bo Peppers plastic bomb on the White House bunker door for a controlled blast. The President and everyone else took cover across the room behind the large upturned conference table along with stacks of other furnishings and then awaited the blast. Unfortunately, Bo's bomb had a suicide fuse that when pulled would ignite instantly. The two men who set the explosive knew this but refused to make it known. Knowing that one of them would have to set it off. While placing the material the Secret Service Agent quietly convinced the Secretary that it was more important for him to live and that it wasn't his job to protect the President but to protect the entire country. The Secretary reluctantly agreed and Special Agent Thomas Sorenson prepared to lose limbs or at worst, to die.

During this process there was a deep rumble from above that shook the bunker.

"Are they attacking the White House?" asked the President.

"Not likely Mr. President," replied the Secret Service Agent. "It was certainly a massive explosion but not a direct one. My guess is some other government building nearby has just been hit, possibly the Capitol. We won't know until we get out of here. But I have to say, Mr. President, that right now you will be a hell of a lot safer in here then out there."

"With my head in the ground? And for how long? No thanks," replied President Moreno. "We're blind in here. I can't do my job in here so get us the hell out."

"Yes, sir. Just one more minute and we'll see what this thing will do."

The group in the bunker anxiously hunkered down and waited. "Hurry over here before that thing blows, Agent Sorenson," called the President.

"Sorry Sir, can't do that."

President Moreno quickly looked to the Secretary of Defense who returned his glance with a brief, "It's the only way, sir. No fuse."

Just then Special Agent Sorenson triggered the explosives. When the smoke and debris settled, President Moreno rose to find the bunker entrance had been breached enough to be forced open but on the floor next to it laid the lifeless Special Agent Sorenson. The President stared in disbelief until he was interrupted by the Secretary of Defense. "Mr. President, we have to go. I'm sure the tunnel is secure and…"

"No," interrupted the President. "I'm going up to the White House… the Peoples' House, and let the world know we're still here, that we're not down and we'll come back strong."

"But Mr. President we can get out through the tunnel and get transport to a safer location," insisted the

Secretary. "To the Pentagon or a military base, possibly even Air Force One. Damn it, you can't stick your neck out up in that rebellious chaos or you'll get it shot off."

President Moreno failed to respond and just went for the exit. As they returned to the upper level of the White House they found it completely abandoned, an empty shell of what was once a daily bee hive of staff and activity. Through the west wing and into the main house they were surprised to find there was no Secret Service, no augmented security forces, no one at all. Then suddenly there came a tremendous thunder that rocked the walls and shook the floors beneath their feet. "My god!" cried the President as he braced himself then quickened his pace to the front entrance. He threw open the doors and rushed out on to the south lawn where he saw smoke and fire rising from the destroyed Capitol Dome. "Oh. Oh my god," cried the President. "What have we done?"

At that moment a security contingent in two humvees rolled around from the side of the White House west wing and pulled in front of the President and his company.

"Mr. President," greeted their officer in charge. "Sir, we were concerned that we had lost you," smiled Captain Lamont Cory. "What a relief."

"Captain, we are going to need transport to the Pentagon," demanded the Secretary of Defense.

"Sorry, sir," replied Captain Cory. "But the Pentagon is currently under attack."

"Can you get us to Air Force One at Andrews?"

"Yes, sir. We sure can," replied Captain Cory who paused and then smiled, looking directly at President Moreno. "Yeah, we sure can... but we won't." Another pause and then he said sarcastically, "I'm afraid all of your reservations have been canceled Mr. President."

At that moment both guns mounted in the two humvee's turrets opened fire. And moments later President Moreno, his staff, and the remaining members of the cabinet lay slaughtered on the south lawn of the White House.

ABOVE THE GULF OF MEXICO – JAN. 25, 2019

Arisztid Bakos eased back into the large soft leather seat of his custom Airbus Jetliner and turned on the massage function. He had just consumed a lean dinner, downed a small glass of Fernet, and was about to close his eyes when his pilot approached from the cockpit.

"Excuse me sir, but I thought I should let you know that for some reason we have an aircraft trailing us."

"Have they made contact and explained why?" inquired Bakos.

"Brief contact only, sir. We have hailed them and asked their intentions. They replied by asking us to identify ourselves. We replied. They acknowledged the reply then went silent."

"Have you seen them?" asked Bakos.

"No, sir. Caught them on radar only, but I'd say from what we can pick up that it's some sort of fighter aircraft."

"And they're keeping their distance?" inquired Bakos.

"Yes, sir."

"Well, there's a bit of a war going on right now so my guess is they're just escorting us out of their combat zone. Most likely assigned as protection by General Lewis, wouldn't you think?"

"To be honest, sir, with what I've been hearing lately, I wouldn't know what to think."

"Well, Captain, they know who we are and haven't done anything aggressive so I wouldn't be too concerned. Let's just stay on course and not look for trouble where there is none."

"Yes, sir," replied the Captain as he returned to the cockpit. Just as he arrived and settled into his seat, the cockpit instruments began to light up and flash, followed by an intermittent alarm.

"Oh shit!" exclaimed the Co-pilot. "We've been targeted. That bastard back there is going to take us out."

"Switch all controls to manual. Prepare for evasive actions."

"Roger," replied the Co-pilot. "Switching to manual." Moments later after altering the controls, "We are now fully manual. It's your bird, Captain."

"It won't do any good," said the Captain. "That bastard's got us if he wants us. Tell all those folks back there to buckle up and brace for the worst."

At that moment the pilot of the F18 that was trailing Bakos made a final call for confirmation of action. "Base, this is Javelin One requesting a final repeat of orders. Please confirm."

"Javelin One, do you have target lock?"

"Affirmative base. I am locked and loaded."

"Roger that, Javelin One. You have a go as per General Lewis directive. Do you copy?"

"Affirmative Base. Copy that base."

The pilot pushed his thrusters for more speed to close the distance between his F18 and his targeted aircraft. He wanted to get closer to the target to permit him a better visual of the strike. "Fox One away," said the pilot. "Fox Two. Two shots away."

Less than a minute later he could see the blast of the large custom Airbus filling the sky with fire and debris. He pitched right to avoid contact then left, orbiting the scene until he witnessed all of the burning debris fall into the waters of the Gulf. "Javelin One to Base."

"Copy Javelin One. Go."

"Confirmed, target is down. No possibility of survivors. Over."

"Copy that Javelin One. Well done. Bring it home."

"Roger that. Javelin One, out."

Arisztid Bakos wanted to remake the world to accommodate his desires for greed and power. Fortunately for him he didn't live long enough to see the results of his efforts. The United States would no longer be united. Both black and white citizens fought each other for longer than anyone cared to remember. In doing so they destroyed the nation's industry, expired most all of the machines and craft that were necessary to make war and defend against war, killed millions of people, created a desperate homeless starving populous, destroyed the economy and the currency, turned the cities into burned out ruins, and, with the involvement of neighboring countries, created a divided landscape.

Farin Dupré had managed to gain control over most of the south's urban areas and was now calling himself the President of the new America. As such he negotiated a deal that awarded the state of Florida to Cuba. Part of the deal was that Cuba would join forces with Mexico, which had been taken over by drug lords, and together they would focus on taking the southwestern states. Cuba agreed and the two countries joined forces and took all the states along the Mexican border including California, Nevada, and Colorado. Their army almost doubled as it rolled into the states where it was joined by millions of Hispanics already residing there. In some towns they were actually welcomed with parades.

Dupré paid little attention to the success of the Hispanic union. He knew it was a bad deal to simply forfeit installations like NASA on Cape Canaveral and the Central Command at MacDill Air Force Base, Tampa. Dupré had already had these critical sites stripped then damaged to the extent they could not be useful or repaired for many years. And there were the losses of the Navy bases in Jacksonville. He did however hold on to the pan handle and the Naval Air Base in Pensacola. There he had too many much needed assets and aircraft to surrender. He had it in mind to simply take Florida back when the big fight was over. His thinking was that by then he would be controlling an overwhelming military force with more than enough power to evict the Cubans. Now however, he would depend on Cuba to watch his back.

As soon as he closed the deal with Cuba he ordered his aircraft to attack the Houston Space Center and not stop until it was left in ashes. It was critical he thought, to take out almost all of the US satellite capabilities even though he wasn't quite sure how. So he chose his most available method, overkill of destruction, sending air armadas of aircraft and bombing them out of existence. The same methods he used on most of the other military installations in Texas, Oklahoma, and California, leaving the door wide open for the Hispanic invasion. What he didn't expect was just how fast Cuba and its allies would turn on them. Cuba threatened to invade Mississippi and Louisiana, knowing that now the newly formed US rebels had little taste for more fight or had the current resources for an adequate defense. The Cubans however, were poised for the fight, busily amassing a large contingent of Cuban and Venezuelan military on Florida's Gulf coast and the border of Texas.

The states of Oregon and Washington avoided the war with the Hispanics altogether by succeeding from the union and declaring themselves Canadian citizens, a can of worms the Hispanic allies chose not to open. Those states became refuge destinations by yuppies and peaceniks that refused to fight and defend their homes and they fled the war. England and Canada joined forces to salvage the central farmlands of the US, knowing that this was where a great deal of the world's food was produced and that a hungry world would lead to worldwide chaos. So for now the United States bread basket belonged to the United Kingdom but was desired by the Hispanics. The Canadian efforts toughest fight was retaking Chicago, not that there was that much left to take. Chicago was in ruins and had first been taken and occupied by African Americans after the riots. They deserted the city when they migrated to what they presumed a safer existence in the southeast, mainly because they disliked being militarily isolated and defenseless. After their departure Chicago was taken by Muslims, both passive and radical, immigrants and terrorists who migrated there from all over the country and the world, coming over the now open borders to escape the war in the Middle East. They arrived by the thousands like flies on a dead carcass. Their goal was to start their own country in Illinois and use Chicago as their national capitol. They were more than willing to die for it and at the hands of the British and Canadians and many stubborn Americans, they did exactly that.

The bloodiest and most destructive portion of the war was, of course, east of the Mississippi. Bloody merciless conflicts were fought to occupy or destroy military bases and confiscate the weapons and resources. America's young soldiers fought beside experienced career men and against angry ex-military rioters, and mercenaries. With each victory the rebels recruited already trained military sympathizers and brainwashed others to join their cause. Many of those taken prisoner who refused to join them were executed which created a standard of conduct by angry Americans on both sides.

Eastern towns and cities were burned to the ground and millions of people became homeless, many forced into the fight just to survive and support and protect their families who were herded into stadiums, large office buildings, college campuses, and any place that would accommodate the masses. The best hotels that weren't destroyed became the domiciles of the fighter elite as they were formed into an organized military. The holding pens eventually turned into work camps and farms. Promises were made and broken and the war continued until both sides began to run out of willing participants and resources. Eventually a truce was negotiated. Blacks and whites fought on both sides, some because they were forced and others because they believed in the cause but it was far from equal. Most of the African Americans in the country migrated south, not always because they justified the cause but because they were black and knew they would suffer facing the vengeance and hatred by surviving whites. Also many of America's finest in their fields and other just angry rabble were beckoned by the deceitful words of Farin Dupré. He was like a new age Adolf Hitler, flooding the airways with propaganda and lies, and playing with the hearts and minds of his race, all the while generating hate and prejudice.

Friends and families became enemies, families and entire communities were torn apart and became lost and separated. The truce however, now afforded anyone from either side to temporarily travel freely without obstruction or interference to the side of their choice. Families could return home if it still existed or to what they assumed would be a safer better life somewhere else. Organizations were formed that would collect them and give them shelter and placement. Many from both sides traveled to the safety of Canada.

The one sticking point of the treaty negotiations was the exchange of prisoners. The still existent elements of the United States military that was for the most part running what was left of the country insisted on keeping prisoners who were former active duty military, claiming they were deserters or worse, outright traitors. Discovering that some had even been tried and put before a firing squad, Farin Dupré began doing the same with his military captives. This brought the truce to an end but not before much of the population had migrated either north or south. It was during the truce that Farin Dupré brought the elements of his side together and formally formed The American Socialist Union.

With the United States in chaos, weakened and broken, aggressor countries jumped at the opportunity to strike and claim lands and countries that could not be championed or defended. The first to fall was South Korea when its neighbor to the north bombed and nearly destroyed the south's entire infrastructure then rolled nearly a half-million troops across the border.

Next came China. After they decimated the United States Pacific fleet with tactical nuclear weapons they immediately invaded and took Taiwan and Japan and were in the process of occupying many of their neighboring Asian countries with little resistance.

On the other side of the planet Russia strutted right into all the countries that had broken away at the fall of communism. Russia was now preparing to fight the countries of the European Union and NATO if they opposed their actions. Likewise, Iran moved quickly to overcome most all of the Middle East and was heavily engulfed in conflict with Turkey, Saudi Arabia, and India. In desperation and to hopefully insure their survival, the NATO countries quickly formed a new nation called the United States of Europe.

In essence the world was falling apart simply because one man who desired a world of his own making, destroyed the very heart of his existence and source of his wealth, the Crystal Empire, that by example and blood, brought democracy, liberty, and prosperity to a planet where it had never before actually succeeded. Now, by example, the world saw just how delicate such a republic can be.

EPILOGUE

CHESAPEAKE BAY, MARYLAND - 2039
20 YEARS LATER

Boxer Bernhardt sat beneath the old oak tree trying to sum up some semblance of humanity that had taken place in the past 19 years, but it seemed to him there was none to be found. He had spent most all of that time flying combat missions, fighting, and surviving, and eventually helping to keep what remained of the United States military intact. The war had taken his grandparents, his parents, his sister and her husband and his son... and of course his country. He was now left with only his sister's twins and their children who had grown up knowing only war and faced a grim future. His nieces, the twins, had also lost their young husbands in the war.

Was the war over? he wondered. *Can we all now embrace our families and rebuild our homes?* He wasn't sure. He only knew they would have to try.

The recent reports from Free Radio came to mind. Reports that claimed the American Socialist Union was cutting back their aggressiveness. That the day of the big battles were over, and that the remaining fighting existed only along the Appalachian Mountains where many die hard US citizen fighters had formed into numerous guerrilla warfare groups. They were causing the opposition mayhem up and down the southeast, striking and then retreating into the mountains. Fighters comprised of all races, religions, and ideology whose differences had vanished in the face of a common enemy. They were now all simply American citizen soldiers defending their homeland and trying their damndest to preserve the freedom and liberty they had begun to take for granted. They were supported by others based at Fort Knox with a goodly sized mobile armor force to defend the base and escort supplies from the Midwest. Though they had no air power, that eventually proved to be of little consequence being the fuel and armaments of the Socialist Union had dwindled and were being kept in reserve to fend off a possible invasion from Europe, the Middle East, or even Cuba and South America. For the most part the Socialist Union was now run by a loose knit hand full of Generals. They were realistic men who based their interest and judgments on the reality of their situation and capabilities rather than a near religious fervor based on some ill conceived and ill perceived outdated hatred.

Boxer had heard a few years prior that their self-appointed president, Farin Dupré, had been assassinated by his own generals because he was insistent on reneging on his deal with the Cubans. The Hispanic Union was now fully supported by Russia who had pulled Venezuela and Columbia into the mix. The Generals were unanimously opposed to Dupré's desires, concerned more about Cuba invading Mississippi and Louisiana than themselves invading Florida or anywhere else. They were tired of war and were of the mind they had achieved their goal. When they were overridden by Dupré and threatened with dismissal they revolted, killed him, and took over. It seemed Caesar had lost his throne.

When Boxer tried to look into the future he saw only despair and was grateful to have the family farm. There he and the children could be self-sufficient and hopefully not be concerned about being caught up and assaulted in an obscene senseless war. And there the Bernhardt family tradition of fighting in wars would end. But Boxer was forcing himself to be an optimist. He knew but refused to think of the real future, the one where the new dominant powers of the world would look on his country as a wounded animal and they would surround it like hungry lions waiting for the right time to strike. They will watch and when the time comes they will strike and in doing so, enslave, restrict or kill the people all for the rewards and resources of this once strong productive land of liberty.

The evening rolled in carrying a slight hint of fog with the darkness. Boxer Bernhardt mounted his prized old Stearman and flew off to the north, to his farm, to where he hoped he could live out the rest of his life in peace.

ABOUT THE AUTHOR

Frank Mosco is the author of ten books which include eight novels. He is a native of Annapolis, Maryland, who now lives and writes in Florida. Frank began collecting awards for writing while still in high school, then again as a journalist in college where he majored in Broadcast Management & Media. He went on to produce material for all forms of media as a reporter, columnist, producer, director, and photographer, as well as media and communications work for the Federal Government and the White House. After many years on the beaches of Florida, which influenced a number of his books, he now produces mostly fictional novels of which he says, *"...can be just as strange as reality but far more convenient and definitely more fun."*